For James

Anna Hoyt
A Novel of Colonial Crime

More by Dana Cameron

Fangborn Novels
Seven Kinds of Hell
Pack of Strays
Hellbender

Emma Fielding Archaeology Mysteries
(now on Hallmark Movies & Mysteries)
Site Unseen
Grave Consequences
Past Malice
A Fugitive Truth
More Bitter Than Death
Ashes and Bones

Also from DCLE:
Pandora's Orphans: A Fangborn Collection
Exit Interview: an a.k.a. Jayne novel

Anna Hoyt

A Novel of Colonial Crime

Dana Cameron

Anna Hoyt:

A Novel of Colonial Crime

DCLE Publishing LLC

ISBN-13: 978-1-7371536-4-1

Cover Art by Errick Nunnally

Content Warning
This is a crime novel, in the noir style, set in a tavern in colonial Boston: the criminal violence (including murder) is explicit and there are references to the cultural and legal discrimination against anyone who is not a white, cisgendered, straight, Protestant man of property. There is domestic and gender-based violence, brief suicidal ideation, crude language, and some sex.

Chapter One: "Femme Sole"
November 1745

"A moment of your time, Anna Hoyt."

Anna slowed and cursed to herself. She'd seen Adam Seaver as she crossed Prince Street, and for a terrible moment, thought he was following her. She'd hoped to lose him amid the peddlers and shoppers at the busy market near Dock Square, but she couldn't ignore him after he called out. His brogue was no more than a low growl, but conversations around him tended to fade and die. He never raised his voice, but he never had a problem making himself heard, even over the loudest of Boston's boisterous hawkers.

In fact, with anxious glances, the crowd melted back in retreat from around her. No one wanted to be between Seaver and whatever he was after.

Cowards, she thought. But her own mouth was dry as he approached.

She turned, swallowed, met his eyes, then lowered hers, hoping it looked like modesty or respect and not revulsion. His face was weathered and, in places, blurred with scars, marks of fights he'd walked away the winner. There was a nick above his ear where he'd had his head shaved. Seaver smiled; she could see two rows of sharp, ugly teeth like a mouthful of broken glass or like one of the bluefish the men sometimes caught in the Harbor. Bluefish were so vicious they had to be clubbed when they were brought into the boat or they'd shear your finger off.

He didn't touch her, but she flinched when he gestured to a quiet space behind the stalls. It was blustery autumn, salt air and a hint of snow to come, but the smell of sour milk nearly gagged her. Dried leaves skittered over discarded rotten vegetables. Was it that even the boldest rats fled when Seaver approached?

"How are you, Mr. Seaver?" she asked. She tried to imagine that she was safely behind her bar. Ever since she'd taken possession of the tavern, signed the papers carefully as her father hacked and coughed, Anna felt she could manage anything with the bar between her and the rest of the world.

"Fair enough. Yourself?"

"Fine." She wished he'd get on with it. "Thanks." His excessive manners worried her. He'd never spoken to her before, other than to order his rum and thank her.

When he didn't speak, Anna felt the sweat prickle along the hairline at the back of her neck. The wind blew a little colder, and the crowd and imagined safety of the market seemed remote. The upright brick structure of the Town House was impossibly far away, and the groaning ships anchored at the nearby wharves might as well have been at sea.

He waited, searched her face, then looked down. "What very pretty shoes."

"Thank you. They're from Turner's." She shifted uncomfortably. She didn't believe he was interested in her shoes, but neither did she imagine he was trying to spare her feelings by not staring at the bruises that ran up the side of her head. These were almost hidden with an artfully draped shawl, but her lip was still visibly puffy. It was too easy to trace the line from that to the black and blue marks. One mark led to the next, like a constellation.

One thing always led to another.

"What can I do for you, Mr. Seaver?" she said at last. Not knowing was too much.

"I may be in a way to do something for you."

Anna sighed. She heard the offer five times a night.

"Nothing like that," he said, showing that rank of teeth. "It's your husband."

"What about him?" Gambling debts, whores, petty theft? Another harebrained investment gone west? Her mind raced over the many ways Thomas could have offended Mr. Seaver.

"I saw him at Clark's law office this morning. I had business with Clark...on behalf of my employer—"

Anna barely stifled a shudder. Best to know nothing of Seaver or his employer, Mr. Oliver Browne. The latter had created a vast fortune so quickly, it could only have come from piracy or the brutal trade in human beings and contraband. If Seaver was rightly feared, Browne's name was never spoken in anything above a whisper, lest he appear. Thick Thomas Hoyt was well beneath the notice of Oliver Browne, praise God.

"—and your husband was still talking to Clark."

"Yes?" Anna refused to reveal surprise at Thomas visiting a lawyer. He had no use or regard for the law.

"He was asking how he could sell your establishment."

"He can't. It's mine."

This time, the words were out before she could stop them, but Seaver showed no surprise at her vehemence. "Much as I thought, and exactly what Clark told him. Apparently, Hook Miller wants the place."

"So he said last night. I thanked him, but I'm not selling. He was more than understanding."

Seaver tilted his head. "Because he thinks the way to acquire your tavern is through your husband."

The words went through Anna like a knife, and she understood. Her hand rose to her cheek. The beating had come only hours after Miller's offer and her refusal. Thomas had been blind drunk, and she could barely make out what had driven him this time.

"If I sell it, how will we live? The man's an idiot."

She was shocked to realize she'd said the words aloud, was having a conversation, *this* conversation, with Seaver.

"Perhaps Thomas thinks he can weasel a big enough price from Miller."

"The place is *mine*. No one can take it, not even my husband. My father said so. I have the papers." 'Feme sole merchant' were what the magistrates called her, with their fancy Latin when she came before them. The documents allowed her to conduct business almost as if she was a man. At first, it was only with her father's consent, but as she and the tavern prospered—and he sickened—it was accepted that she was responsible for the business on her own, the community unwilling to lose a favorite tavern. Very nearly independent, almost as good as a man, in the year of Our Lord 1745. And though she could never say so aloud, better than most.

"I think Clark will be bound by the document," Seaver said. "At least until someone more persuasive than Thomas comes along."

The list of people more persuasive and smarter than her husband was lengthy.

"It's only a piece of paper." Seaver shrugged. "A fragile thing."

Anna nodded, trying not to shift from one foot to another. Eventually, Hook Miller would find a way. As long as she'd known him, he always had.

Anna swallowed. "Why are you telling me this? Why are you helping me?"

He shrugged. "I like to drink at your place."

She almost believed him. "And?"

She knew what was coming, was nearly willing to pay the price that Seaver would ask. Whatever would save her property and livelihood, the modicum of security and independence she'd struggled to achieve. What were her alternatives? Sewing until she was blind, or following behind some rich bitch and carrying *her* purse, running *her* errands? Turn a sailor's whore? There was so little space between thriving and the thrall of poverty, and Anna had no desire to revisit the hard times her family had escaped. The Queen's Arms provided an unthinkable measure of safety, and she'd sworn to her father that she'd never sell it.

"And?" she repeated, wanting to know the worst.

"And." He leered. "I want to see what you will do."

✳

The bad times were hard for everyone, but the good times were what brought real trouble, she thought. A pretty young lass with no family and a thriving business on the waterfront? She might as well have hung out a sign.

Anna hurried back to the Queen's Arms, shopping forgotten. No one had ever paid the property any unusual attention when her father ran the place. It was only after she'd taken over the tavern, within sight of the wharves that cut into Boston Harbor, that business grew and drew attention her way.

The Queen was a neighborhood place on Fleet Street. "The burying ground up behind you, and the deep, dark sea ahead," her father used to say, but in between was a place for a working man to drink his beer after work—or before, as may be the case—the occasional whiskey, if he was feeling full and fat. Or three or five, if he was broke and beset.

She tripped over the cobbles in the street, but recovered and continued to hurry, needing to reassure herself the place was still there, that it hadn't vanished, hadn't been whisked away by magic from the crowd of buildings that lined the narrow streets above the Harbor. Or burned to the ground, more likely. She never doubted her husband, stupid as he was, would find a way to rob her for Miller, if that's what Thomas imagined he wanted.

Had Thomas Hoyt been content with hot meals twice a day, too much to drink and ten minutes sweating over his wife on Saturday night with church and repentance Sunday morning, Anna could have managed him well enough. She wanted a more ambitious man, but Thomas came with his mother's failed shop next door, and when Thomas agreed to sell Anna the empty shop if she married him, Anna accepted his proposal as soon as the sale was made. After all, by expanding her tavern into the new space next door, she also enlarged her business, and thought that transaction a fair enough trade for Thomas's lack of ambition.

Until she discovered Thomas *was* ambitious, in his own way. While she poured ale, rum, and whiskey, he sat in the corner. Ready to change the barrels or quell the occasional rowdiness, he more often read his paper and smoked, playing the host. His eyes followed his pretty wife's movements and those of all the men all around her. The dock workers and sailors—mostly white, a few brown and black, but all worn by the sea and aged by hard life—were eager for a modicum of ease at the end of a back-breaking day.

There were two men Thomas had watched with peculiar interest, and Anna now understood why. One was Hook, named Robert Miller by his mother, a ruffian with a finger in every pie and a hand in every pocket. Hook's gang was first to take advantage of all trade on the waterfront, from loading and unloading ships to smuggling. But he did more for the local men than he took from them and was a kind of hero for it. Of course Miller appealed to Thomas: Hook was everything Thomas imagined he himself could be.

The other man Thomas watched was Seaver, but even Thomas was smart enough to be circumspect when he did it. When one of Miller's men drunkenly pulled Seaver from his chair, claiming his looks were souring the beer, Seaver left without a word. But he came back the next night, and Miller's man never did. Three fingers from his right hand were broken and his nose bitten off. According to the gossip at the well over the next few days, he now drank at another house, well away from where anyone knew him.

The other men left Seaver alone after that. Anna smiled as she served his rum, but it stopped at her eyes. He was content to sit quietly, alone with who knew what thoughts.

✳

Thomas was scrubbing the bar when she arrived. He looked up, smiled as though he remembered nothing of what had happened the night before. Maybe he didn't.

"There's my girl. Marketing done?"

"I forgot something."

"Well, find it and I'll walk you to the dressmaker's myself. It's getting dark."

He said it as though the dark brought devils instead of the tradesmen who came regularly to her place. Who worshiped her. She had married him hastily, a year before, after her father died, for protection—it was safer all around if it was thought she were governed by a man in her enterprises. She ran her tongue along the inside of her cheek, felt the swelling there, felt a tooth wiggle, her lip torn a fraction.

"I won't have you be less than the best-dressed lady in the North End," he said expansively, as if he emptied his pockets onto the counter himself. Anna and Mr. Long, the dressmaker, had a deal: Anna borrowed the latest gowns, and wearing them, showed them to perfection, the ideal advertisement with her golden hair and slim waist. The men at her place either sent their wives to the dressmaker's so they'd look more like Anna or spent more money at Anna's just to look at her, a fine, pretty thing amid so much coarseness. If her hands were roughened by a life of work, she yet appeared a delicate creature, seeming out of place in her tavern.

She pretended to locate some trifle, and Thomas wiped his hands on the seat of his britches. She forced a smile into her eyes; her mouth still hurt. Better to have him think she was stupid or in love. Even better, afraid.

"The best news, Anna," he said, taking her arm as they went back onto the street. "Rob Miller has added another ten pounds to his asking price. We were right to wait."

It was still less than half the value of the place. Under no circumstances would she consider selling to Hook Miller and give Thomas the money to invest and lose.

She nodded, as if her refusal to sell had been a joint decision.

"I think we'll wait until Friday, see if we can't drive the price a little higher," he said, patting her hand. His own hand was heavy and rough. She saw the faint abrasions along the knuckles, remembered them intimately.

She nodded again, kept her eyes on her feet, shoes peeping out from under her skirt, as she hurried to keep up with Thomas. He raced across the cobbles, she a half pace behind.

Friday, then. Three days. Between Miller's desire for her tavern and Thomas's wish to impress him, she was trapped.

✳

Friday night came despite Anna's prayers for fire, a hurricane, a French invasion. But the place was as it always was: a wide, long room, stools and tables, two good chairs by a large, welcoming fire. The old windows were in good repair, their leads tight, and decent curtains kept out the drafts. The warm smells of fine Barbadian rum and local ale kept the world at bay.

When Miller came into the tavern, Thomas got up immediately, offered him the best upholstered seat, nearest the fire. Miller dismissed him outright, said his business was with Anna. She tried with all her might to divert his attention back to Thomas, but Miller could not have made more of a show of favoring her in front of the entire room, who watched from behind raised mugs. Thomas glowered, his gaze never leaving Anna.

"Why won't you sell the place, Anna?" Miller's words and tone were filled with hurt; she was doing him unfairly.

Anna's eyes flicked around the room; the men who were paying attention were curious. Why would Anna cross Miller? No profit in that, they all knew.

"And if I did, what would I live on then?" she asked gaily, as if Miller had been revisiting a long-standing joke, like a proposal or an elopement. "No house, no means of support?"

"Go to the country, for all of me," he said, draining his glass. It might as well have been, "Go to the devil."

As if she had a farm to retire to, a home somewhere but over the barroom. "I promised my father I would not," she said, trying to maintain the idea of a joke, but the strain was audible in her voice, her desperation a tremor in her answer.

"Well, come find me—" He set his empty glass down. "—when you're ready to be reasonable." He tipped his hat to her, ignored Thomas, and left.

After that, the other regulars filed out, one by one. None wanted to see what they all knew would come next. Anna tried to entice them to stay, even offering a round on the house on a flimsy excuse of someone's good haul of fish. But it couldn't last forever, and eventually, even the boy Silas, who helped serve, was sent home. Only Seaver was left.

It was late, past the time when Thomas generally retired. It was obvious he wasn't going to bed.

Seaver stood up. Anna looked at him with a wild hope. Perhaps he would come to her aid, somehow defuse the situation. He put a coin down on the counter and leaned toward her.

She glanced hastily at Thomas, who was scowling as he jabbed the fire with a poker. Anna's face was a mask of desperation. She leaned closer, and Seaver surreptitiously ran a finger along the back of her hand.

"Better if you don't argue with him," he breathed, his lips barely moving. "Don't fight back too much."

She watched his back as he left. The room was empty, quiet, save for the crackle of the fire, the beating of Anna's heart in her chest.

Thomas straightened, and turned. "I thought we had an agreement."

Anna looked around; there was no one to help her. The door...

"I thought, any man comes in here looking for a piece, you send him up to that fancy cathouse on Salem Street. And yet, I see you, a damned slut, making cow eyes at every man in here, right in front of me."

She ran for the door, but as she touched the latch, she felt the poker slam across her shoulders. She cried out, fell against the door. The next blows landed on her back, but Thomas, tired of imprecision and mindful of leaving more visible marks that would make the punters uneasy, dropped the poker and relied on the toe of his boot.

After a while, his rage diminished, Thomas stormed out. Anna remained on the floor, too afraid and too hurt to get up. She measured the grain of the wood planks while she thought. Thomas would go to Miller, reassure him the sale was imminent. Soon she would have no choice.

Eventually, she forced herself up, pulling herself onto a stool. No bones broken, this time. Anna had long since given up the hope that each successive beating would hurt less, or that she would become inured to the bruises and cuts. Increased familiarity with Thomas's habits in violence bred only a dreadful prescience of the rhythm of his blows, and she tried not to flinch and anticipate the next, lest she infuriate him further.

In her quest to find security, independence, she put her faith in her husband's strength. Now...she wasn't sure what would work, but knew she would be damned if she gave in. Not after all she'd done to make the place her own. Anna had been raised on the horrific tales told by her parents about the plague only a few years before her birth. Half of Boston contracted the pox, and of those, nearly one in ten had died. Her father had repeated the value of a business, and the strife his family had gone through to keep the tavern, over and over, as she held his hand while he died. Property, a business, distinguished man from animals, and more, brought safety against uncertain times. He'd said there were only two books she needed to mind, her Bible and her ledger, but now the latter had her in deep trouble. She moved stiffly to the bar, poured herself a large rum, and drank it down neat, exchanging the burn of the liquor for the searing pain in her back.

✳

Thomas didn't return in the morning, but Anna hadn't expected him to. He often stayed away after a beating, a chance for her to think over her sins, he'd told her once before. But never for more than a day or two.

She moved stiffly that day, easier the next. But late the third evening, when Anna was about to bar the door for the night, a man's hand shoved it open. Maybe Thomas had a change of heart, had come home—

It was Hook Miller.

She didn't offer a drink. He didn't ask for one.

"Why not sell to me, Anna Hoyt?" he said, warming his hands at the fire. "I want this place, so you might as well save yourself the trouble."

"I told you. My father told me never to. Property—it's the only sure thing, in this world."

Miller didn't seem bothered, only a trifle impatient. "There's nothing sure, Anna. Wood burns, casks break, and customers leave. And I've had the lawyer Clark make your rights over to Thomas. Take my money, leave here."

She said nothing. Felt the paper she kept in her shoe, the copy of the papers that gave her the Queen's Arms, the property, the right to do business. Now he was telling her they were worthless. After all her work, all she'd done to keep this little scrap of security...

Suddenly, Anna had a dreadful thought. "Where is Thomas? Have you seen him?"

"Indeed, I've just left him." Miller stood straight, smiled crookedly. He continued, mock-serious. "He's...down by the wharf. He couldn't persuade you to sell, but he's still looking after your interests."

The blood froze inside her. Thomas was dead, she knew it. All her supposed cleverness in protecting herself, the prices she'd paid for it...and it was if she'd been hiding behind a stalk of grass. She couldn't feel anything but a raw vulnerability as if her skin had been flayed away, leaving her exposed to the universe.

Miller tilted his head and waited. When she couldn't bring herself to respond, he left, closing the door behind him.

The paralyzing cold spread over her, and, for a blessed moment, Anna felt nothing. Then the shivering started, brought her back to the tavern. Anna's first thought was that her knees would give way before she reached the chair by the fire. She clutched the back of it, her nails digging into the upholstery. When she felt one of them snap, she turned, took three steps, then vomited into the slops pot behind the bar.

Better, Anna thought, wiping her mouth. *I must be better than this.*

Still trembling, but at least able to think, she climbed the stairs to her rooms. She saw Thomas's good shirt hanging from a peg and buried her face in it, breathing deeply. She took it down, rubbing the thick linen between her fingers, and considered the length of the sleeves. She stared at the peg, high on the wall, and reluctantly made her decision.

Everything was different in her new shoes. Used to her lighter slippers, the cobbles felt oddly distant beneath the thick soles, and it took her a while to master the clunkiness of the wider heels. She relied on a population used to drunken sailors and foreign sorts to ignore her, relied on the long cloak to conceal most of her blunders. Thomas's clothes would have been impossible, but she still had a chest full of her father's things, and his boots were a better fit. Best not to think about the rest of her garb. She needed to confirm what Miller had hinted, and she couldn't be seen doing it. Anna was too familiar a figure to those whose lives were spent on the wharves, and most of them would be friendly faces. But not if she were caught. If they caught her, so scandalously dressed in britches, well... Losing the tavern would be the least of it.

Somehow, her need to know for sure was stronger than fear, than embarrassment, and the bell in the North Church chimed by the time she found her way to the wharf that Miller currently managed. The reek of tar and wood fires made her eyes water, and a stiff breeze combined drying fish with the smells of spices in nearby warehouses, making her almost gag.

The moon broke through the clouds. She walked out to the harbor, feeling more and more exposed by the moment. Nothing on the wharf that shouldn't be there.

She stopped, struck by the realization. Hook would never lay the murder at his own doorstep.

The urge to move a short way down to the pier and wharf that belonged to Clark, Miller's detested rival in business, was nearly physical.

At first, Anna saw nothing but the boards of the pier itself. She climbed down the ladder to the water's edge, hooked one of the dinghies by its rope, and pulled it close. She boarded, cast off, and rowed, following the length of the pier. Though she preferred to be secret, there was no need to muffle the oarlocks; the waterfront's activity died down at night, but it was never completely silent along the water. Sweat trickled down her back even as thin ice crackled on the planks of the boat beneath her feet.

The half hour rang out, echoed by church bells across Boston and Charlestown, and Anna shivered in spite of her warm exercise.

Three-quarters of the way down the pier, Anna saw a glimpse of white on the water. She uncovered her lantern, and held it up.

Among the pilings, beneath the pier, all manner of lost and discarded things floated, bobbing idly on top of the waves: broken crate wood, a dead seagull, an unmoored float. There was something else.

A body.

Even without seeing his face, she knew it was Thomas, his light hair floating like kelp, the shirt she herself had patched billowing around him like sea foam. A wave broke against the piling of the pier and one of his hands was thrust momentarily to the surface, puffy and raw. The fish and harbor creatures had been to feast.

Anna stared a while, and then maneuvered the boat around. She rowed quietly back to the ladder, tied up the dinghy, and went home. She brought the bottle of rum to her room, drank until the cold was chased away, and she could feel her fingers again. Then she drank a good deal more. She changed back into her own clothing and, keeping her father's advice in mind, opened her Bible. In an old habit, she let it fall open where it would, closing her eyes and placing a finger on the text. The candle burned low while she read, waiting for someone to come and tell her Thomas Hoyt was dead.

✳

Hook Miller came to the burial on Copp's Hill. As he made his way up the hill to where Anna stood, the crowd of neighbors—there were nearly fifty of them, for nothing beat a good funeral—doffed their hats or bobbed a curtsy out of respect to his standing. Miller's clothes were showy but ill-suited to him, Anna knew, and he pretended concern that was as foreign to him as a clean handkerchief. He even waited decently before he approached her, and those nearby heard a generous offer of aid to the widow, so that she could retreat to a quieter life elsewhere. The offering price was still an affront. When she shook her head, he nodded sadly, said he'd be back when she was more composed. She knew it wasn't solicitousness but the eyes of the neighborhood that made him so nice. The next time Miller approached her, it would be in private. There would be no refusing that offer.

When Seaver came in for his drink later, she avoided his glance.

She'd already made up her mind.

The next morning, she sent a note to Hook Miller. No reason to be seen going to him, when there was nothing more natural than for him to come to the tavern. And if his visit stood out among others, why, she was a propertied widow now who had to keep an eye to the future.

He didn't bother knocking, came in as if he already owned the place, and barred the door behind him. She was standing behind a chair, waiting, a bottle of wine on the table, squat bodied and long-necked, along with two of her best glasses polished to gleaming. One was half-filled, half-drunk. The fire was low, and there were only two candles lit.

He bowed and sat without being asked. His breath was thick with harsh New England rum. "Well?"

"I can't sell the place. I'd be left with nothing. I have no special talent with a needle and none with children; no one will hire a lady to keep their accounts. This is all I have. All I know." She wouldn't tell him about the nightmares she had, rooted in the stories handed down from her parents about calamity and poverty: Anna's mother had lost her parents, and with no support was forced to travel to the north, to Lynn, her place of birth. With none there to help her, she was forced to return to Boston, where her father had been born, only to be traded back and forth between cities, hungry and unwanted, until Philip Sommers married her.

When her father signed over the Queen's Arms to Anna, he reiterated its importance, that life was uncertain, and the tavern was the source of their security and continued existence, lessons she took to heart.

Miller said nothing, but his eyes narrowed. "And?"

Anna straightened. "Marry me. That way...the place will be yours, and I'll be...looked after."

"You didn't sign it over to Thomas."

"Thomas Hoyt was as thick as two short planks. I couldn't trust him to find his arse with both hands."

Thomas's absence now was not discussed.

Miller pondered. "If I do, you'll sign the Queen's Arms over to me."

"The day we wed." Her father had given her the hope and the means, but then slowly, painfully, she'd discovered she couldn't keep the place on her own, not the day to day heavy work, not the expansion and renovations expanding into the Hoyt's abandoned shop next door. She swallowed. "I can't do this by myself."

"And what benefit to me to marry you?"

Her hours of thought had prepared the answer. "You'll get a property you've always wanted, and with it, an eye and an ear to everything that happens all along the waterfront. More than that: respectability. This whole neighborhood is getting nothing but richer, and you'd be in the middle of it. What better way to advance than through deals with the merchant nobs themselves? To say nothing of window dressing for your other...affairs."

Miller laughed, then stopped, considered what she was saying. "Sharp. And a clever wife to entertain my new friends? It makes sense."

"Those rich merchants, they're no more than a step above hustling themselves. We can be of use to each other," she said carefully. She'd almost said "need," but that would have been fatal. "Wine?"

He looked at her, looked at the bottle, the one empty glass.

"Thanks."

She poured, the ruby liquid turning blood black in the green-tinged glasses, against the dark of the room.

He stared at the glass, his brow furrowing. "I've more of a mind for beer, if you don't mind."

She looked disappointed, but didn't press him. "You'll have to get a head for wine if you expect to move up in the world," she said as she rose and slid a pewter mug from a peg on the wall. She filled it from the large barrel behind her bar.

Miller smiled, thanked her. She raised her glass to him, sipped. He saluted and drank, too.

It was then he noticed the large Bible on the table next to them. He reached over, flipped through carelessly.

"Too much theater, for one about to be so soon remarried, don't you think?" He flicked through the pages, as if looking for something he could make use of. "Devotion doesn't play. Not around here, anyway."

"Don't you touch that!" Anna felt a flame ignite in her, seeing him handle the book so roughly. She shut it firmly, moved it away, barely kept from striking Miller with it. "My father said it was the only book besides my ledger to heed." She knew that it was a weak excuse, and that he'd find piety unexpected, especially after her reaction—or lack thereof—to her husband's murder. She relied on him to assume—as so many did—that women were inscrutable.

"Suit yourself." Miller shrugged.

Her reaction aroused him, however. Any resistance did. "Let me see what I'll be getting myself into. Lift your skirts."

Anna had known it would come to this; still, she hesitated. Only a moment. But before Hook had to say another word, she bunched up the silk, slippery in her sweaty palms, and raised her skirts to her thighs. Miller reached out, grabbed the ribbon of her garter, and pulled. It slithered out of its knot, draped itself over his fist. He leaned over, reached a finger over the top of her stocking, then collapsed onto the table. His head hit hard, but he never said another word.

Repulsed, Anna unhooked his finger from her stocking, let his hand fall heavily, smack against the chair leg. She straightened her stocking, retied her garter, then picked up the heavy Bible. She hesitated, gulping air, then, remembering her father's words and the fourth chapter of Judges, nodded.

I must be better than this. I must manage. It's the only way to survive.

She reached into the cracked binding of the Bible and withdrew a long steel needle. Its point picked up the light from the candle and glittered. Her breath held, she stood over the unconscious man, then, aiming carefully, she drove it deep into his ear.

Shortly, with a grunt, a shudder, a sigh, Miller stopped breathing.

✳

She'd been afraid she'd been too stingy, miscalculated the dose, unseen in the bottom of the pewter mug, not wanting to warn him with the smell of belladonna or have it spill as it waited on the peg. Her father had been frailer, older, and when she could stand his rasping, rattling breathing no longer, could wait no longer to begin her own plans for the Queen's Arms, she brought him tea laced with a smaller amount. No matter. Either the poison or the needle had done its work on Hook Miller.

Anna threw the rest of the beer onto the floor, followed it with the last of the wine from the bottle. No sense in taking chances. She had a long night ahead of her. She could barely move Hook on her own. Slender though she was, she was strong from hauling water and kegs and wood from the time she could walk, but he was nearly two hundred pounds of dead meat. She'd planned this, though, with much meticulousness. She'd learned early on that it didn't pay to be unprepared, so she considered her moves like a general on the field—everything that could be anticipated, that is. Thomas's ill-conceived greediness she hadn't counted on, nor Miller's interest in her place. These were hard lessons and dearly bought.

She would be better. She would manage.

She went to the back, brought out the barrow used to move barrels. With careful work, and a little luck, Anna tipped Miller from his chair into the barrow, and, struggling to keep her balance, wheeled him out of the public room into the back kitchen ell. She left him there, out of sight, and checked again that the back door was still barred. She twitched the curtain so that it hung completely over the small window.

She lit a taper from the fireplace, considering her plan. A change of clothes, from silk into something for scut work. She had hours of dirty work ahead of her, as bad and dirty as slaughtering season, but really, it was no different from butchering a hog.

A small price to pay for her freedom and the time to plan how better to keep it.

Holding the lit taper, she hurried up the narrow back stairs to the chamber over the public room. When she opened the door, her breath caught in her throat. There was a lighted candle on the table across from her bed.

Seaver was sitting in her best chair.

Anna felt her mouth parch. Although she'd half expected to be interrupted in her work, she hadn't thought it would be in her own chamber. But Seaver had wanted to see what she'd do—he'd said so himself. She swallowed two or three times, before she could ask.

"How?"

"You should nail up that kitchen window. It's too easy to reach in and shove the bar from the door. Then up the stairs, just as you yourself came. But not before I watched you with Miller." He pulled an unopened bottle from his pocket, cut the red wax from the stopper, opened it. "I'll pour my own drinks, thanks. What is the verse? 'After she gave him drink, Jael went unto him with a peg of the tent and smote the nail into his temple?'"

"Near enough."

"A mistake teaching women to read. But then, if you couldn't read, you couldn't figure your books, and you wouldn't have such a brisk business as you do." He drank. "A double-edged sword. But as nice a bit of needlework as I've ever seen from a lady."

Keep breathing, Anna. You're not done yet. "What now?" She thought of the pistol in the trunk by the bed, the knife under her pillow. They might as well have been at the bottom of the Harbor.

"A bargain. You're a widow with a tavern, I am the agent of an important man. You also have a prime piece of real estate, and an eye on everything that happens along here. And, it seems, an eye to advancement. I think we can deal amiably enough, and to our mutual benefit."

At that moment, Anna almost wished Seaver would just cut her throat. She'd never be free of this succession of men, never able to manage by herself. The rage welled up in her, as it had never done before, and she thought she would choke on it. She thought of the documents that made the tavern and its business wholly her own, and how she'd fought for them. She'd be damned before she handed it over to another man.

But she saw Seaver watching her carefully, and then it came to her. Perhaps like Miller not seeing that the obvious next move for him was civil life and nearly legitimate trade—with all its fat skimming—she was not ambitious enough. Instead of mere survival, relying on the tavern, she could parlay it into more. Working with Seaver, who, after all, was only the errand boy of one of the most powerful—and dangerous—men in New England, she might do more than survive. She saw the beginning of a much wider, richer future ahead of her.

The whole world open to her, if she kept sharp. If she could learn as she had done. If she could be better than she was.

She went over to the mantel, took down a new bottle herself, opened it, poured herself a drink. Raised the glass.

She would pour her own drinks, and Seaver would pour his own.

She would manage.

"To our mutual benefit," she toasted.

Chapter Two: "Disarming"
January 1745/46

It took Anna two days before she left her small room in her inn at Southwark. She had not been ill a single day during her voyage to England, despite the late season and the January roughness of the Atlantic; some passengers had never left their cabins. Nor was it the distressing contents of the letter she kept in her Bible that paralyzed her. It was the sheer size of London, looming beyond her window, shrouded by icy fog. Even her life near the hectic activity of the Boston wharves hadn't prepared her for the tumult she encountered by the waterfront, slippery with stinking, briny mud. She was nearly run down twice before she found a carter willing to take her and her luggage. The driver incomprehensibly cursed her when she asked him a third time to repeat his price; at length she understood he was speaking English, but with the thickest Welsh accent she'd ever heard. He urged his horses into the gloom, muttering to himself as Anna clung to her seat, miserable and shivering in the frigid January rain.

That last mile on land had robbed her nerve. Once in her room, Anna locked the door behind her, and sat trembling on the bed. Feeling small and alone, she huddled there, not even venturing as far as the tray of food the landlord left on the table. It seemed too distant, too dangerous to cross the floor from the square yard of bed she claimed as her own.

After time alone, however, she was propelled not only by boredom, but the pressing knowledge that she did not travel on her own behalf. That letter, with its red wax seal, along with drafts for a small fortune, served to remind her. While Anna had never known good news to come in a letter, it was possible this terrible threat was mingled with opportunity.

✳

Two months before, in November of 1745, she'd been summoned to the country house of Mr. Oliver Browne by his agent, Adam Seaver. When he brought the request, Mr. Seaver had smiled, showing his broken teeth; Anna had barely contained her shudder. Seaver made a good enough figure when he tried, and he always tried with Anna, and she was grateful. Anna could not imagine why the monstrously powerful Browne wanted to see her, or why he did not come to her tavern. Seaver's appearance at the tavern was always terrifying, but when he was acting on direct orders from Browne, it was as if he was an emissary from the devil himself.

Stomach churning, Anna waited for the carriage Browne had promised. As she departed the Queen's Arms, Venus stepping from a seashell, the flash of the finery beneath her cloak a shock of loveliness against the rough wooden exterior, she considered flight. She did not like leaving the boisterous North End, where everyone knew her. Stiff in her new dress and her pretend calm, Anna rode as if to her own trial, blotting her sweating hands on her handkerchief.

The name "Browne" figured in her family's whispered stories of trouble and danger, though she never knew if it was more particular than the local legends about him.

A few miles outside Boston, in the calm countryside of Medford, she viewed Browne's home: two and a half stories of pleasing brick symmetry with five bays of glass windows overlooking gardens, orchards and fields, impressive even as they were bedded down for the winter. She knew it was tended by a staggering number of servants and even a few Black slaves. Her confidence rose as she descended from the carriage and Anna was gratified by the size and splendor of the house, recognizing its taste and modernity. If she could not meet Browne without fear, she could tell much about him from his property.

This inclination grew as Browne, a well-fed and well-dressed little man, welcomed her into a parlor furnished with relics from earlier generations—perhaps even his own family's inherited goods. Silver plate and China-ware in blue and white gleamed from an ancient cupboard. The walls were well-plastered and painted and hung with stern portraits. If outward appearances reflected inner truths, this did not seem to be the abode of an evil man.

Seated at a table covered with an immaculate white cloth, Anna sighed with a kind of relief. Perhaps there was nothing to fear. Perhaps all would be well. Perhaps the rumors were untrue.

"I am delighted to meet you, Mistress Hoyt." Browne eased himself into a fashionable chair too dainty to comfortably accommodate him. He poured wine. "Do you know London, I wonder?"

As she took the proffered glass, Anna jerked. The garnet wine met the edge of her glass but did not spill over. Of all the topics she might have expected—her recent widowhood and the disappearance of a local tough only ten days before—London was last on the list. London might as well have been the moon.

She examined her glass, as if admiring it. "I have never been, sir."

"I would like to send you there."

Her astonishment could not have been greater. She looked up.

"Why, Mr. Browne?"

"I think you can be of use to me, if you would. A voyage would help distract you from the grief of your husband's murder—"

"Murder? My husband met with accident, drunk on the wharf," she said, as if by rote.

He paid no notice. "—and distract you also from feelings that surely must follow the perplexing disappearance of Hook Miller."

She felt her jaw tighten. "What's Miller to do with me? He wanted to buy my tavern, and I refused."

Hook Miller is gone, she thought. *I managed Hook Miller.*

"Indeed," Browne continued, "he was last seen leaving for your place, and never seen after."

She shrugged, her heart racing now. "Anything may happen between one place and another."

"Never seen again, save by my man, here." He nodded to Seaver. "Who watched you haul Hook's carcass to your kitchen to carve him up. For bait, I hope."

Anna said nothing, couldn't have if she wanted. She noticed her hand shaking and pressed the glass to her lips to conceal it. Seaver watched her from behind Browne's chair; she drank anyway. The wine seemed wholesome and tasted of honey.

"With these...tragedies...so hard on the heels of your father's illness and death, but a year or so ago, I would like to help you," Browne said, leaning forward. "If you were not to go, I would turn aside, should you ever find yourself in need. For whatever reason."

"I've survived much, without you knowing my name. Why *me*?" Anna asked bluntly. She jerked her head at Seaver. "When you have so many already at your command?"

"I could send Seaver, but he's known in London." Browne grimaced. "And look at him: He refuses to wear the perfectly good false teeth I bought for him. No, a workman needs a variety of tools, each suited to its particular job."

Browne tapped his fingers. "Obviously, I can compel you by virtue of my knowledge. But how much more interesting that you kept your appointment today. You remain calm, even now. And you are curious."

Anna could barely breathe. "You make vile hints and threats— why should I trust you?"

"Do or do not," he said. "Decide quickly, though, for speed is of the utmost importance. The ship I mean you to sail on leaves next week."

His presumption was too much. The room closed in around Anna. Her late husband, however, had taught her well the virtues of concealing emotion and speaking cautiously. "Mr. Browne, why should *I* go to London for you?"

"For no reason but to oblige me. And to gain my friendship. Think carefully, Mistress Hoyt."

The idea that he believed he could command her so easily, turn her from her business to his own with so little care, blindsided Anna. A black rage threatened to swallow her up with an urge to do violence.

He sets the tune, and I must dance because he has the power to reveal so much. Will I never be done with those who seek to use me?

She dragged her eyes from the corkscrew Browne had used to open the wine to the bottle itself and took a deep breath, mastering her emotions. The wine bottle was marked with his own seal and filled, no doubt, from private barrels in his cellar. A silver teapot and its attendant service caught her eye on another table covered with a Turkey-work rug. She considered the small army of servants it took to run such a household, to give him such ease.

With a jolt, Anna realized her beloved home was dark, crude, in comparison. After all she'd done to protect it, the security of her tavern was an illusion.

Browne's good will was not to be dismissed lightly, she thought. Rumors were rampant—his fortune arose from piracy, slavery, and smuggling; judges were swayed by his presence in court; politicians cast nervous glances his way before voting. His responses to those who crossed him, swift and terrible.

He might keep the law and local rascals away from me, this favor for him done. He might even leave me alone.

She took another sip of wine, and raised her eyes to Browne, surprised to find her face still in softly pleasant lines. "Perhaps I shall go."

"I am very glad of it."

"What is my errand?"

He paused delicately. "I have a rival in affairs, Mr. Edward Earle. He won't be reasoned with and his actions threaten to ruin me. His heir will not be such impediment to my business."

Anna's brow creased; this was entirely beyond her. "And how do you think I might... remove him?"

"I merely want you to make his acquaintance, learn his vulnerabilities."

"Nothing more?"

Browne showed the edge of impatient ill temper. "Meet him. Observe him. Report to me how I may use his weaknesses against him. Only it must be soon; the bill that interests us both goes before Parliament in the spring, and I yet lack his influence there. You have three weeks, after you arrive, to leave a report with the captain of my ship, *Indomitable*."

If I fail, he loses nothing, she thought. *If I succeed, he still has his grasp on me.* "I, alas, cannot leave." She glanced around the room. "My business requires constant attention or I starve."

He smiled and gestured to Seaver, who handed him several pieces of paper, a sealed letter, and a purse.

"If you have one you trust to watch your establishment for a few months, I will supply all you need. More."

When she returned home, Browne's purse was heavy—with gold—in the pocket under her skirt, his papers tucked into her shoes. Anna surveyed the common room of the Queen's Arms, gave instructions to the barmaid, and retired to her chamber. She sat down at her desk and began to study her Bible.

✳

Each day for the next week after she arrived, Anna set herself a new destination to overcome her intimidation. The scale of London was like nothing Anna could have imagined, teeming—and stinking—with seven hundred thousand souls. The bad roads, clogged with every kind of traffic, made travel by foot perilous. Once she hired a sedan, which was jostling and expensive, but most often she paid one of the astonishingly vulgar watermen to ferry her across the rank river and walked from there. The sheer noise of so many people acquiring the means for life—and support of an empire—was daunting. Even away from the wharves, the variety of nations and languages represented there varied more than they ever did outside the waterfront of Boston. And each neighborhood was like a different village: This one was more fashionable, the next, devoted to business and craftsmen, this one to law, and so on. She marveled at the grandness of St. Paul's cathedral, and when she viewed the Tower menagerie and other merrymakers baiting the great lions with dogs, she noted how Londoners loved a good brawl. She learned which coffee houses were frequented by artists, merchants and foreigners and which taverns were best for news or for politics.

As she became familiar with the city and read its papers, Anna began to observe the more elevated society, its modes and manners, the people most likely to have access to Earle. During the weeks spent crossing the Atlantic, she'd made herself frantic with one question: How did one meet Edward Earle? She made inquiries, and after learning the names of the best inns, she moved to one on the north side of the Thames, in the western part of London, without giving up her room near the great stone bridge in Southwark.

Installed at this finer inn, she learned where to go to scrutinize the gentlemen and the ladies of the higher ranks. She knew she could not penetrate Earle's circle from above, but not from too far below, either. She was a little disappointed to discover she was as comfortably anonymous in her dress—neither too rich nor too shabby—as any local lady of means. Boston was not so far behind London, then, but a pretty, modish gown was not enough.

From time to time, Anna had a distinct sensation of being observe...stalked. Her skin crawled, whenever it happened, and she would hurry back to her room.

Each night, she pored over newspapers. She scanned them for word of Earle or his associates, and found he was very much a public gentleman, devoted to pleasure as well as his business. Just before bed, she also reread the letter given to her by Mr. Browne, the copy of the red-waxed and sealed letter in his possession:

"Mr. Justice Harcourt: You must inquire with Mistress Anna Hoyt of the Queen's Arms about the murder of Robert Miller, called Hook."

One day, when asked by a young man in the street, Anna was gratified to be able to give directions.

Knowing the place was where travelers with business gathered to exchange news, she impulsively said, "Perhaps you would see me there?" She touched his hand, and watched him color. "I believe I almost recognize your voice, for are you not also from New England?"

"New York, Madam. It would be my pleasure to escort you." He made a decent leg, then offered her his arm. "Faith, it is good to hear familiar accents. London is a filthy maze and a veritable Babel."

She smiled kindly. "You prefer the countryside, perhaps?"

"I am sick for the sight of homely places and friendly faces. When my ship leaves, I shall be thankful."

This reminded Anna of the Indomitable, its departure date two weeks hence, her letter about Earle still unwritten.

She banished the thought. "We are here," she announced.

"Thank you, Madam. I never fail to lose myself in this warren."

He offered her coffee, then introduced her to his friends, all American merchants. Soon, Anna was the center of attention. It was no different from her fishermen and sailors; she fixed a pleasant look over her boredom, and let them show off for her with their talk of business and politics. She almost fell asleep, smothered by the smoke of their interminable pipes, but revived when they mentioned names she recognized. Men close to Earle.

Finally, encouraged by the enlivening coffee, one of them asked her purpose in London. Taking her cue from their stories, Anna instantly fabricated a husband with a claim against Mr. Earle, and how she, now a widow, sought the money for herself.

"I wish I had better news for you, Mrs. Hoyt," said a reed-thin gentleman. "Mr. Earle has been the source of all my hope, and lately, all my discouragement. He has avoided my calls to his home and ignored my letters. An acquaintance of mine arranged an introduction, once; Nicholas suffered for that kindness to me, I fear. Mr. Earle is not only hard in business, but very cruel to those who displease him." He took a deep sip. "I was very rudely received and plan to return home next week, for London has eaten my funds."

"Perhaps you would introduce me to this friend?" Anna said. "I would be happy for any advantage in my endeavor."

He glanced at her. "I am certain Nicholas would be charmed to meet you," he said.

✳

After Anna left, she wandered very late, thinking. Suddenly, Anna felt herself shoved into an alley. A second man pulled her in deeper and slammed her head against stone wall.

"Money," he said. "Now."

She slapped her attacker. She'd had enough of the demands of men and would not suffer his impudence.

Then the first man appeared next to his fellow, and Anna's outrage was replaced by fear. The chances of her escaping unharmed evaporated, and she screamed.

"None of that," her attacker said. A strong hand clamped over her mouth.

She bit at the hand and struggled, nearly wrenching herself free. A curse, followed by a cold, sharp pain as a knife glanced across her shoulder.

The man with the knife suddenly jerked back, and she was free.

A stink of rotting teeth, then a familiar voice said, "Run, woman."

Anna heard sounds of fighting deeper in the alley as she fled. Not until she was within sight of her inn, did she slow, her breathing constrained by the boning in her bodice.

It had been Seaver who rescued her. Anna now knew she was being tested. If she failed in her errand, she would be killed as surely as Seaver was killing the two cutpurses.

That evening, Anna counted money drawn against Mr. Browne's letters of credit. She studied the papers for boats leaving England. She considered her options—fleeing with the money, to abandon her home, or obeying Browne—and turned to her Bible. It fell open to St. Luke. She read what one must render unto Caesar and unto God.

✳

The next morning, Anna arose later than usual. After she examined her shoulder—the wound was painful, but shallow—she went downstairs and was greeted by the innkeeper.

"Ah, here is another of our foreign ladies!"

Before Anna could correct him—she was an Englishwoman—he asked, "Will you break your fast with Mrs. Western?"

"Sit with me, and never mind him," the lady called. Anna recognized the woman's Bristol accent from the sailors who frequented the Queen's Arms. "Londoners are insufferable."

Luck and study and her choice of inns had finally helped Anna. Mrs. Western was "the particular friend" of Mr. Upton, a gentleman who spent most of his time in London. Anna tried to conceal her excitement as the woman prattled on: Mr. Upton was a close acquaintance of Edward Earle.

Mrs. Western was overjoyed to gossip and show herself in every way Anna's superior, so Anna sifted each grain of useful information from a great deal of chaff. She forced herself to be patient and not think of Browne's commands nor Seaver's presence.

"I understand Mr. Upton to be a close friend of Mr. Edward Earle," she said. "What is that gentleman like?"

"Well. He's very handsome. Very rich..." Mrs. Western studied her chicken stew intently.

"Isn't handsome and rich good enough?"

"You'd hope so, wouldn't you?" After looking around, she leaned in, lowered her voice. "It's not enough for him to get what he wants. He's not happy until he's taken someone else's happiness away."

Anna also whispered, her interest completely genuine: "Mr. Earle sounds very wicked."

"Perhaps. He's also generous enough...with his acquaintances. Ladies, I mean." She regarded Anna with a sisterly eye. "You are interested."

Anna decided the truth would serve. "I seem to collect scoundrels."

Mrs. Western was thrilled at the chance to enlarge herself in Anna's eyes. "Edward—Mr. Earle, I mean—hosts a gathering, a week hence. Join us, why don't you?"

"How very kind! Thank you."

The landlord's boy coughed quietly then and handed Anna a note. She read it, folded it and put it away.

"He'll meet you in the small parlor," the boy said.

Anna nodded.

Mrs. Western said, "Notes and meetings in private. At breakfast."

The woman's words were painfully arch, and Anna straightened herself. "I have business with this gentleman. I do not discuss my business in public."

Mrs. Western shrunk at this, and Anna realized she'd scared the woman. She'd never known herself to be intimidating on such short acquaintance, and found that information useful as well.

"I meant no harm," Mrs. Western said stiffly.

"None was taken. I merely wish to be clear. A lady's reputation is all she has."

Mrs. Western looked away. "Certainly."

✳

The gentleman in the parlor—so marked by his elegant shoes and excellent deportment—had not taken off his hat or cloak. His face was largely concealed by a scarf, still damp from the outside. Anna saw gray eyes that were quick, yet weary.

"Mr. Nicholas?" She made her courtesy, and he his. He still did not remove his wet cloak.

"I understand you have business with Mr. Earle," he said, his words somewhat muffled by his scarf. "I would dissuade you, if I could. No suit you bring would be worth it, and the only reason he might entertain it would be to indulge his more destructive appetites."

Anna folded her hands. "You have a distaste for the gentleman."

A barking laugh came from the scarf. "I would see him in hell, if I could."

His enmity toward Earle was genuine, Anna was certain. Emboldened by this frankness, she asked, "And if I said I had no interest in meeting him but to discover how best to ruin him?"

The gray eyes appraised her. After a moment, he said, "Call the boy and order coffee." He shrugged off his cloak and unwound his scarf.

*

Her business with Mr. Nicholas concluded, Anna found her way to a tailor he suggested. The tailor was examining his account books, and Anna felt a stab of homesickness. As she paused to examine a doll dressed in a miniature of the latest fashion, Anna understood the man was nearly drunk.

"I need to insinuate myself into a discerning circle," she said. "A party, at the home of Mr. Edward Earle."

"Would that Mr. Earle was as prompt with his payment as he is with his newest orders," the tailor said, closing his ledger. "Liberal beyond belief with friends, he makes me wait for my money until it is almost a shame to continue to ask for payment. His servants live well but hate him; the slums are filled with his cast-off maids and their bastard children. He loves only who he fears, and none of them pay, either."

The man was very drunk, Anna thought, to be so forthright. "I will give you an advance, and more than you ask, if the dress is what I require, and in time. Make me look like any of the best of them."

He slowly smiled. "No."

Her eyes narrowed. "You will not?"

"Not entirely," he said. "If I dress you like them, you will appear ridiculous in borrowed plumes. The trick is not to ape your betters, nor to appear purely countrified or provincial, but...exotic. So well informed that you acknowledge fashion and yet make it your own.

He was warming to his subject. "Embrace that difference, and you will disarm them with your novelty. Make them love you for it."

Anna didn't understand completely, but after looking around the beautiful shop she decided to trust him. She nodded. "If you are sure you can accomplish this..." She pulled out her purse and set coins, one by one, on the counter.

He eyed the gold and was instantly her accomplice. "I will make you fascinating."

Having agreed on a pattern, materials, date and price, Anna turned to leave. She stopped, again captivated by the elegant doll, which was composed, mute and immobile, and yet dictated fashion. Anna found this power admirable.

✳

Anna now had one week, and only one chance, to observe Earle. Anything else she gave Browne would be hearsay, which she knew would disappoint him. That she dared not do. In her room, she weighed that disappointment against the last of Browne's money and a fast ship for Holland. Even if she managed to slip away from Seaver—who no longer bothered to conceal his presence much—she knew she would never be able to forsake the Queen's Arms. It was either success or a noose.

The afternoon of the party, she dressed then met Mrs. Western. She sat up at the sight of Anna transformed by the tailor, as did Mr. Upton. Mrs. Western marked this attention jealously as she made the introductions.

"I have a carriage and would be more than happy to show you the metropolis this evening," Mr. Upton offered.

Anna watched Mrs. Western bridle as she accepted.

Night revealed more than daylight. Torchlight illuminated the Ranelagh rotunda and the music and diversions there, but Anna also noted the whores and beggars outside. She saw carriages manned by liveried footmen lined up outside Bedlam, as their masters—and the well-off from around the world—viewed the cells, seeking spectacle in the filthy and desperate inmates.

Mr. Upton, thinking to further impress Anna, pointed out Coram's Foundling Hospital. "It is not five years old, built by subscription by our most fashionable ladies, great men and not a few lords. Children may be left there, who might otherwise starve in the street."

Anna recalled the tailor's talk of Earle's bastards. "Better they might save themselves the expense, and everyone else a great deal of trouble, if the 'great men and lords' would only keep their breeches closed in the first place," she said without thinking.

Mrs. Western hooted at Anna's audacity; Mr. Upton's jaw dropped. Anna had the sense to make a jest of it. "Such is the case in Boston, anyway."

Then Anna saw Earle's home, a veritable palace of new sandstone with its own small park, all enclosed by iron fencing. Mrs. Western took Anna aside.

"While Mr. Earle can be very agreeable, he's keenly aware of rank. You could be the Princess Royal of all the savage Americas, and it would mean nothing to him."

Anna forced herself to nod.

"I mean, I would not recommend the same familiarity with him as you showed Mr. Upton in the carriage."

Anna nodded again, understanding the threat in Mrs. Western's tone was not only with regard to Mr. Earle. But now, her eyes were dazzled. Inside, Earle's house was ablaze with candles reflecting against gilt and mirrors. She felt dwarfed by what she saw: twenty-foot ceilings painted with classical scenes and walls covered with hand-painted Chinese paper and plaster ornaments. The guests were dressed in glistening silks and velvets, shining from head to toe. The ladies' coiffures were bedecked with jewels, the gentlemen resplendent in gold and silver embroidery and braid, and even their well-heeled shoes had silver buckles. There was carved furniture and rugs on marble floors of a sumptuousness Anna could scarcely believe. The livery of the servants was superior to many a gentleman's suit she'd seen in Boston. If London had showed her its sharp edges, this was a world beyond. Anna groped for the language to describe it, but had none.

All she knew was, compared to this masterpiece, Mr. Browne's brick house was an inelegant barn. What had seemed so rare and lovely to her was now quaint and ungainly, contrived by rustics. She could not bear to think of the Queen's Arms, its low-beamed ceilings and clean, whitewashed walls and two good upholstered chairs.

And yet, she recalled the tailor's advice. Anna did not try to appear other than she was. She was unfamiliar, so she evinced an air of quiet mystery and spun that into allure. She acknowledged Mr. Earle politely when introduced but did not seek further conversation. She made herself agreeable to Mr. Upton and his friends, who had not the least objection, and when she saw herself in one of the mirrors, she didn't recognize the fairy-like creature she'd become. Her turquoise silk stood out against a sea of demure cream satin. An ornament of tiny feathers—an emblem of the Americas—in twinkling French paste adorned her little lace cap, matching the needlework on her stomacher. The side-hoops in her skirts were narrow, permitting easier, more graceful movement and allowing gentlemen nearer. If other ladies had gowns embroidered with flowers, Anna was herself a flower.

Mrs. Western was unhappy with Mr. Upton's attentions to Anna. "This is Mrs. Hoyt's first time in London. She has been viewing the city," she said loudly near Earle. His annoyance was tempered by his curiosity about Anna: he was not used to such disinterest from a lady. Earle took Mrs. Western's cue and turned to Anna.

"You have not been in London very long?"

"Scarcely a month," she said.

"Let me show you everything the city has to offer."

"What a very friendly gesture! Mr. Upton has already been kind enough to do just that this evening." She bestowed a smile on Mr. Upton, and was gratified by the displeasure she saw in Earle. The company might be elevated, but men were easy enough to manipulate.

"Mr. Upton should spend all of his time with Mrs. Western; she has so little time away from her cows, and he from his wife," Earle said. "That is what they share in common, a familiarity with the barnyard."

Mr. Upton, overhearing this, took Mrs. Western's arm and retreated. Anna watched Earle casually malign one woman's livelihood and another's character while their friends laughed.

They make fun of Mrs. Western who's done nothing they do not do, she thought. *They make the rules, but even if you follow them, you cannot survive their game.*

"She's common as muck," Earle announced, "and he's become tedious. I won't invite him again."

His secretary said quietly, "But you're backing his venture to the—"

Earle frowned. "Enough, Brady. There's always someone else."

"But—"

"Brady, who are you to judge your betters? You've racked up massive gambling debts, and failed to pay them!"

Anna flushed; her father had always warned her that gambling and debt of any sort was a shortcut to ruin.

Earle attempted to kick Brady, who stepped away. The other gentlemen and ladies exchanged glances of repressed amusement. Anna understood Earle's rages were as much a diversion as those who inhabited Bedlam.

"But rumor has it you do not pay your tailor, Mr. Earle," Anna said. "Or your wine merchant, or your butcher, or your cabinet maker, or your…"

This was met by universal laughter. *None of them pay*, she recalled.

Earle waved a dismissive hand. "Ah, I pay the wretches every quarter. Perhaps not as much as they'd like…"

More laughter followed. "You are very bold," Earle said.

Anna tried to take that as a compliment, and dipped a curtsy. "What is that room over there, I wonder?"

"Let me show you," he said.

Anna was aware of the eyes on her as she left with Earle. No sooner had the door closed behind them than Earle took her hand.

Anna stepped back. "Mr. Earle, I would like to address a certain matter…"

He sighed. "You're not going to bore me with business, I hope. You're far too pretty.

"Business of benefit to us both, I hope."

Anna could see his interest fading and decided that her boldness had paid off once already. "I was sent to spy upon you."

"Oh, yes?" He was intrigued now.

"Mr. Oliver Browne of Boston has no love for you. He sent me to find out your weaknesses."

Earle's face hardened at the mention of Browne. "And what shall you tell him?"

"You have a weakness for fine things." She gestured to the room. "You are vulnerable about the heart, with regards to my sex. Word in the coffee houses is you have too many connections in the City and Westminster, in all the world's ports, to be taken unawares. A man with information, and the stomach to use it." She took a deep breath, and offered the last tidbit of information from the invaluable Mr. Nicholas. "Item: your confidential secretary, who owes so many debts, was once your partner."

"You are quick, Mrs. Hoyt." When Earle's face went bland—not bored, not lustful— Anna she knew she'd calculated correctly. "How have you found London?" he asked.

"Very much to my liking. Were it not for my obligations at home, I should be quite happy here."

"Of course, moving from a backwater to the beating heart of the world. What if I were to give you a full and complete list of my weaknesses, which you would convey to Mr. Browne? Perhaps he would be so pleased, he would send you back again. A lady like you could be of use to me."

Anna sighed now. "I should find it hard to live without the means of my...income at home, which is contingent upon me being there."

"You mean you run some kind of shop or public house, you mean. A rum barrel in a hut catering to the Indians in a palm-treed wilderness."

Anna was about to correct him—Indians were not allowed within the city limits of Boston without an armed guard—but realized it didn't matter.

He watched her, and when she did not respond, shook his head. "Never worry, Mrs. Hoyt. I would assist you in your new life. You would know my generosity, and my favor. Think on that. We shall meet later to discuss the particulars. Brady!"

His secretary appeared, and Earle whispered to him. Brady left, only to return with a purse, which Earle handed to Mrs. Hoyt.

"A token of what you may expect, should you decide to stay."

She bowed her head, concealing her triumph.

Business done, he led her to his coach. She extended her hand, and he kissed it.

"Good night, Mrs. Hoyt."

"Thank you, Mr. Earle. I hope we shall meet again soon." She smiled brilliantly.

He nodded thoughtfully, and the coachman clucked to the horses.

＊

Anna clutched the upholstery as the carriage rocked and bounced across the cobbled roads. At first, she could feel nothing, then a throbbing seized her head, numbing it to any other sensation. Her ears rang and her nose ached, as if she'd been punched.

After an eternity, the coach stopped outside her inn. She nodded to the driver, directed the sleepy boy to send hot brandy punch to her room, and then climbed the stairs, holding her skirts carefully.

Once in her room, Anna was ill, her insides griping with panic. When her drink arrived, she forced composure upon herself, and that, with the hot brandy, helped.

She drank deeply, burning her tongue, thinking of Browne and Earle, and her shock at the behavior of her so-called "betters." *The rich have no grace save to the extent they may indulge their depravities,* she suddenly realized. *They create manners and laws to enslave those beneath them with no consequence. They are nothing but silvered tin, but because of a trick of birth I, despite my excellent clothes and modest behavior, am nothing to them.*

One last time, Anna counted the money left from Browne's investment, adding Earle's purse to it. She could leave with Browne's ship, hoping Earle would not follow. She could betray Browne, praying Earle's protection would be enough. Or she could flee them both, forsaking the Queen's Arms, and live comfortably out of the reach of anyone who might ask about Hook Miller. A comfortable life no longer enough, its perceived safety too tenuous. She understood she must constantly improve herself, or she would never survive her dealings with men like Browne and Earle.

She opened her Bible, reading in the Second Book of the Kings about debts. She had been raised to frugalness, to avoid indebtedness at all cost. The story of how the tavern came to her family's possession because of another's financial obligation was a parable engraved on her heart.

After a few moments, she decided. She washed her face and changed into a simple robe, charming in its dishabille. She slipped her small, very sharp clasp knife into her pocket, then checked her looking glass.

She whispered to her reflection, and it was with a fervid vehemence she felt to her bones: "I abjure their power over me. I renounce the illusion of their superiority. I refuse to submit to their order that demands I offer up my survival for their aggrandizement.

"My will," she told her glass, "or none at all."

✳

She had the boy find her a carriage, and just before she arrived back at Earle's house, she reconsidered her intentions. Then she pulled up the hood of her cloak, opened the door and stepped into the dirty snow. Wetness soaked through her thin embroidered silk shoes, but she never felt the cold outside for the cold within.

She knocked softly, the door opened and she was gathered inside. Whiskey-breath and slurred words as hands wandered over her flaxen hair.

Every man exactly the same, she thought.

"My beautiful conspirator," he said. "Welcome."

She could have borne it better if he hadn't spoke. Anna gathered her courage, raised her hand.

Anna undid the knot at her throat, turned her head away and thought of the dress-maker's doll as she felt the silk slip from her shoulder.

✳

"Mistress Hoyt—Anna," Earle said, seated in his parlor several days later. "It's been too long since our last meeting."

Anna found it in herself to blush.

"As you asked, I've sent the rest of my servants away. And Brady can be trusted to keep your secrets." He signaled to the secretary, who poured two glasses of wine. Anna lowered her eyes as she accepted one.

Earle dismissed the man. "What have you decided? I'm not one to stand and wait."

"Thank you, sir." She gathered herself. "I cannot accept your offer."

"No? You've made a bad mistake." He stood and rang a small bell. "And you've made a fool of me, not to answer so before. I should take great care on your way home. The streets can be treacherous—"

Earle grunted and clutched at his back as if with cramp. He winced, lunged forward to his knees, as Mr. Nicholas Brady pulled back his master's hair and plunged his dagger again.

Earle's screams echoed through the empty house. Nicholas Brady sweated and grunted, muttering unintelligibly through clenched teeth as he repeatedly stabbed the other man. Earle twitched and drooled, provoking Brady to use the dagger once more, a sweeping coup de grace.

Blood sprayed in an arc. Anna watched transfixed as it flowed down the hand-painted wallpaper and the marble mantel, running vividly against the pale yellows and whites. The Chinese rug, a veritable flower garden, was forever marred as blood soaked into its fibers.

Without a word, Anna stepped back from the spreading stain. Her shoes were new and embroidered. It would be too great a shame for them to share the fate of the rug. A fortune in that room lost with just a few ounces of blood. Suddenly, the whitewashed walls and dark timbers of the Queen's Arms seemed much more practical than the expensive painted walls.

When Brady raised his hand again, Anna broke from her trance. "Enough, Nicholas. He's dead. You've written the letter?"

"Dated two days ago."

"And you're quite sure the house is empty?"

He glared at her, wiping his hands on the jacket of his dead master. "The rest of the household has been already left for the country house—we were to decamp there to avoid debt prosecution—and they believe me away on another errand."

"And the money you owed him? Your unpaid debt?" She nodded to the dead man on the floor.

Brady scowled, his gray eyes clouded. "Surely he has no use for it now?"

Anna tried not to show her annoyance. "If you wish it believed you discharged your debt and left two days ago, you'll leave that money with the letter."

Brady looked away first, and then pulled a large portion of the money Earle had given Anna from his pocket. "You are right." She watched him leave it in a desk drawer. When he came back, he held out his hand. "The rest of our money?"

Our money. She handed him a bag of Browne's gold, transmuted from the last letter of credit. "We must hurry."

He pulled her close. "We're alone."

"Let us make the most of that, then." She allowed him to kiss her, but she stared, entranced by the blood on the wall. She shrugged out of his embrace. "I will meet you at the Antelope, in Plymouth, in a week."

"And then the world is ours."

She nodded. "It is a long way between us and safety. Do not fail to follow every step of our plan."

He kissed her hands, and she pulled away impatiently. Time was slipping away.

Anna had already packed her trunks and left the west London inn.

After considering how much she'd already spent, and how much she must hold in reserve for her journey, she went to the tailor to pay her balance and make one last purchase. Aghast at her spendthrift use of money and time, she hurried back to the Southwark room and barred her door. Two days before she must leave, she longed for home. She crept onto the bed and pulled her feet tight under her, striving for calm, creating distance between herself and the hateful city.

A knock woke her the next morning. She uncurled painfully, her heart beating loud in her breast. "Leave me be."

"It's your brother, come with urgent news from home, madam," the girl called.

Her two brothers were in the ground next to her parents on Copp's Hill, one killed in a brawl, the other dead of an infection.

Another knock. It had to be Brady. She cursed the love-struck fool for ignoring her instructions. How had he found her?

"A moment," she said, arranging herself. She clutched her Bible close to her. "Come."

It was not Brady. It was Adam Seaver.

"Brother," she said, rising. "What news?"

The maid, satisfied, closed the door behind her.

"You've done Mr. Browne a great service," he said. "News is Earle is dead. His brother, weak-willed as he is, is in the Commons and more partial to Browne now Edward is dead."

"I never touched Mr. Earle, Mr. Seaver."

"Mr. Browne would never ask you to do such a thing, Mrs. Hoyt." It was a gentle reproof.

"Earle was struck down by a vengeful servant, I understand. Mr. Browne asked nothing. I did nothing."

Seaver sat back. "And yet all worked out perfectly well. What a pleasing situation for us all, Mrs. Hoyt."

She bowed her head, praying she'd chosen correctly.

"I'm sure you have expended all the money you were given—to effect so much with so little effort. Browne would not have it said he is ungrateful."

"I am happy to bring Mr. Browne such good news."

"You will be rewarded for it." He handed her a piece of crisp white paper, a letter of credit against Mr. Browne for a sum of money so great she grew dizzy.

Anna smiled a little numbly, ran her thumb over the black ink. Both Earle and Browne were gross monsters, she thought. But she needed one of them, and Browne at least paid his debts. She recalled the instructions in the Book of Kings: *pay thy debt, and live.*

He rose. "You are ready to depart?"

She nodded. "I wish I were home now."

"I have a carriage; gather your things." Seaver paused at the door, surveying her. "That dress suits you admirably. It is entirely disarming. We shall all be very good friends, shall we not, Mrs. Hoyt?"

"I hope so, Mr. Seaver."

Anna waited until the door closed and she heard his footsteps fade. She opened her trunk and saw her last purchase, the tailor's golden-haired model, frozen in a miniature perfection of carriage and dress. She hid the letter of credit under the manikin's dress and leaned over to whisper:

"No need to tell Adam Seaver, Dolly. Nothing I did was for Mr. Browne."

Chapter Three: "Ardent"
March 1746

Having reached a despairing state en route from London to Boston, Anna, as a last resort, found herself in church.

Her legs betrayed her, and she sat down heavily, the roll of heavy winter seas having taught her a different way of walking in the weeks during the passage from London. At least the salt air in the meeting-house was mingled with freshness, without the closeness of shipboard life. The hard plank seat of the pew was welcome because it did not move, the silence of the church a blessing after the unceasing roar of wind and waves.

She was no more than hours away by sail from Boston across Massachusetts Bay, in the village of Eastham. She longed to see her tavern after having labored so hard to preserve her livelihood there. Her trip to London had opened her eyes to the restrictions of rank and sex, the power of learning, and the astonishing ease with which men could be manipulated, even to murder. And while she knew in her heart she belonged in Boston, she also knew that her former life pouring beer for sailors and fishermen was now impossible. She had money, and a glimpse of the wider world that fed a kind of ambition, but for what, she did not know. The question had plagued her over the weeks of travel: If she could not be what she had been, and was not allowed to be what she might want, what would she do?

Once, she'd actually climbed the stairs from her quarters on Mr. Oliver Browne's ship *Indomitable* and gone to the railing, looking at the waves' angry white-capped slate, imagining she might throw herself into the ocean. She hesitated, then would not jump. Why harm herself, when she might turn her anger at those who'd placed her in this position? The men who conspired for her property, the men who would use her quick wit for themselves, the men who made the laws that constrained her as a woman.

The welcome rage sustained her, though she remained desperate.

Just before dawn on the last day, within sight of land, she saw an unholy light. Beautiful tongues of orange and pink and green stretched out into the sky, and Anna realized she watched a building burning.

"Someone's lost money tonight," said Adam Seaver. "We must stop here, to attend business. They'll put us ashore."

No doubt the business was on behalf of their mutual benefactor and employer, Mr. Browne. Still answerless, Anna was neither relieved nor angered by the delay; she merely nodded.

But the Sunday morning bustle at their inn reminded her of her own establishment. She glanced at the exquisitely dressed manikin on her room's table, but Dolly had no comfort for her. And when she turned to her well-worn Bible for instruction, her eyes so blurred she could not read. Denied this, she pulled on her blue velvet cloak and left.

The village was set against sandy dunes on a sheltered harbor created by a spit of land that curled protectively against the bay. Outside the inn, she saw a crowd standing around the burnt ruin of the building she'd seen from the ship. No more fiery beauty here. Heavy timbers burned to charcoal jutted out from the collapsed wreckage against the clear sky, like so many black marks on a blotter. The oily smell of the fire raised the hairs on the back of her neck: the destruction of fire was too common an occurrence in life. Turning away from the gathered townspeople, Anna saw a man in a towering fury shaking a boy half his size. The child's thin arms and legs practically rattled with the movement, and tears streamed down his filthy face.

"You little shit of a liar!" Flecks of spittle flew from the man's lips. "First you say you saw a man, then a girl. Which is it?"

"Both!"

The man dropped the boy, and kicked him until his anger was dissipated and the boy stopped moving.

Anna shook her head. She walked until she found the meetinghouse by the creek.

She did not pray over her questions. And she didn't have it in her to ask for favor. The church was only another container for her emptiness. She went through the rituals absently, without solace.

But there was information to be had. The vehemence of the sermon, drawn from Leviticus, about the land turning to whoredom, alerted Anna. The red and sweating face of the preacher, and his steadfast refusal to look anywhere near the lovely lady in the third row confirmed it. The preacher would have chosen a milder topic if he hadn't been caught doing something he shouldn't.

Two women in front of Anna barely concealed their amusement. "Come Monday," one whispered to the other, "she'll be right back at it. Where else would our betters get their release?"

Their gossip ceased only when the churchwarden raised his eyebrows. Anna added this observation to her present perplexity. The lady who seemed to be the object of the sermon hadn't asked permission to ply her trade. She was in church, nodding with the best of them, free to ignore the implications. She was certainly prosperous, in one of the better pews, modestly but finely dressed.

She makes her way well enough, asking no leave of anyone, Anna thought. *If it is my will I am determined to serve, what do I want?*

As the preacher delved into the exact nature of the hellfire that awaited sinners, Anna stood, ready to leave. There was nothing for her here, only more men with more words to shape the world for themselves. She had to leave or go mad.

Something stopped her, and she almost rebelled against it, but pausing showed her the reason. Out the window, she saw him peering in furtively. Blond hair, more ash gray now, but the same face. The same cant to the shoulders, an old injury never healed, but so recognizable, so dear.

Anna sat, smoothing out her gown, as if it was all she'd meant to do. She put her head down on clasped hands.

Her eyes closed, she had but one thought, as urgent as prayer, over and over:

Look at me.

She tilted her head, still on her hands, and opened her eyes.

He saw her. The intake of breath, the widening eyes revealed his recognition, and confirmed her suspicion.

Not dead. Not lost.

Restored to her. A miracle.

Emotions in a flood of memories, good and sweet and sad. Suddenly, Anna had a reason to keep searching for her answers.

✳

After the final hymn, she got up and walked away from the congregation, moving in the direction he'd indicated. She saw him vanish into a slender stand of trees by the churchyard, beyond sight of the parishioners. Slowing by the gravestones to see whether she was observed, she followed him through the late winter snow.

He was hunkered down against a tree, waiting for her. His face, like his calloused and work-stained hands, was older, and browned with the sun. His face kept from fae beauty due to the scars of his work and weathering, but well-formed, nonetheless. Once they had been thought a match for each other: her blonde hair fine and light, his thick and unruly, until a misunderstanding with an employer sent Bram far away, never to return.

Anna stepped forward. He rose and clasped her shoulders, peering into her face.

"It is you."

She nodded. "It is."

"I thought it was some dream, seeing you."

"I thought you were a thousand miles away, Bram Munroe, making your fortune. How do you come to be so close to home?"

"Ill fortune at every turn kept me tethered here, Anna, and betrayals kept me from returning to Boston. I would not let my bad luck follow me to you."

They embraced. It started to rain, with heavy, cold drops, and she shivered. They both laughed.

"I'm a respectable widow, now. There's no shame in being seen together near a warm fire." This much freedom she had, at least. The gift of a kingdom.

He nodded, but didn't move. "I'd not tarnish our meeting— a public disagreement with my former employer. A trifle, but seeing him would sour the moment."

"But...you are well?"

"The better for seeing you, Anna."

A shadow moving beyond the trees. Seaver, walking to the inn.

Anna collected herself; he could not have seen them. "I cannot stay. Tell me where to meet you, and I'll find you later."

"There is a shack just off the road on the beach. Meet me there, late, tonight." He pressed her hand to his lips. "Oh, Anna."

"Tonight."

For the first time in many weeks, Anna smiled.

✳

Here, then, was what she'd been waiting for, the reason she'd continued when all seemed lost. A fresh start with an old love, plenty of money, and new ideas. The Queen would not be a coffin confining her; Bram and her fortune would transform her old life.

These happy thoughts fled as she entered the inn. Adam Seaver was sprawled out before the large fire, boots off, a pewter mug large enough to stave in a man's head on the table by his side. It was a cold day and there was room enough around the fire for the other patrons, but they found places away from Seaver. Perhaps they knew him, perhaps not, Anna thought. Knowing Adam Seaver personally was not necessary to understand how dangerous he was, if one had eyes to see and a brain to reason.

He seemed to sense her arrival, for he opened his eyes to slits, then sat up. "Mistress Hoyt."

There was no avoiding him, now. On the ship, she'd kept to herself, pleading illness, and he had been satisfied with that.

"Mr. Seaver."

"You look very well." He stretched and looked more closely. "Sermons agree with you."

He couldn't have seen us, she thought. She looked straight at him. "I'm glad to be off the ship."

"You'll dine with me tomorrow. We have business."

"*We* have no business. Mr. Browne asked for you to stop."

Seaver raised an eyebrow at this bald rebellion. Before, when he had spoken to Anna, it had been as Mr. Browne himself had done so. He shrugged. "I would consider it a kindness, then, if you would."

There were no manners from Adam Seaver that did not conceal worse things. Anna understood she'd gone too far, too quickly. "Of course."

"I stop to collect on a debt, but the gentleman we dine with has many problems that keep him—repeatedly—from paying Mr. Browne. I admire your ability to understand people. And I know Mr. Browne does."

"I am happy to help," she said.

"Tomorrow evening, then. Across the harbor, the old tavern on Great Island." Seaver flashed a brief, broken smile, no more warm than it was lovely, and settled back to doze.

I'll help, this one last time, Anna thought. *Then we're done. I'll be my own woman, with the man I've always loved, and I'll no more of you.*

✳

She arrived at the shack after dark, her heart aloft. She carried a large jug, filled with rum, which swung heavily against her skirts. She tapped lightly on the door and let herself in.

Bram was on her in an instant, sweeping up high, so her gown brushed the narrow walls and her hair grazed the ceiling. He stumbled, his boot causing a clank of glass bottles to roll on the tamped earth floor, and nearly overturned the candle that lit the small room.

"Anna, Anna, 'tis the very fates bring us together now." He set her down and restored the candle carefully with a kind of reverence, then kissed her wrists.

The mere touch reminded her of the days before he left Boston. The very sight of him sent Anna's head swimming and made her heart giddy. A brush of his lips was enough to drive every thought away. If it had not been for his abrupt, necessary departure, they would have been married.

She found herself eager for him. With her husband, intercourse had been the price for protection and enlarging her business. Although there had been no one of consequence since Thomas, she'd long ago forgotten the act might be for other than bargaining.

*

Later, he sighed. "You're the only one who's ever understood. No other man or woman could see me for what I am."

"Surely there've been others who've recognized your qualities."

"Never. Every time, every place, I found nothing but louts, ignorance, a desire for the mediocre. No appreciation for artistry."

"Such brilliance, to be ignored!" She put her hand on his shoulder, suppressing a smile. "They little knew they abused a lord among smiths!"

He pinched her hand playfully. "You mock me, I fear."

"I don't! I know the excellence of your hinges and bolts."

"I am Vulcan! My hammer and tongs forge miracles! The coals and heat are quick to obey me!" He laughed with her. "Drink to me, now, my love!"

Tilting the jug to Anna's mouth, he sloshed the liquor over her lips. The dark spirits ran over her chin, sharp, sweet and sticky. With his tongue, Bram traced its path across her jaw and down her throat, burying his face in the lace at the top of her gown.

She shifted under him, trying to find a comfortable spot in the lumpy pallet. Anna sighed with happiness, intoxicated with love.

*

They woke in each other's arms. Bram rolled over, cradled his head, moaning, but made a brave show of it when Anna looked at him.

"It's nothing. A pounding head is a small price to pay for such a reunion."

"We'll be in Boston in two days," she said. The hopefulness that attended the thought was a sensation virtually forgotten since he'd left so abruptly five years ago. "I'll set you up there in a shop of your own."

He nodded eagerly. "It will be good to be back where I belong, back among the embers, bending metal to my will." He hesitated. "Anywhere else but Boston, though. I have enemies there."

"How so?" she said, smiling. "It's not possible. An age since you left, and all unpleasantness long forgotten, I'm sure."

"Alas, my former master—in title only!"

"Who is this man? I'll have him run out of town." She was proud to realize she had some influence, a way to solve his problems for him.

"Bah, a bully of the first order, and he is dead, thank God. But his cousin, the one who threatened me, has a long memory, and a longer reach. A wretch the name of—Owen? Oliver. Oliver Browne."

Anna's heart seemed to stop beating for a long moment, before it resumed with a painful thump. She almost laughed: once again, Browne stood between her and happiness. Always Browne between her and what she wanted most, and he held what he knew about her actions to keep her in thrall.

"But it is no matter," he continued. Anna barely registered that Bram was talking as she forced her anger down. "We can go anywhere else, and be happy."

She thought again of her tavern. Must she choose between the Queen and Bram? Impossible; there was nothing to be gained by asking aloud. Anna nodded, smiled and dressed, and with a heavy soul and a newly-aching head, she made sure no one was about as she slipped away to her room.

✳

Had Samuel Stratton walked into the Queen's Arms, Anna would have nodded welcome, as to anyone else, and offered him one of the better chairs. Then she would have signaled her man, Josiah Ball, who would address the more volatile regulars, finding pretext to send them home. She would go about her business, pausing only to make sure the cudgel she kept behind her bar was at hand when violence broke out. Something in Stratton's carriage, and that of men like him, alerted her, like dark clouds and a drop in the barometer told of a storm. If Adam Seaver was a man to rely quietly on his reputation, retaliating privately and viciously, Samuel Stratton wore his aggression as a cloak, flourishing it at every opportunity, spoiling for trouble.

She recognized him as the man who had beaten the boy.

Stratton looked well enough—tall and hale and dark—and he seated her with a gruff and rusty courtesy. This she understood was a rarity, a gesture to Seaver's presence and Browne's influence. It extended only that far, for as soon as the tavern-keeper's wife deposited their dinner on the table and left, he ignored Anna and turned to Seaver.

"My works have been bedeviled of late. My still and stores were destroyed in the fire, and I can't supply Mr. Browne nor pay him his interest until I rebuild. If you'd convey that to him, I'd be obliged." Stratton used his knife to joint the roast bird, and then forswore cutlery as he ate the wing, using the table cloth to wipe his fingers. "I may be delayed for months."

Seaver helped Anna to a plate of oysters but took nothing for himself. "And the nature of this devilry?"

"Petty theft, and worse: arson and murder. My head distiller, Goodchild, was burned alive, trapped in the building when it went up."

Suddenly Anna was reminded of another fire long ago. Just before Bram had left his place of work, his master's dwelling. Remembered the smith's scientific obsession with fire, the principal tool of his trade.

"Someone has a grudge against you," Seaver said. The humor in his words suggested this was no surprise.

Stratton only grunted. "Someone will pay for it, when I find 'em." He threw the bones down and rubbed his greasy hands together. The light in his eyes caused Anna to turn to her plate. "I think I know who it is. A little weasel I thought I could get cheap for labor. A smith with ideas too big for him. I'll string him up by his balls, and when I'm done with him, hungry seagulls won't touch what's left."

Bram. Panic seized Anna. Yet another instance in which Oliver Browne was tangled up in her affairs, and always to her detriment.

"Interesting," Seaver said. "I'd like to inspect the site. I'm required in Boston shortly, but I would present a full report of your troubles to Mr. Browne, and your request to—once again—delay payment."

At this invocation of Browne's name, Stratton grew less agitated, more unsure. "Thank you."

❋

Anna and Seaver left shortly thereafter, claiming fatigue, and returned to their inn across the harbor.

"What think you of our host?" Seaver extracted his pipe and tobacco pouch, once they were seated.

"He lacks...economy. I saw him beat a boy almost to death, when he could have had the information he wanted for a piece of bread and bacon fat."

Seaver shrugged. "And the current matter?"

Anna spoke carefully. She had too clear a memory of Bram's former master, who was Oliver Browne's kinsman, watching his house burn down, after he'd crossed Bram. "He's either lying or mistaken."

"How so?"

"Thieves don't set fires; they don't want to get caught. The fire was an accident, or perhaps he set the fire himself, having removed the equipment first, to save paying what he owes Mr. Browne while secretly distilling elsewhere."

"I see." Seaver considered. "The man killed inside?"

"Accidental or intentional, the fire covers the deed. Do you think Stratton cares about anything but his profit?"

"I think you are right, Mrs. Hoyt." He rose and grinned. He did not truly smile, as his teeth were not made to express happiness. "I shall examine the place. Thank you for your opinion."

She nodded good night, not trusting her voice, and climbed to her room.

The door was ajar.

Her heart quickened. *It mustn't be Bram, not here... Too close to Stratton, too close to Browne...*

She rested her hand against the door, as if to discern his presence, then pushed it open.

A movement by the curtain. Anna took two steps to the table and her Bible. She picked it up, and from the recently repaired binding, withdrew a strong, slender blade. The steel was German, sharp and bright, flat for concealment in the spine of the book, something she'd acquired in London.

Holding it behind her skirts, she said, "Who's there? Show yourself!"

The curtains twitched again, and a bedraggled girl, barely twenty, stepped out. "Please. It's only me."

Anna knew the inn's household; this girl was no part of it. "Who are you? What are you doing here? I have no time for thieves."

"I'm Clarissa. Please...I need...take me away from here. "

The smell of molasses and charcoal and sugar burnt to acid assailed Anna's nose. "You're the one Stratton is looking for. You started the fire."

The girl straightened herself, jutted her chin out. "I didn't. I have money, I can pay my way, I just need help—"

Her sureness, her lack of servility, immediately set Anna against her. "Money you stole."

Clarissa shook her head. "My own," she said haughtily. "I stole nothing."

"Show me."

The girl unknotted a stained handkerchief. It was filled with small coins, the sort of sum accumulated with great care over a long time. A pair of new pieces of silver shone among them.

"You lie! You are a thief." Anna took a step forward and slapped the girl twice, hard. "Those two you stole. "

Clarissa's face burned, but she held Anna's glance. "It's mostly my own, with whatever was in the man's pockets. Exactly what I was owed—and if I kept the stillery running while he was sunk in drink, shouldn't I have my wages? Goodchild wouldn't pay me."

"So you killed him?"

"An accident. In defense of my own person, when he tried to take advantage. And when I saw he didn't get up, I knew I'd have to leave here forever. He had no more use for the money."

"And the fire?"

"I know nothing about it, I swear."

Anna waited for the truth. Two lies already...

Clarissa relented. "The door opened, another man came in. I hid. I watched him pull apart the still and strike a light to a barrel of spirits. I got out as soon as I could." She shivered. "I was not certain he would ever leave, he stared at the flames so." She held out the money again. "I only need help. I can pay!"

"Why come here?"

"You stood out, on your way to church. With your fine clothes and cloak, you weren't here to stay. I thought you might need a lady's maid. And you're a stranger."

"I dined with Mr. Stratton tonight. A stranger to these parts, but not unknown."

The girl blanched. "Then let me leave."

Anna turned and barred the door. "Sit. I may have use for you."

She glanced at Dolly, cold and mute, on the table as she opened her Bible. She let the book fall open where it would, and began to read in Proverbs, the twentieth verse of the twenty-sixth chapter: *Where no wood is, there the fire goeth out; so where there is no talebearer, the strife ceases.*

Anna sighed and stared at Clarissa, with her fanciful name, probably made-up or worse, Catholic. The girl had not moved all the while. She'd admitted killing Stratton's distiller and had witnessed Bram setting the fire. She had a grievance against Stratton, but given his temper, she must have been canny enough to hide this and survive life in his service.

Anna needed to save Bram from Stratton, and Browne—who'd been foxing her life even before she knew him. She opened a trunk, studied the bottles there, selected one, and left the girl in the room, locking the door behind her.

✳

Anna could not see for the tears in her eyes, as she stumbled toward Bram's shack, splashing along the sandy shore. The salt water soaked her skirts, making them heavier and heavier, as if clutching fingers were dragging her down. The more she moved, the more difficult it became, but she slogged on until she reached the path. She sat exhausted, on the vertebra of one of the great whales they fished and slaughtered here; the place was never free of the fetid stench. She stared at the moon, wishing it would strike her blind or remove the terrible choices before her. A few miles to the east was the wild ocean, stretching for a world away, seething, chaotic, but ripe to explore. Here, calmer waters separated her and home and all she knew too well. She sat between them to choose.

She could not hand Bram over to Seaver and Stratton.

Could not bring him home to Boston, and the possibility that Mr. Browne would discover him, punish him for his acts against his family.

She could not abandon the Queen's Arms, leave with Bram, forsake what she had. It was little enough, but hard-won and more than she'd ever dreamed of.

She thought for another hour, shivering under the moonlight. She got up, heavily, and walked toward the shack where Bram was sleeping. She unlatched the door, now knowing the trick of keeping it silent, and pulled it closed behind her. She watched him by the light of a guttering candle, asleep on the old pallet, snoring, as she struggled with the hooks and lacings of her sodden clothes. With patient fingers she worked, and then, naked and numb, she slipped under the covers next to him.

He stirred, shuddered awake, but smiled when he saw her. "I was dreaming of you. And now you're here, conjured from the sea." He started. "You're cold as the grave—"

She put her hand on his mouth and climbed on top of him, feeling his warm body beneath her.

An hour later, when it was quiet and they could hear the wintry rain on the roof of the shack, Bram kissed Anna on the back of the neck.

In response, she reached for his hand and kissed each finger. Her lips slid down past his knuckle. He sighed, contented.

She eased the ring off his index finger, slid it onto her own, then looked into his eyes.

"I heard Samuel Stratton is looking for you. I won't let him have you," she said. "We'll run away, to New York. There's a ship tomorrow night."

He sat up. "Let us go *now*! I can find a horse—"

"No, be patient. Did you know Stratton owes a great debt to Oliver Browne?"

Bram clutched his head in his hands. "No. No, no..."

"I must keep them from you forever. Can you trust me to do that? I have a plan, and will come aboard the ship at the last minute, just before it sails."

He stared at her, then dropped his head in agreement. "Anna, you must take care. If anything should happen to you, I'd die." He held his hand over the flame of the candle until a blister raised. "I swear it."

She hesitated, then nodded. "I understand. But you must trust me."

"With my life."

She found the bottle she'd brought with her and offered it. "Drink to it, then."

As Anna left, Bram was still and silent. She hadn't realized what hope did to a person, until this moment. Unrealistic expectation coupled with...something foreign. Optimism.

It was terrible. She wept as she found her way back to her room.

The next day, Anna returned to Boston and the Queen's Arms, and found it much the same as before she'd left for London, under the watchful eye of her man Josiah Ball. He had been devoted to Anna's father since that gentleman had helped him escape a naval impressment gang, out to seize any able-bodied men they could find for unwilling and compulsory service in His Majesty's Navy. Josiah, well aware of his good fortune in avoiding them, had continued to show that same devotion to Anna and handled the heavy lifting and peace-making.

As welcome as its familiarity, the tavern's walls seemed to press in around her, leaving her breathless.

All was well, but not yet to her liking.

If she had given up Bram, not willing to relinquish the small fortune and cupful of power she'd carefully amassed, neither was she ready to return to drawing beer and measuring rum. By choosing to thwart Stratton—and Browne—she'd chosen more than her old life.

There was no certainty in life. She'd learned the power of social barriers in London, but she'd learned how laws could be winked at and public esteem maintained by the respectable whore in church.

So *more* it must be, and by her choice and will, if she could not have *certainty* in her life.

But carefully, carefully. She would never be free of Browne, but she might learn to work...in his margins. Alongside him, if not beneath him.

In the next days, she went to the merchant Rowe about the purchase of a piece of his land outside the city. They shook hands after negotiating; he had a faint smile on his face. Hers was quite determined. It would be the first of many such purchases she'd make. She had plans of her own.

Anna sat at her desk, entered the transaction in her ledger, then drafted a note to the lawyer Clark, giving him a chance to redeem himself for betraying her to her dead husband's friends. She outlined instructions about the purchase, asking him to find a second-hand copper still for her, ordering one new, if necessary. She considered where she might find a small building to house it and who she would employ in her future enterprises. She drew a list. It was short, but every one reliable.

There was a knock at her door. The taproom boy Silas was there, announcing a visitor. His eyes were wide.

Seaver? It might be a short career, then, if he had discovered her betrayal. She looked to the little blonde manikin, and asked, "Dolly, what is the right lie?"

The caller was Clarissa.

The girl looked much better for a change of air and dress. Fresh-scrubbed and the gray under her eyes gone, her cheeks rosy and black hair gleaming, she was more than presentable, the picture of modesty. Better, she was unrecognizable, even in Anna's blue velvet cloak.

"Mr. Munroe took my absence well?" Anna asked.

Clarissa laughed.

Anna shrugged, surprised at how little she felt now, only glad her plan worked. "But he didn't get off the ship?"

"Oh no, he's gone. And he won't dare come to Boston, now that he believes you left his ring at the site of the fire for Mr. Seaver and Mr. Stratton to find. He cursed you, roundly and foully. Even threatened to kill you—I wasn't sure I'd escape his rage—but the money you paid the captain was enough to keep him on board, while I slipped back ashore. He won't show himself here."

Anna nodded, trying not to look at her battered Bible. There was a slight gap between the pages in the middle, where she'd hidden Bram's ring. "Where no wood is, there the fire goeth out."

"What's that?"

"From Proverbs. You can read?"

Clarissa nodded.

Anna hesitated. She needed help to expand her livelihood beyond the tavern, varying her endeavors so that her fortunes would not rely solely on the Queen's Arms. All this was now possible thanks to the money she'd had from Mr. Browne and Mr. Earle. Clarissa had a knack for distilling, owed her much, and was bright enough. Perhaps she would do.

"Start with this, then." She handed Clarissa a new Bible, one she'd bought for public show, rather than her old heavy Bible. It seemed fitting, somehow, that she should outfit her new employee as she had been, with a Bible. Perhaps one day, Clarissa would earn the right to keep a ledger for Anna. "You'll need to read, if you're to work for me, and you'll find many answers here."

Chapter Four: "Declaration"
July 1746

The only notice Anna took of the spring progressing into summer was the need to change from her quilted wool skirts into lighter gowns. She was grateful for the long days and extra hours of sunlight. Her new distillery venture was completed and working; she'd been fortunate to buy a still and shed for a good price from a widow who was leaving Boston for good and had no love for the man who had been her husband's competitor.

"As if I'd sell him the very gear my dear Henry Russell used!" the widow proclaimed. "He'd say the most slanderous things, trying to run down our business. No, I'll gladly sell to you, Mrs. Hoyt, and if you have the chance to do Mr. Ross dirty and get away with it, you do it with my blessing."

Both parties were more than satisfied with the deal. Mrs. Russell was so pleased to leave Boston behind her and do a further disservice to Mr. Ross that she left Anna a few barrels of the last winter's applejack, which Anna sampled with Clarissa to determine whether it could be improved.

To Anna's great delight, Clarissa told her that the equipment she'd purchased was far better than that she'd worked for Mr. Stratton's distiller, and that a few modifications of time and heat would bring an even better result next time. She was brimming with ideas and Anna was elated by the girl's enthusiasm and ambition, agreeing to supply the necessary materials and ingredients.

Clarissa's industry endeared her to Anna, who felt a kindred spirit in the younger woman. Clarissa had been more than happy with the clothing Anna had given her from her own trunks and had expressed gratitude for every little kindness and reward. The shared work and common goals were a true bond between them, and Anna marveled several times at just how much a good example, a little kindness and a little extra money could make in a family's life.

Anna worked harder than she ever had in her life. In addition to the daily operation of the Queen's Arms, she had the distillery to manage and, now, several small pieces of property she'd acquired on her return to Boston. Her outlay for the new undertakings terrified her, sound as they might be, and that drove her harder.

"Why take on so much all at once?" Prudence King asked one evening over a jug of beer. They had been friends since girlhood and took pleasure in each other's company. "You're killing yourself, Anna."

"Prudence, I'm not." Anna leaned back, tired, watching the hot summer sun finally set. "It won't be long now until the distillery shows some profit—small, to start, but it's a game of patience while the spirits age. In the meantime, the properties have been repaired and rented out, so I'm seeing much more income already from them. The start of anything takes dedication, an initial investment of my time, that is all."

Seeing that her friend was not convinced, Anna added, "It will not be much longer before things are running themselves. You're kind to worry about me."

"The tavern isn't in trouble, is it?" Prudence asked. Her dark brown skin glistened with sweat in the candle light. "Is that why you're so busy, doing the work of three men?"

Anna was silent for a long time. Prudence was only a handful of years older than she, nearly thirty, and had grown up in Boston. She too was acutely aware that earthquakes, fire, storms, plagues and any sort of calamity might beset the city in an instant. The poorhouse was filled with those who couldn't support themselves, and neither of the friends had any intention of being one of those poor souls.

"All is well with the tavern. I merely work for my widowhood and old age, to provide against any mischance. We both understand that fortune is fickle, and strive to live." She took a sip of beer and gazed at her friend over her mug. "Not so different from you working by candlelight and firelight, straining your eyes to increase your profitable work."

Prudence slapped her knee, sloshing her beer as she laughed. "You have the right of me, Anna. We are both blessed—or cursed—with the knowledge that we don't know what the future holds and are on guard against it."

"A week or two more," Anna said. "Then I'll be able to rest."

Several days later, news came of an attack upon the distillery. The miscreant took nothing, but Anna's anger could not have been greater.

The intrusion was marked only by the cracked window and the scatter of grain across the floor of the brick-walled distilling shed, along with tools that had been deliberately broken. The grain, spoiled in a most foul way, was gathered up and burned. Still, Anna paced among the barrels of molasses long after she'd set her broom aside and dispatched her boy Silas and Clarissa to find replacement tools and a new pane for the window. Although spring had turned to summer, dry and fine, Anna knew that carefully maintaining the conditions in the distillery was critical.

So perhaps "trespasser" or "mischief-maker" was more apt than "thief," but with her time ill-used and her temper black, Anna felt herself robbed.

She might have been content to consider the vandalism the work of vagrants and drunkards or some youthful prank but for two facts.

First, Anna and her tavern, the Queen's Arms, were protected by the esteem in which they were held. In return for her hospitality, men were quick to take up her part.

But, other men, more powerful than the rest, had been seen there recently.

Secondly, Anna's reliable neighbor, Prudence King, had spied a man exiting in a hasty fashion, leaving the door off its latch. When questioned further, Mrs. King said she had assumed he had early work with Clarissa, else she would have cried out at the sight of him.

If he'd been intending to steal the applejack, he was far too late: The barrels had been in her warehouse since early spring. If the rum, then he was too early, as the molasses were not even measured out. And Clarissa had had no chance to experiment with the rye she had purchased. To steal the massive copper still, the thief had been woefully unprepared, with no horse, no tools, no cart. And yet there were marks, where heavy blows had been struck against the body of it and the cap had been knocked off.

All had been done to interrupt her commerce. She needed to find out who'd been responsible.

Of late, she'd heard rumbles about her keen interest in distilling. All well and good, Dame Rumor cried, if she continued as a tavern-keeper after her husband's death. It was a decent enough trade for a woman—keeping a local tavern open was good for the neighborhood and kept another widow off the alms list. Making real money was another matter. Unseemly.

Anna bridled when the unwary or the uninformed assumed she inherited the tavern from Thomas. The Queen's Arms had always been her family's, ever since her father and his partner took ownership of it.

She might have dismissed the grumbling—there was *always* grumbling, there always *would* be grumbling. A woman was always too bold, too shy, too pretty, too plain, too clever, too dull; she might as well whistle for the wind as satisfy the world's opinion of her. Anna respected the confines of social comment and had always taken care to work within its lists. She also knew a certain leeway existed. Some of her behavior might be winked at in exchange for other considerations.

But the break-in had a different cast than mere caviling or envy; it was direct, personal, and hostile.

Anna did not care for such specific complaint. It drew scrutiny, which was the enemy of discretion, and discretion was as gold to her.

She resolved to address the situation. She needed information.

Two names were offered by Mrs. King. John Griswold owned a nearby establishment and had always offered Anna too low of a price for her tavern in an attempt to drive her out. George Tanner himself was a comparative stranger to Anna, but said by many—including his own brother—to be no friend of hers. Anna shrugged; the deeply religious or anyone else who disapproved of her establishment either left her alone or railed against her—until some friend of hers corrected their opinion of her and her place. Often this correction was made with rhetoric of the gutter, but sometimes, more firmly, with a barrel stave or gaffing hook.

Anna privately added a third and fourth names for consideration. She wondered about Mr. Ross, he who was so eager to purchase the distilling equipment himself from the widow Russell.

And finally, Anna saw no reason for Mr. Oliver Browne to have any quarrel with her new occupation. Indeed, he should know nothing of it, for Anna had worked to conceal it from him, deliberately going to other merchants for her supplies. While he had many spies, why should he take an interest in the small efforts she made? And if he did, he had no cause to dispute them, so long as she took care not to intrude on his matters or trammel his sensibilities. Moreover, this paltry vandalism was so far from his familiar signature of studied violence as to be ridiculous.

However, Anna had recently learned the virtues of considering Mr. Browne a factor in everything she did: He simply was not to be trifled with. Anna had learned this to her profit and to her fear. While she could not fathom his potential interest in her property, she knew it wise to consider that it might exist.

On her way back to the Queen, Anna cast an eye to the bar to see that all was well, and being satisfied, climbed to her chamber. She drew out her Bible and, closing her eyes, let it fall open where it would. The binding was cracked and deteriorating. Pages were nearly transparent, so thin and old, and they fell with a dry flutter. The holy book had an odor of aging leather, polished with a century of handling, and some hint of a spice Anna could not quite identify. She accounted the odor as being a relic of the past before her family's custodianship of the Bible.

The passage she opened her eyes to was the last verse of Proverbs Thirty-One.

She shook her head and glanced at the tailor's model on the table. Dolly, as blonde as Anna, and perfectly turned out in the latest fashion, was regally disdainful in the half-light. Anna had been as well dressed as the doll, indeed, as well as any lady in London, but on her return to Boston had resumed her usual dress: pretty, but tidy and decent rather than grand. Although she'd changed a great deal in recent months during her travels, Anna had found she slipped back to her customary roles with as much ease as a seal slid into the harbor. None observing her in her daily affairs would suspect how her travels had affected her, inside and out. Anna had risked much, won and learned a great deal. It would not do to have her neighbors suspect that she saw the world through different eyes, that she viewed them as something apart from her. Best to keep her secret to herself and make of it what she could while she could.

"Dolly, what is this? 'Give her the fruit of her hands, and let her own works praise her in the gates?' I made a fine show of myself in London, and might have stayed, happily situated, there. But now home, I work my fingers raw, and none yet sing my praises but thirsty men for all my modest work. Indeed, more are now against my efforts, it seems. That was no praise today in my still house, certainly."

She slammed her Bible shut, her mouth creased in a frown. "Nothing but riddles for me here."

Dolly remained impassive. Anna envied her the proud bearing of the doll: None would doubt she intended to rule all who saw her. Anna wished for the same lack of hesitation.

No satisfaction in her book, Anna turned her mind to more

worldly themes and her ledger. If John Griswold or George Tanner was responsible for the damage to her still, she knew how she might proceed. If it was Mr. Browne or his agents who had disrupted her work, she was uncertain.

Easiest to address the first two gentlemen. No need to draw Mr. Browne's attention unless absolutely necessary.

✳

Mr. George Tanner was not hard to find. His vegetable stall was the last, at the far end of the row, not far from the market's waste heap, which was even now attracting a swarm of buzzing flies that multiplied as the sun rose in the sky.

"Mr. Tanner."

Tanner, bone thin with wisps of gray hair across his head and in tufts at his ears and nose, was occupied culling the rotten vegetables. He grunted and turned to Anna, with a handful of moldy potatoes. Recognizing her, he grunted again, and returned to his work.

"Mr. Tanner, did you have some business near my establishment this morning? Early, before full light?"

He continued to ignore her and turned only to fling the potatoes to the growing refuse heap.

"Mr. Tanner!"

"Why would I bother with the likes of you and the poison you sell? You're responsible for all my earthly woes!"

Anna, who had been prepared for a great many responses, was taken aback. "And how do you count that, when you've never been to my tavern?"

"My brother Roger stops by your place to get a skinful. If he hadn't been drunk—on your wares—I wouldn't have had to take the cart home that day. If I hadn't been driving, it would have been *him* tipped over on the road, *his* foot crushed under the wheel."

Anna followed his eyes down, to a grimy bandage over a stump where the greater part of his left foot had once been. She was quite perplexed by this outpouring of vitriol and illogic.

"The doctor says I was lucky to keep the leg," he said. "So the misery of my house is on you—"

Anna held up a hand. "More like it's on your brother for drinking too much. I'm not his conscience, and not yours, neither, but he told me the story—even *he* knows I've nothing to do with your problems. If you were so worried, why didn't you come get him an hour earlier? And what makes you such an infant, you can't handle an old horse with a vegetable cart? My old ma could manage one of those, and she was no bigger than a child *and* missing an eye. Or why not spend the night in the cart, under canvas? Wouldn't be the first time, from what I've heard of the two of you, because if you're too good to step inside the Queen, you're not above keeping a jug of cheap rum next to you. No, 'the misery of your house' is square on you, and no sensible person would say otherwise."

A crowd was gathering, eager for spectacle.

"I can only sit here and sell my vegetables." He snuffled. "I've no life at all now."

"Another man might have traded for a better spot, or gotten up earlier, or fought for a stall closer to the center of the market and farther from the rubbish heap," Anna said, before she could think. "You're a man, aren't you? You've a limp, is all, but also land and a house, and that's more than most. So you're as much as you want to be, and that no fault of mine."

Having no other answer, Tanner threw a handful of moldy potatoes at Anna.

Anna, too familiar with the intentions of the maudlin and the angry, skipped back and dodged the barrage. The potatoes landed hard on the uneven ground, spattering one or two unwary souls with rotten muck. They answered with curses. This was all to the amusement of the growing crowd of spectators.

"You were ever the wit," Anna said. "I cannot match you. Good morning to you, Mr. Tanner! Always a pleasure to pass the time of day."

She made a shallow curtsy and retreated, followed by scattered applause and whistles of derision for Tanner. She glanced about the assemblage: The majority took her part. It never hurt to consider the market and take its gauge, for one's reputation was a commodity and worth measuring. Like any good, its value rose or dipped with the times.

Her eyes caught those of the tavern owner John Griswold and found no friendship there. She ducked her head as he approached her and put three stalls' distance between them in an instant as she hurried away.

Avoiding Mr. Griswold, Anna slowed her pace to normal. Glancing back, all eyes were turned on George Tanner, who was now at odds with those who'd been in the way of his vegetable salvo.

She was almost to the door to her tavern when Adam Seaver stepped out from the alley into her way. The impact of his body was so great it stole her breath. Anna would have tumbled into the street had he not caught her by the elbow and steadied her.

Perhaps he had meant to jostle her; Anna was not certain. She was always uncertain when it came to Adam Seaver, but Seaver had saved her life at least once and had been the instrument of much of her good fortune in spite of Mr. Browne.

His surprise and concern were equal to her own, or else he was the best actor who ever lived. If Anna hadn't been so accustomed to the occasional acts of violence in her tavern, fights that broke out with the abrupt speed of lightning cracking and the force of a gale, she might not have noticed his other hand snaking under his coat, replacing a knife there.

A sharp voice cut through the noise of the street. "Mistress Hoyt! Mind those cobbles, with your pretty new shoes!"

Anna looked up. Mrs. King, waved from the window across the way, her face contrasting against the crisp white linen and bright ribbon of her dainty cap.

"Mind you, those cobbles are slick as cat shit!" Mrs. King hooted, waved again when Anna indicated all was well, and withdrew from her window.

When Anna turned to Mr. Seaver, she found him staring at Mrs. King's window, peculiarly vexed. "Your neighbor follows the doings of the street and is free with her advice," he said.

"Yes." Suddenly Anna wondered if the knife hadn't been meant for her and Mrs. King spoiled Adam Seaver's plans. She'd seen it before; a man walks past another, and appearing to bump into him, leaves the first man gut-stabbed and dying before anyone is the wiser. Perhaps his surprise was at seeing Mrs. King's sudden appearance. "Yes, she is a widow, vigilant to the neighborhood, and a sterling seamstress. She makes good use of that window for her needlework as much as for her spying and honest gossip."

Anna was about to tell Seaver that someone had been seen depart-ing her stillhouse, then did not, for fear it had been Seaver himself on behalf of Mr. Browne. Mrs. King was a close confidante, and Anna had no desire to turn Seaver's attention to her neighbor any more than necessary.

"Come inside, if you have a moment," she said. "Were you looking for me?"

"I was not, but I would be happy to stop with you briefly." He didn't smile.

Again, Anna wondered if he was telling the truth. It seemed too much a coincidence that he should appear so shortly after the break-in and her encounters with John Griswold and George Tanner, all in the same morning.

She led him to the better, upholstered chair. She bade Clarissa stay behind the bar with a small wave, and taking a moment to shake off her confused thoughts, asked her to pour two measures of good Bar-badian rum. Anna observed with approval that the girl went about it as quickly and neatly as she would have done herself.

She returned to the table, saluted Mr. Seaver and swallowed deep-ly.

"How have you been, Mr. Seaver?"

"Very well, thank you." Seaver drank off his own rum, and Anna gestured for Clarissa to fetch the bottle over. "And you?"

"Well, thank you." She sipped and paused, staring into the liquid, dark at the bottom of the green-tinged glass.

Seaver exhaled impatiently. "Mrs. Hoyt, is there something I can do for you?"

She started. "Why do you ask?"

"You and I...pardon me, but we do not converse. You are always politeness itself, a quick and capable hostess. But we do not make pleasantries. We are most often about business." He looked at her. "Until now."

"I..." Anna closed her mouth. "No, we do not—we have not. That does not mean we *may* not."

"No."

"No. But..."

"Yes?"

"Only, I did wonder if you were here to see me," she blurted out. "On some errand for Mr. Browne."

He raised his eyebrows. "I have already said I had other objectives," he replied.

"Perhaps..." Anna's thoughts were still a jumble, disordered by her worries over the damage done to her new business and what might follow. "I fear I have in some small way displeased Mr. Browne."

She drank swiftly. It was precisely the wrong thing to say.

"Mrs. Hoyt, we have both made acquaintance with Mr. Browne, his manner, and his reputation. While you have known him—and me—for a few months only, I feel quite confident you understand: Mr. Browne would make no mystery of it if he were displeased with you. There could be no mistake. You would immediately be aware of his disposition toward you."

"Of...of course, you have the right of it."

He glanced at her, and Anna knew now she must hide all her worries and suspicions. She had not spoken to Mr. Browne of her undertaking; it interfered with none of his concerns. She could not, however, dismiss the notion that she should have informed him because of their particular relationship.

She put on the best face she could—it came quite readily, after long years of practice—and took the bottle and poured. "I have not heard from him in some time. I was not sure...of my standing in his regard. Whether I ought not to communicate with him."

Her lie was weak, but Seaver could not gainsay it. It was easy enough for Anna to feign uncertainty; she was immensely uncertain of her dealings with Mr. Browne. She felt sure that if she was not still indebted to him, they would still always have a connection, and not for the good.

John Griswold's public house barely warranted a name, but it was called the Ship. The remains of a weather-beaten plank that had once held the image of an East Indiaman under sail swung dispiritedly from its hooks. The exterior of his tavern was no better, having been battered by wind and rain and neglected for twice as many years as Anna had been alive. There was no pride in its upkeep and Griswold was as ill-favored as his establishment, raw-boned, red-faced, ill-tempered, in a filthy apron and an even dirtier set of clothes. Anna knew that the Queen had a reputation for unpolished behavior and rowdiness, with the odd moments of violence that might bedevil honest men sunk deep in their cups by ill-luck and the vicissitudes of life. But The Ship's customers never expected anything but mayhem, and that was all to be found there.

The other tavern was shut down by the watchmen, occasionally, to cool the choleric temper of the place. It served a purpose, however, as everyone knew: A sinkhole was invaluable for catching the worst of society and keeping it from spilling over into better neighborhoods. If you took that away, where would they be so easily found elsewhere? It was a boon to the law and law-breaker alike and preserved the better part of society from their stain.

Anna knew better than to go alone. She set the boy, Silas, to work at the bar, left Clarissa to the maintenance of the distillery and sought out her man-of-all-work Josiah Ball. His devotion to her was unquestionable, and he arrived almost as soon as she called. Once well-built, Josiah had gone to hard fat about the stomach and the pockmarks from a youthful illness made his face sag so that he always appeared sad.

She held up a coin. He was on his feet with a quickness surprising for his bulk. His eyes, following the coin, were bright amid his lumpen features.

"We go to the Ship," she said. "I don't want trouble. You're to mind yourself carefully."

He scowled and reached for a hooked piece of wood, like a shepherd's crook or a bishop's crozier.

"Josiah?"

He dropped his eyes expectantly.

"You carry a knife?"

"Yah."

She nodded her satisfaction, turned and left, Josiah following.

The Ship was no more than a few steps from the Queen's Arms but was a world away from Anna's sailors and tradesmen. She stepped into the darkened room, catching her breath at the stench of unwashed bodies and stale tobacco while noticing a floor sticky with years of spilt beer and spirits and blood. Winter was marginally better, as snow melted from boots and diluted the mess, and the chill air seemed to cut through the reek like a clean knife. Summer was worse, the heat in the tight space stifling, breeding every pestilence. Even the rats thought twice of seeking their dinner there, as those who frequented the Ship developed cruel traps to claim the bounty of rum for each furry carcass.

The room went quiet at the sight of Anna. A few looks were exchanged, elbows alerting neighbors to the proximity of a lady. There were angry murmurs at the intrusion, some tinged with lust, and she found herself the unwilling center of attention. No chance for a quiet conversation with Griswold now. Anna began to wonder if even Josiah, with his taste for a brawl, would be enough to protect her should things turn ugly. She fingered the handle of the knife commonly hid in the spine of her ancient family Bible, now in the pocket beneath her skirts. She took no more than one or two steps from the open door—and the comparative safety of the street—and cleared her throat.

"Mr. Griswold, a friend saw you stop by my distillery this morning, very early. Before anyone was about. I've come to repay the call and find out what you wanted to discuss."

"That Black old besom, Mrs. King, had better keep her nose indoors," Griswold said. He flicked a dirty cloth at a fly on a tun. "I was nowheres near your place this morning nor any other."

Although Mrs. King had a well-earned reputation for keeping an eye on the neighborhood, Anna would not have said her name to John Griswold for the world. Anna suppressed her anger at the implied threat to her friend. "No, it was a passing sailor on his way to his berth gave me the news. If you've come to press your suit to buy my tavern, my answer is the same."

"To the devil with your answer, and damn you, too. You take bread from the mouths of hardworking men, men with families, persisting as you do in trade."

"Do you then have a family to keep, Mr. Griswold?" Anna knew he did not.

"My men do, some of 'em." He inclined his head to a jaundiced-looking man seen often in his company, as lanky as Griswold was thick. "Houseworth here, for one."

"And I haven't the right to keep myself fed and off the public rolls as much as any of them?" Anna retorted. "More right, because I've no husband to keep me?"

"You've no right to dabble and steal my business."

Anna knew it wasn't his trade if their potential patrons were at the Queen and not the Ship, but knew better than to say so. "We find ourselves at an impasse. I'll bid you good day."

"'I'll bid you good day,'" Griswold mimicked. "Get back to your whoring and take that sorry, limp son of a bitch with you. I've honest work to do."

Anna had heard worse, but the venom in John Griswold's tone was comprehensive. She understood in that moment, as she had not before, that like George Tanner, Griswold had made her the emblem of all his troubles when his failures were rooted elsewhere. The principal difference between the two men was Mr. Griswold, like his tavern, was tenacious, active and violent. She shook her head at Josiah, who was eager to answer Griswold's insult, and they left.

✻

The night passed without further incident, and after closing the door, Anna sent Clarissa to her attic room and Silas to his bed in the kitchen. She counted out the takings, and being satisfied, entered the notes into her ledger. Closing the book, she took it and the money up to her chamber, locked them in the cupboard and hung her apron on the peg on the wall. She unhooked and unlaced herself, and after blotting a small stain from her gown, folded it away into the chest at the foot of her bed. She checked the pistol she kept loaded and primed at the top of the chest and carefully arranged on old toweling so it would not stain her clothing.

She knelt and prayed, then opened the shutters on the window overlooking the alley. There was no air stirring. It seemed every noise carried in the warm, still night.

Anna got into bed, throwing the coverlet aside, and extinguished her candle.

Sleep eluded her. It was not the heat—Anna's days were so full, she'd never had trouble sleeping. The wakefulness itself troubled her, but after a restless hour, she dozed off.

She came awake moments later and sat upright. Something drove her out of bed and she used the pot, hoping that would ease her mind. More awake than ever, she paced a while, then retrieved her gown, pulling it over her linen shift. She began to lace it loosely, then another impulse seized her and she again threw open the chest. She took the pistol and put it on half-cock. Stepping into her shoes, she hurried downstairs to the kitchen.

Silas roused himself, was up on his elbow, rubbing at his pale, freckled face, ginger hair wildly untamed. There was little difference between Silas awake and Silas asleep, with his drowsy eyes and gaping mouth. "Umm...aye. What is it, missus?"

"Did Matthew Brink arrive this morning? With my new barrels?"

"No, missus. He stopped by, day before, to say he'd be by later, as he was behind on his orders." He scratched his cheek. "It's still dark out."

"Yes." She retrieved a candle stub from the box and lit it from the hearth. "Go back to sleep. Get the fires going in three hours."

Silas nodded, his eyes closed even before his head hit the pallet.

Anna paused, envying the boy the order of his life, the simplicity of his desires.

She hurried down the street to the building where she housed her 'stilling equipment. The door was locked, as she'd left it that morning, and there had been no more intrusions. She unlocked it, entered and barred the door behind her. Anna raised the candle and looked around warily.

Nothing.

She set the keys and pistol down, while she inspected the copper still. The seams and connections were sound, not so much as a speck of dust had accumulated, the apparatus no worse than before. All was well.

There was nothing to her fears that the distillery was upset, nothing to the fancy that had driven her from house and bed. She raised the candle, unbarred the door and saw it.

Not a mark on the lock. She was rigorous in her habits and always locked up tight, but Mrs. King had said—

The door came crashing in on her, knocking her flat. As she hit the floor, the impact took the pistol from her hands. The rush of air put out her candle. She cried in surprise.

John Griswold came from behind the door, followed by Samuel Houseworth, whom Anna had seen at the Ship. They paused, reeling, addled by cheap spirits and the surprise at finding someone else in the still house.

She had no doubt the spirits perfuming their breath inspired this visit, as well as their earlier one.

She pulled herself up to sitting, feeling dizzy. There was something wrong with her knee; it shrieked agony when she tried to use it. "Get out of here! What do you mean by this?"

Griswold pulled Houseworth in, stumbling, set down a lantern and barred the door. He put down the pry bar he carried and walked to where Anna sat on the hard-packed earth.

Anna tried again. "Don't you know—"

"Griswold," Houseworth warned, nervously looking around. "Get the copper and molasses, if you've a mind to 'em, and we'll be off."

"Shut up."

Anna screamed. It echoed within the thick walls of the building and she knew they were isolated. She dragged herself a few more feet, then seeing Griswold advance, braced herself and raised her arms.

Griswold kicked Anna, hard in the side. Breath stolen, she doubled in pain and vomited. Her head exposed, he aimed another kick at her face. The whiskey made him unsteady and made Anna lucky. She felt the sharp heel of his boot graze her shoulder, tearing through cotton and skin, even as the toe grazed her cheek.

His blow going amiss, he tripped, crashing into a stack of barrels. It would have been better if they'd been filled and stood firm. Instead of a bruised but solid landing, he knocked them over. As he fell, another rolled over his hand, crushing it.

Griswold roared.

Samuel Houseworth, in weaving steps, tried to help him up but only unbalanced both of them.

Her hand to her face, Anna gasped in anguish. Reassured her eye was intact, she rolled over and crawled as far from Griswold as she could. She spat bloody filth from her mouth and felt a tooth wobble sickeningly. She cast about in desperation. The broom she'd used in the morning was across the room. The orderliness of the distillery left her few options.

There, a wash bucket, a few paces from her. She didn't trust herself to stand, but if she could reach the bucket, she'd have a weapon of sorts.

As she tried to crawl away, she felt a sharp yank on her foot. The pain in her knee exploded, and she saw bright dancing lights as Griswold pulled her back. Even as her head hit the floor hard, her eyes opened wide with surprise.

The shock of such treatment drove outrage through her, fueling her anger. "How dare you!"

Griswold's response was to kick at her again, but so ineffectually, he missed entirely.

As Houseworth steadied his friend, Anna's thoughts turned to Dolly and her calm, quiet, imperiousness.

It came to her at once. *Of course he dares,* she thought. *Everyone might. They have no idea.*

Through the blur of pain and angry tears, she saw her pistol behind the bucket.

Salvation was within inches.

Gasping, she stretched to reach it, feeling muscles strain and tear.

Her knee was nothing but hellish torment.

Suddenly, the breath was forced from her as Griswold's boot landed on Anna's stomach. His full weight was unsteady, but it pinned her. She heard the soft rustle of wool as Griswold unbuttoned his britches.

"Johnny-boy, we've no time for that," Houseworth said, his voice echoing something of Anna's desperation. "Let's leave."

"Bah, her noise won't get through these walls. No one's coming," Griswold said. "We've all night. But before I use a woman, she better know her place. This one doesn't, yet."

She felt wet warmth soaking through her gown. A sour smell confirmed Griswold was pissing on her.

Anna did not scream again. She never stopped straining for the pistol. As the stream lessened, she knew what would follow.

As her fingertips brushed cold, welcome steel, the final answer to her confusion came: *These men would never have offered such violence to Mr. Browne.*

She was at fault, in this matter.

A kind of calm settled on her.

Houseworth pulled on his friend's shoulder. "This ain't the easy money you promised me. I'm leaving."

Griswold started on him, a snarl on his face. The surprise reflected on Houseworth's face made him turn back to Anna.

She had raised the pistol and cocked it full. "Get out," she said, and spit out another mouthful of blood.

Before either man could say anything, she fired.

She felt the kick of the explosion. John Griswold screamed. Blood spread, instantly bright, on his threadbare shirt. A brief glimpse of something pale amid the crimson told her she'd broken his collarbone.

Griswold reeled back, moaning. Houseworth caught him, barely. With a look of horror and regret, Houseworth said, "Don't...we're..." He nodded at the door and helped the sobbing Griswold, tripping over his lowered breeches, away.

Still dazed, her ears ringing, Anna wondered whether the noise of the shot being discharged would bring anyone and what she would tell them if they appeared. She deemed the matter a private affair; she felt herself blush at what had happened—at what had almost happened. Assuring herself there was no significant clue to reveal what had just transpired in the room, she pulled herself up. The anguish of her cheek and jaw was excruciating and waves of nausea made movement difficult. Her knee seemed even worse now than before, and she wondered if it had been broken.

She found the broom, and using it to steady her, made her way to the door. She left the candle extinguished. She wanted no one to see her; she could not stand the humiliation. After a deep breath, she locked the door behind her.

Her halting progress across the cobbles was a nightmare. If she tripped, her stomach rebelled. If she jarred her distressed knee, her teeth clenched shut, which sent a new shock through her jaw.

At last, she saw the sign of the Queen's Arms and almost wept for joy.

A light appeared in a window across the way from her tavern. The door opened there, and Mrs. King beckoned. Anna cursed her bad luck again, but even in her humiliation, she would not ignore the grace of a friend who was looking out for her.

Mrs. King held the door to her home open, then waited to make sure no one had seen them. Only then did she help Anna to a stool, squeezing her hand. Anna sat down with a hiss, her bad leg outstretched before her.

"Merciful God, Anna! Who did this to you?" Mrs. King found a pitcher of water and soaked a cloth in it.

Anna shook her head. "I cannot say, Prudence. I must not."

"You must! Look at you, oh, your poor face!" Mrs. King wiped a drying crust of blood away, and then examined the angry cut on Anna's bruised shoulder. Her nose wrinkled, as the disgusting smell from Anna's gown filled the small room. "Wait here. I'll find you something decent to wear."

"Help me stand, please."

Anna gritted her teeth—her leg was stiffening and swelling now—and Mrs. King did as she asked. When Mrs. King left, Anna stripped off her filthy clothing, leaving it in a heap. She picked up the cloth and continued to wash herself.

Anna knew she might bathe every day for a week, and the smell of vomit, urine, and molasses would still fill her nose.

Mrs. King returned, with a clean shift. Without a word, she helped Anna pull it on.

"What will you do with them?" Mrs. King asked, glancing at the garments on the floor.

"Burn them." She nodded at the pile of disgusting rags. "Please, don't try to wash them or mend them, Prudence, though you know I admire your handiness with a needle. Don't keep them, even for rags, either: I'll give you five new silk gowns, but on my life, I'll never let *them* see me—or anyone—wearing those again. I'll just burn them."

Mrs. King knew the worth of the gown and shift, torn and soiled or not; she might have turned it into someone's workaday gown and turned a handsome profit. But she also recognized what Anna had been through, and knew how she felt.

"Let me." Holding her breath, Mrs. King picked up the sodden gown and threw it into the fire, her fine and generous mouth compressed and down-turned at the smell. "Anna, let me call the night watch. This gross insult cannot go unanswered—"

Alarm filled Anna's face. "No! You must not! It's—" She grabbed for her friend's hand "They didn't know...if I had only...please, don't! The fault is mine."

"Your fault?" For a moment, Anna thought Prudence King would choke on her rage. "Not even Thomas Hoyt used you this ill!"

Anna clutched at the woman's shoulder. "Please...they couldn't have known...I hadn't..."

When Mrs. King saw that Anna would not be swayed, she said, "Not even a complaint to the constable?" She shook her head. "It's almost day and Hugh Williams is an honest man. It would be a sin to let these monsters go unpunished, and you and I know that well."

Anna's excellent aim and handiness with a broken cobble had saved Prudence from an attacker years ago. The man had been a pest to every woman who approached the well—including Anna herself—but ceased his foul mischief after that. It was the origin and source of their friendship.

"I know, but not a word, *please*, Prudence. You must not. I...beg of you." She swallowed and said again, as clearly as she could. "It is not on them; I had not made myself clear. Please, say nothing."

Mrs. King frowned but nodded, pursing her lips. She washed her own hands, her eyes on Anna. She dried her hands on her apron and found Anna a blanket. She made a cup of willow-bark tea and watched until Anna finished it. Finally, she said. "As you say, Mrs. Hoyt. I would not go against you, knowing you wish otherwise."

Anna's eyes went wide as she understood completely now what she must do. Her heart was filled with gratitude, and she clasped the other woman's hands. "Yes, Mrs. King—oh, thank you!"

"Will you stay here? Come to bed," Mrs. King said.

"No, I..." Finally, Anna could no longer form a coherent thought.

"Shall I help you home, Anna?"

Anna could only nod.

Promising she would look in on her in the morning, Mrs. King departed the tavern.

Anna stared into the dark, long after the candle's flame guttered and died. No sleep was possible, her mind awhirl. She gave orders to Josiah and Silas with a look that said they must not ask questions and left them in charge.

Before she could take to her own bed, there was a knock at her chamber door. Clarissa placed a bowl of warm water, along with some clean rags, on the desk. She left without saying a word, but the women shared a knowing glance of recognition.

Anna spent the entire day in her chamber. Much later that night, only after the crowds had left the Queen and the watchman had passed on his rounds, Anna rose and washed herself carefully and drank another dose of willow-bark tea left by Mrs. King. She was stiff from her abuse, with fresh aches from lying still for so long. She found the bottle of rum she kept in her chamber, and her hand shaking, poured a glass. She drank it down, the alcohol burning the cuts on her mouth, biting deep where her tooth stood proud from the gum. She winced, stifled a cry and poured another, drinking until her muscles loosened and the pain faded, or she imagined it so.

She limped down the back stairs, through the kitchen. She stopped at the bar, and considered, finally choosing an unopened bottle of the strongest whiskey she had, the quality of which she hoped to imitate in her own wares. Using a pair of small tongs, she took a red earthen cup full of nearly dead embers from the hearth, blew on them to revive their heat and found an oily rag behind the counter, smiling painfully at a memory of Bram Munroe and his love and understanding of fire.

She found her way to the Ship and studied the windows, noting the way the wood had dried and cracked in the early summer drought. She sluiced whiskey along the ancient door frame in front; the dry wood sucked up the liquid thirstily. She arranged the embers along the doorway with the tongs, as carefully as if she were preparing to cook a meal. It took little for the dry wood to catch. A slight breeze fanned the flames high and quick.

Having chosen her second objective, she stuffed the rag into the bottle of whiskey, making sure the wick was well-drenched, and then set it alight from the fire now consuming the door.

If he's so interested in my distilling ventures, he may taste my ambition now.

She threw the bottle through an open upper window. One of them was bound to mark the chamber of John Griswold, and if not, he could as well suffocate as burn, for all Anna cared. There was a faint sound of breaking glass as the bottle hit, and a faint flush of light was visible against the darkness. The fire seemed to diminish a moment, then with a slight breeze, leapt up, visible behind the window, soon spreading along the top floor, along curtains and bedding.

Anna watched, amazed at the speed with which the building was consumed. A noise inside, not the fire, caught her ear, and she tossed the cup, now empty, into the harbor and shrank back into a doorway to avoid observation.

Anna heard a screech like nothing she'd ever experienced before, not like an owl caught in a chimney, not even like a prisoner at the first application of hot tar. The door, now merrily ablaze, shuddered once, twice, then shattered. Griswold slammed his way through, jagged splinters of wood dragging at his clothing and spreading the flames over him. Blood from his bullet wound soaked his nightdress. He forced his way out and staggered, gasping, to the cobbles, and then a little farther.

Mingled with the overwhelming wood smoke and sweet smell of burning alcohol, Anna would have stood in church and sworn, hand on her Bible, that she smelled roasting pork as he passed.

Another unearthly scream, and John Griswold stumbled forward and pitched himself into the harbor.

For a moment, Anna remained frozen, too stunned to move. She took a ragged breath, surveyed the road along the wharves. Lights were only beginning to shine in other windows. One shout raised others, and the cry of "Fire!" began to rouse the neighborhood to action. A long length of rope was neatly coiled nearby.

She needed to know.

Anna hastened to the side of the wharf and peered over. At first, she saw nothing and wondered if he'd already drowned, then realized he was farther away from the wharf than she expected, the tide slowly working against him.

"In the name of—!" Griswold's head bobbed under and the water drowned his words. Desperation drove him and his thrashing renewed, but weaker, as he struggled against the waves, the weight of his clothing and his broken collar bone. He sputtered and gagged. "God help me, I cannot swim!"

He seemed very small in the water to Anna, and very far away, though she knew he was still within help's reach.

His gasping coughs were all she heard now, no air left for speech, nor the lungs to use it, she reckoned.

Around her, shouts were growing in number and volume. Soon rescuers would be here.

She shook herself, shocked by her actions.

Enough of this, Anna. Enough.

No time to lose. Anna seized the rope. It was heavier than she expected and she stumbled as the coils slid from her grasp, pulling her off balance. Her knee was a torture, a blade through her body that no drink or tea would lessen. She gathered up the loops resolutely and twisted, using the rope's weight to help her as she flung it as hard as she could.

It landed high up the street, almost as far away from her as she was from the wharf.

Well out of reach.

John Griswold was no longer to be heard, no more splashes audible against the fire and noises of the night.

She cast another glance around, and reassured she would not be seen or recognized by the men—half-asleep, half-dressed, buckets in their hands, quenching the fire their only thought—she fled back to the shadows of the warehouse just up the street. She cut behind it and hobbled, undetected, the long way around back to the Queen.

A light across the window. Prudence caught Anna's eye, cocked her head.

Anna nodded. Once.

Prudence nodded back. The women shared a moment of understanding before Anna unlocked her door.

She stole into the kitchen just as Silas was stirring on his pallet by the hearth.

"What is it?" He rubbed his eyes.

"There's a fire," she said as she climbed the stairs to her chamber. "Go help the men."

Anna kept herself behind the bar at the Queen's Arms until the bruises faded, the swelling reduced and she could walk easily. Then she dressed in one of her plainer London gowns and kept the appointment she'd requested with Mr. Oliver Browne. She made a point of greeting several acquaintances, that they might notice her entering Mr. Browne's place of business in the city.

"I cannot fathom your reasoning," he said, once tea was poured. "We have served each other well in the past. There is no reason why you should not ask assistance of me."

He conveyed a gentle reproof, a small grief at her negligence. Anna knew this veneer of hurt friendship was the least of her worries. Her way past his immediate displeasure was everything.

She chose her words carefully. "My thought, my *every* thought, sir, was not to trouble you with the inconsequential. You are burdened with worldly cares beyond my ken; you hold the business and livelihood of a thousand men in your hands. In the face of that, my efforts are nothing. It would be impertinent, even selfish, to distract you, seeking such basic instruction despite all the evidence of your previous kindness to me."

"Oh, Mrs. Hoyt!" He put his hand over his heart, as if to swear an oath or calm himself. "I would not have you believe that. Any help I can give you is my pleasure to offer. I would not be so churlish as to insist, but it is my fondest wish you would always consider me first when you undertake a new operation, to ask my advice, my aid. It is yours, of course." He smiled warmly and took her hand.

The merest pressure, barely felt through the fine kidskin of her glove. He could not have made himself more plain: Once she'd given Seaver reason to suspect she was hiding something, Browne had determined to discover it. She'd have to pay him for the pleasure of expanding her own trade.

She had been a fool to think he'd ignore her or that he'd willingly sever their connection. Her trip to London on his errand was not repayment of her debt to him but a heavier chain, binding her to him even more tightly. He had even more information with which to keep her biddable. But she knew now, if she could not exist away from Mr. Browne, if she must give him some of her profit to continue, she would make sure to benefit from his acquaintance, wealth and connections.

And she would not hesitate to use his reputation to add luster to her own.

"Do not deny me this small pleasure," he said, with a pat on the hand. "I beg you."

There was none of the benevolence of his words in his face.

"Mr. Browne," she said. Her demure smile belied her still-bothersome tooth. "I would not for the world."

That matter settled, she made a point of detouring through the market on her way home to oversee the evening rush. A new ship at dock, full of men thirsty for fresh ale and the sight of a pretty face—all these were good for the tavern.

She stopped by George Tanner's stall and, before he could do anything, she stepped in, placed her hand gently on his shoulder, and whispered into his ear.

"I killed Hook Miller, in my place, last autumn. He crossed me, so I poisoned his drink, drove a knife through his ear and fed him to the pigs. Last month, Mr. John Griswold interfered with my business, so I stole into his room, cut his throat, then stuffed a rag into his mouth and set it alight while he was still breathing. I watched *him* watch—helpless, bleeding, and too weak to move—as the fire ate his hair, clothes and bed. At least three others died in the conflagration. They still can't put a name to some of those greasy, burnt bones."

Before Tanner could verbally express the horror that erupted on his face, Anna tightened her grip on his arm.

"You're a weakling and a runt, and you've shown yourself willing to cross me. I hope that never comes to pass, for God alone knows—" She shook him, gripping him even more firmly. "God alone knows what would befall you. You, already well known for accidents and now so unable to avoid them, hobbling on your half-foot as you do. And then there's your drunken brother."

She paused, waiting for Tanner to dare to speak. When he did not, she said, "But you've stayed alive this long—you have some knack for it, and keeping your mouth shut some of the time, apparently. So, you are going to continue to sit here in your stall and sell your bruised vegetables, and you're going to keep your eyes open for me. Because if anyone comes for me or mine, for any reason, ever, with intent to harm or cross me, I'll assume you were involved. That you pointed them my way. And I'll make you pay, and worse than the others, because I've given you fair warning. Do you understand me?"

Tanner nodded. A familiar sharp odor assailed Anna over the rot of the composting vegetables. The man had soiled himself.

Anna smiled, sweet as honey, and pressed a coin into his hand. "I pay those who work for me. There'll be another, every week, and maybe sometimes I'll stop by and you'll tell me of anything, anything at all, that might interest me from what you hear of those around you. And maybe, in time, you'll get a better stall, and you'll profit, and everyone will be the happier for this conversation."

Her eyes were dead and dark behind, the same sweet smile still on her face.

"But if anything should happen to me, if you should suddenly grow the stones and if luck blesses you, and you do somehow contrive to kill me?" She shook her head. "There's no safety even after I'm dead, because Mr. Oliver Browne—oh, you've heard of him, I can see it by your look of fear—he backs my plans. What I know, he knows. And *he'll* come looking for you. Because if you hurt me, you hurt him."

"Mistress Hoyt, I would never—"

She held up her hand. "All I want for you to say is that you understand and that we have a deal. Nothing else. Is that clear?"

"Yes. I understand. We have a deal."

"Excellent."

As Anna picked up her skirts and found her way to the main avenue of the market, she nodded. While she'd determined to make her own way in the world, she'd neglected to let the world know so that it might avoid her.

Now they understand, she thought. *Now they know not to trifle with me.*

My work will speak for me now, inside my gates and out.

Chapter Five: "An Obliging Cousin"
September 1746

Several months after the incident in the distillery, there was no reason for Anna to feel so abominably ill. The early autumn day continued as it had started: calmly, with no demands above the daily requirements attending a tavern and a few scuffles before the evening crowd settled into its equilibrium. Clarissa Jones reported that all was well at the distillery before she left for the evening.

"I think we shall exceed your initial expectations," the girl said. Anna poured her a small glass of rum, and one for herself. "Your willingness to give me what I asked for to start has ensured this."

Anna nodded, her satisfaction with the project, and with Clarissa's abilities, was unmatched. "I have great hopes for our continued efforts," she said with a fond smile.

In the public room, the brisk business increased with the late setting sun. Anna found herself in the comfortable rhythms of serving her customers. Her acts were meditative—find a bottle or a barrel, fill a glass, take money or chalk up an account, make small talk and occasionally glance around to assess the mood of the room. Only one incident marred the time: Her old chatelaine failed, the number of keys Anna now carried too heavy for the slender hook. As she retrieved the keys and implements that had scattered across the floor, Anna considered the day. She did not believe in heaven—in her life, she had found far more evidence for the other place—but if heaven did exist as she was told, she imagined something like this particular day closest to it.

As the evening went on, Anna's head began to ache. Her skull felt as if it was filled with shattered glass and a pain stabbed rhythmically behind her left eye. The throbbing was echoed by a toothache so fierce, she thought she may have an abscess from Griswold's beating. Yet, when she touched her cheek, there was no swelling and no obvious hurt, though the sensation remained.

The next morning it was worse. She broke her fast with porridge and beer, and though she found it did not actually hurt to eat, the pounding in her head and jaw persisted. She drank some willow-bark tea, laced with rum, and the ache eased somewhat, though she was left feeling sick and out of sorts. She snapped at Clarissa over a simple question and hastily apologized, seeing the girl's stricken face. She was short with her man Josiah when he struggled with a cask of ale, hoisting it right herself. Eventually Anna's inability to concentrate forced her to withdraw to her chamber, where her accounts refused to tally correctly and her correspondence swam before her eyes, communicating nothing of sense to her.

"Enough!" She slammed the book shut, making the inkwell's lid rattle. "What is the matter with me? Is this some new effect of advancing age, or the frailties of the feminine condition? If so, I shall plunder all the herbals and medical schools in the world for its cure, for I am not ready to succumb to either. Until then, more willow bark, more rum, and a darkened room."

She pushed back her chair and stood. Unhooking her gown, Anna tripped over a raised nail head in the floorboard and fell down, hard. She cried out and tears spilled instantly down her cheeks. Her knee was a riot of new hurts and old ones summoned up.

I am afflicted at every turn! I will not tolerate this infirmity, she thought. She tried to lift herself but her arms buckled beneath her. Filled with rage, she fell back to the floor. Anna had seldom felt so miserable in her life. The other times—

Lizzy, her maid of all work, rushed in. "What's happened, madam?" She knelt and helped Anna to her feet.

As soon as she was steady, Anna shook off her arm. "Your sluttish ways will kill me! How is it a lady cannot even walk across her chamber without your inattention causing confusion and injury! This nail should have been fixed before it laid me low."

Confused, Lizzy stepped back. "Yes, madam."

"Get away from me and better attend your other duties or I'll sell you to a brothel. Close the shutters and get out."

Lizzy opened her mouth to reply, but Anna held up a hand and looked away from her. The sound of the closing shutters followed by a small click of the latch told her Lizzy had gone, pulling the door closed behind her.

Anna hobbled over to her bed and, grimacing, climbed onto it. She loosened her stays, and after a few endless moments of pulsing pain, fell into an uneasy sleep.

She awoke with a start. It was fully dark inside the room and out; hours must have passed. Anna rubbed her swollen and salt-crusted eyes. She had been dreaming of Thomas Hoyt and being unable to escape him, even though he was as she had seen him last: sea-bloated and tangled with cast off ropes and seaweed, dead, but pursuing her still.

Why did he plague her when he'd been dead for almost a year? She presently had more troubling concerns than Thomas had ever provoked and far more to fear these days than his ill-temper and beatings.

Just months ago, she had fought for her life at the hands of John Griswold and Samuel Houseworth...

The memory brought back the pains in her head and jaw and knee, fresh as if they were newly inflicted.

"I am going mad," she said to herself. She turned to the well-dressed porcelain figure on her desk. "Dolly, I cannot bear this unwarranted upset. Is it some nervous malady? A knife in my heart, rather than this unbearable—"

A discreet knock at the door. "Anna, it is Clarissa. I wanted to ask you about ordering more barrels."

Anna swung her feet off the bed with a groan, pulled the bed curtains back and made her way to her desk by the fire. "Come in."

Clarissa handed her the notes and Anna glanced at them. She could barely focus her eyes to read. "Very well, order twenty more barrels, and do not forget we have five empty waiting to be used or sold." Anna suddenly found herself unable to turn away from her assistant.

Clarissa stood as she always did, in a reasonable imitation of good posture. Her dress was unremarkable, a serviceable light wool in a pretty plum color, her dark hair carefully dressed. There was no sign of anything unusual in her oval face and nothing about her at all out of the ordinary. Then Anna's gaze lighted upon something twinkling on Clarissa's wrist.

Anna recognized it immediately as the key to the still house.

The untouched lock plate, the cracked but unbroken window, all the things she'd observed directly before she had been assaulted by Griswold and Houseworth. Anna felt the world swim around her.

Time appeared to stop for Anna.

"Yes, Anna?"

The sound of the woman's voice seemed to come from a great distance, but the understanding of what had actually transpired the night of her attack raised Anna's every instinct to preserve herself. It came easily, after long years of practice in schooling her emotions and controlling her face to avoid one of Thomas's beatings.

Instantly Anna shook her head, smiling a little. "I have lost myself again. I apologize. I have not been my right self this week."

"It is of no consequence," Clarissa said, bobbing a small curtsy. "It might happen to any of us. If there's nothing else...?"

"No. Thank you."

The door closing behind Clarissa, Anna got up and barred it. Returning to her desk, she sat down heavily, though not with pain—that had all fled in that blinding moment of insight.

Clarissa had betrayed her. Clarissa had used her key to let in Griswold. Clarissa had known she'd been beaten by him and said nothing.

"'Of no consequence', she says," Anna murmured as she met Dolly's fixed gaze.

※

Anna stayed in her room the next day. She didn't trust herself not to reveal her emotions and intentions. She was so outraged at Clarissa's actions—and indeed, angry with herself for not paying better attention— that everyone would know her thoughts the moment she showed her face. She had her meals brought up as she wondered how Clarissa had come to conspire against her with Mr. Griswold and whether there was another suspect.

But she knew what she'd seen. So much had happened, immediately after the attack and since her discussion with her new patron and some-time employer, the powerful Mr. Browne, it had fled her mind before greater concerns. But Anna's memory was as good as it ever was.

When she had examined the lock on the door to the distilling shed, she had seen no trace of tampering or prying. One window was cracked, but not broken through. She'd had her own key; it never left her chatelaine, which was either on her waist or locked away. Clarissa had the other, under strictest orders to never loan it to anyone, for any purpose. So either she'd disobeyed Anna's direct order or she'd actually let John Griswold and his accomplice in that night.

To destroy the still Anna had worked so hard to make productive. To ruin her enterprise and humiliate, perhaps kill, Anna.

Her motive? Clarissa might have had a thousand, but Anna could not for her life imagine what would be the cause of such betrayal. She'd rescued Clarissa, hired her, taught her some accounting and left her in charge of the distilling and brewing, for which Anna paid her handsomely. She gave the other woman the gowns in which she was no longer interested, which were better quality than anything Clarissa might have had—a few even from London. They had shared bread and drink and the satisfaction of mutual cooperation more as friends, sometime, than benefactor and delivered. There was no fathoming what caused this treachery.

Anna resolved at last to find a method to deal with Clarissa if she was the traitor within the household. Once her rage subsided, she knew how to keep her face in polite and common society, to go to church regularly enough, pay taxes and debts promptly, and behave civilly with everyone she met until she was given reason (and the opportunity) to behave otherwise. But just as she'd discovered with the nobility in London, there was a trick to finding the right bearing in every sort of society, within every shade of respectability. She had learned, that terrible night of the assault, that she also had to embrace a direct and brutal persona, at once more aggressive and more discreet, with those involved in her other commerce. By doing this, Anna had made it abundantly clear with whom she was aligned and that she meant to continue, more boldly, as she'd begun accidentally.

The lesson had been well-learned, if dearly bought.

Anna finished her midday meal and pondered her choices. If the removal of Clarissa from her situation as distiller became necessary, who would replace her? Anna had learned the rhythm of the distilling process from observing Clarissa, but now had no time to devote to it herself. She would need to find another distiller, which might not be easy, as she had no idea to tell whether someone was qualified or talented. She needed more information before she could proceed.

She also knew she must appear soon in the tavern or begin to raise suspicions. So she dressed, and, reassured she looked well enough—her earlier pain was completely vanished now that she had a name for the suspicions dogging her—Anna descended to the common area to survey the foundation of her small but growing empire. All being well, she went to the distillery building.

"I have the chance to acquire another still," Anna said to Clarissa. "Do you think you could manage that as well, or would you require an assistant? Or two?"

"I am running from dawn until dusk as it is, with just Silas to help me and the men when the heavy lifting comes necessary," Clarissa replied, adjusting a knob on the apparatus. "When might this happen? And might I have the time beforehand to visit my people in Hartford? You know I've been patient."

"Very soon now—we've done good work to be so well-established this summer," Anna said. She fought to keep her face still, giving away nothing of the turmoil she suddenly felt. *Was that it? So little? All that trouble and anger, over...nothing? That could not be why she sold me out to Mr. Griswold? It wasn't possible.* "I cannot spare you just yet. And how many more assistants might you need, and suited for which skills, if I were to go ahead with this plan?"

As Clarissa outlined what was needed, Anna wrote notes absently, attending other thoughts. Ignoring Clarissa's transgression was now impossible, especially as Anna had already dealt with her attackers. Worse, if Clarissa had believed she'd been able to fool Anna and get away with it, there was no telling what she might imagine possible. If she was willing to help rob Anna and subject her to cruel usage, then she was capable of anything. Anna forced herself to smile and nod.

No, Anna could not stay her hand when it came to Clarissa. *Best to do it quickly,* she thought, *now that I know what I will need to replace the girl.*

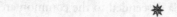

"Clarissa, would you help me?" Anna called from the cellar several days later. "I need another cask of brandy."

As soon as Clarissa was down the ladder and in the far corner of the cellar where the brandy was stored, Anna stepped forward and slapped her so hard, Clarissa's head hit the stone wall. The girl's lip split and bled, her eyelids fluttered and she was close to insensibility. She moaned and staggered to her feet, grasping the wall for support.

Setting down her lantern, Anna picked up her pistol. Shadows danced on the uneven surface of the cellar's stone walls and a brackish smell wafted up from the damp dirt floor. "How dare you break trust with me! Aiding my enemies, who would not only ruin me but murder me? I know it was you who gave them the key—do not dare to deny it."

Clarissa gasped and her eyes focused. "What—?" Then she seemed to recognize where she was now, and what had just happened.

"I know you sold me to John Griswold! How much was it? What did he promise you?"

As she steadied herself, Clarissa's eyes narrowed and filled with hate. "Not so very much. More money. My own still, with him backing me, and the running of your tavern, when you finally decided to sell it to him. The chance to visit my family."

Anna raised her hand to slap her again, but this time, Clarissa caught her by the wrist, not heeding the pistol now jammed under her chin. "No more of that. Never again. You get that first one, because I was stupid and unwary. But no more. How did you know?"

"It was the key on your wrist that reminded me. The distillery door had been unlocked by someone. My key was with me. That meant it was your key." Anna stared. "I asked you only to delay your visit, that is all. This is a sad turn, Clarissa. I am hurt. I cannot find it in me to forgive this."

"I have done nothing that you yourself have not done." Clarissa spat blood on the floor. "You are no model for any creature, and in no way my better."

"Have I ever harmed you?" Anna cried. She felt an anger filling her anew, overflowing. "How have you suffered at my hands? I took you away from that wretched town of Eastham and that fool Mr. Stratton when I needn't have. I gave you food, clothing, a life you might never have had and work you take some pride in. I thought of you as a—have I ever asked you to do more than I would myself?" Anna shook her head. "I have never treated you like this. You have had nothing but good will from me and you've repaid me as a viper would."

Clarissa laughed unhappily. "I've seen how *you've* repaid people, o queen of vipers, and have learned well enough from your example. So you need not think you can kill me as simply as you imagine. We will make a new arrangement regarding my service right now."

Anna pointed the pistol at Clarissa's face. "You are in no situation to give me orders or dictate terms."

"If I die, you are destroyed. I left a letter in the safe of Mr. Marsh, the merchant. It details all your activities, legal and illegal."

"Liar!" Anna said.

"If you doubt me, look at this." Clarissa reached into her bodice.

Anna shoved the pistol closer. "If you produce anything that I think threatens me, I'll shoot you and the consequences be damned."

Clarissa raised her eyebrows. "No threat but this." She removed a slip of paper, much creased, and handed it to Anna. "Read it."

"You read it. I prefer not to be distracted at this moment."

Clarissa shrugged. "As you like. 'I have received of Clarissa Jones this day a sealed note to be opened at the moment of her death or by her order.'" She held it before Anna, then threw the note to the floor. "You may examine the seal and the signature at your leisure."

Anna, having recognized both, could not for the life of her conceive a response.

Clarissa continued. "So we shall go on, you and I, as we have done. I shall work until I decide I want to open my own place, when you will back me. It will appear that I'm working for you, but all the profits of the distillery will be mine now. You will not strike me or I will call for the letter. If anything happens to me, it returns to you a hundredfold. Unlike so many of your adversaries, I have come into this prepared. I know your ways, I know your mind. Whatever happens now, it rests with you, Anna Hoyt. What is your answer?"

Anna was silent still, her mind awhirl with thoughts of Bram with his hammer and fire, Thomas with his brawling fists. She finally lowered the pistol and stepped aside.

"Thank you." Clarissa pushed herself away from the wall, rubbing her jaw. She was halfway to the ladder when she paused and turned back. "I know I said that you earned that first blow, or rather, I failed to avoid it, but I think a test of our bargain is in order. For the marks I shall bear on my face—and say nothing about their origin—I would like twenty shillings. Today, I think, please."

Anna's jaw dropped. The sum was outrageous, a week's wages to many.

Clarissa tilted her head. "I will not make a habit of it, being satisfied with what I intend and relying on your desire to preserve yourself and your business. But I think that much, in earnest and in compensation for the other times you have ill-used me, is not unreasonable. If you please."

There was nothing to be done. Anna nodded and preceded Clarissa up the ladder. As she reached the top, about to emerge into the kitchen, Clarissa jostled the ladder, causing Anna to gasp and grab for the edge of the trap door's opening.

"Mind you!" Clarissa called from below. "Remember, your situation is very precarious, mistress. You must take heed."

Anna shot her a look of pure hatred and scrambled out. She retrieved her purse from her locked box and handed Clarissa the money without a word.

Clarissa smiled broadly. "Now, shall I begin the day's work?"

Anna could barely make herself speak. "If you please."

"Of course." And Clarissa hurried away, reaching for the back of her head to check for bruises and blood.

Anna climbed to her chamber, brushing off Lizzy's questions and, out of sheer habit, ordering Silas the boy to wipe down the tables in the tavern room. Locking her door and barring it, she took up the bolster, bit onto it and screamed. No noise but a high-pitched whine escaped the thick upholstery and feathers. Long ago she had declared to herself that she would rather die than show the world such weakness but found the unobserved expression of emotion necessary still.

To be at the mercy of such a creature was unbearable. She had to find a way to extricate herself from Clarissa's snare. And yet she found herself helpless, with only the memory of the girl's smile, bland and treacherous, taunting her. Anna felt a contraction in her chest, her breath short. She had long ago sworn she would never be caught up in an impossible situation again, and yet...what could she do?

It was hellish, secretly being held at the will of another. She bore it because she had to. Her dealings with Mr. Browne sat less odiously on Anna now that she knew the explicit terms of their relationship—and she knew what he was and how he might hurt her. Her partnership with Browne was not one of equals, but it was agreed upon. This problem with Clarissa was no deal, no agreement. Anna felt as if she'd been taken hostage with no hope of redemption.

Anna had no reason to believe that Clarissa, cagey as she was, would ever abandon such a valuable asset. Anna would never be free until the other woman's natural death, and perhaps not even then.

She remembered her father telling stories of how his business partner—and equal owner in the Queen—had betrayed him, and how that led to them parting ways. She felt doubly humiliated for not having recalled that sooner.

Anna knew she could not bear this situation for long. Proof of that came on a busy morning when bad weather and a leaky window and an empty beer keg added to the bustle and confusion.

"Clarissa, bring up another keg," Anna called as she tried to sop the water from the stools and floor beneath the broken window, Silas working to repair the frame.

"Get Josiah to do it," Clarissa replied as she collected the mugs from one table. "Dozy old sow," she added, not lowering her voice to the seated drinkers. "Thinks I have six hands."

Titters and a few guffaws from the customers had Anna on her feet and in front of Clarissa so quickly, she dropped one of the mugs. It landed with a sharp crack, and fragments of red earthenware scattered across the floor.

In a fit of rage and forgetfulness, Anna went to slap her. Her hand stopped only an inch from Clarissa's cheek, and only when she saw the light in Clarissa's eyes, revealing the hope that she'd pushed Anna into a public display of violence.

"I will not brook impertinence in my establishment," she said, aware that every eye was upon her. Anna could not let herself give in to her impulse, but she also could not let the company see Clarissa being so disrespectful. She would lose her reputation, which was so important to every aspect of her work. "Do not let it happen again."

"No, missus."

She nodded to the broken red mug. "That will come from your pay."

"Yes, missus."

"Clean it up."

Anna did not dock her pay, of course, and burned under Clarissa's scorn when she asked Anna if she would find it all there.

But it grew worse as Clarissa pretended to be all sweetness, obedience and industry, fostering the admiration and sympathy of those around her. Anna was often forced either to pretend to be more unjust than she was or be thought to be too indulgent of Clarissa. There were whole days when she might have forgotten the sword hanging over her head, only to have Clarissa remind her in some way, overtly or secretly. It was excruciating.

At one point, when Clarissa had taken a ribbon Anna had purchased in London and particularly favored, Anna considered simply killing her outright in her sleep, making it look as though it were an accident. Anna had poisons; she knew how to use them—any householder did, her mother notably talented among them. And yet she dared not for fear of what Clarissa's letter might hold. Twice, upon seeing the blue and gold ribbon in Clarissa's hair, she moved toward her store of herbs and chemicals she kept carefully hidden. Both times, she stopped and turned away before she reached the place.

Anna also contemplated seeking help from Mr. Browne but knew too well that she could not afford to lose face in front of him lest she also lose his favor in their joint enterprises. There was no way to find help without showing weakness, no way to solve the problem finally.

No way, but to endure.

Until one chilly evening, when the door opened and shut and the atmosphere shifted in the room as palpably as a change in the barometer. Anna looked up from her evening's accounts. A current ran through the crowd, eddies and flows of men rearranging themselves in groups or leaving altogether. The movement left a space open nearest the fire and the two best chairs in the room.

Anna did not need to turn around to know that Adam Seaver had entered the tavern. But sensing trouble, as she always did in his presence, she did anyway. He stood just inside the closed door, as if pausing a moment to unbutton his coat. A faint smile—no, not even so much as that, a ghost of barely perceptible satisfaction—crossed his face, and Anna knew he was giving lesser men the chance to avoid him. He accepted it as his right, a lion among jackals, and let their surreptitious scurrying serve as a warning to those few men not familiar with him.

With a deliberation more commonly found in judges and preachers, Seaver greeted Anna before moving to the chair miraculously vacated for him.

Anna pulled down the bottle of rum Seaver preferred and poured a generous dram. She found herself vaguely pleased she'd worn one of her better work-a-day dresses and presented more than a tidy and trim figure as she set the glass before him on the bench between the chairs.

"Thank you, Mrs. Hoyt. Would you join me for a moment?"

Anna was taken aback. Her conversations with Adam Seaver usually took place far from other ears and were best left that way. He was not one for frivolous talk or gossip, and his attention was the sort that she preferred not to enjoy within the public eye.

She nodded and sat, wondering what could have occasioned such a gesture on his part.

"How do you fare, Mistress Hoyt?"

"Very well, thank you, Mr. Seaver, and I hope you are also well?"

"I am." He drank deeply. "I admit to being somewhat foxed in matters of business and was hoping you would spare me a moment of your time after you've closed shop for the evening. Will you?"

"Certainly, Mr. Seaver. We are just an hour shy of closing. If you'd care to wait?"

"Thank you, I will."

Anna returned to her work, acting as if nothing was unusual. And it was with a shock that she realized nothing *was* unusual. Once upon a time, not so long ago, the sight of Adam Seaver in her establishment would have been a cause of great fear and anxiety. While she still understood just how dangerous a man Seaver was, she now thought of him as an associate: Each of them knew precisely what their relationship was. And she noticed additionally that the general demeanor of some patrons in the barroom had changed as well. Benjamin O'Shea, who had no more use for Anna other than to fetch his beer and take his money, touched his brow as he left for the evening. She had no doubt this rare bit of respect was because he feared Adam Seaver more than anyone, and by extension, that courtesy was extended to her. Jonathan Jordan did the same, mumbling "good night" as he left, though he did not meet her eyes. Anna understood that it was not only her campaign of forthrightly ensuring that others knew what her commerce was about; it was the fact of her acquaintance with others that accorded her this new status in the community. As she extended herself, others responded to the change in her behavior.

The calmness with which she worked slowed but did not stop the early abandonment of the tavern by its usual complement of patrons. Adam Seaver might evoke respect, but that was born of fear, and fear made men prefer home and bed to drink and conversation.

So it was a good half hour early that she followed the last man out and barred the door.

"Ah, this is timely," Seaver said with satisfaction.

"And expensive," Anna replied as she replaced several bottles and sent Silas to sleep in the kitchen for the night. "If you make many more such appearances, I shall be a bankrupt within the year."

Hearing what she'd said, and how unwisely, Anna was about to qualify her statement with some nicety, but Seaver erupted in laughter. It was an unfamiliar sound, and it took her a moment to recognize the noise as mirth rather than mockery.

"My apologies, Mrs. Hoyt, but *surely* you no longer are scraping by on the few pennies the last orders would have brought in. *Surely* the tavern is no longer your most profitable undertaking."

Although she used the tavern as her overt means of support, Anna thought of the distillery, and the small lots of land she'd acquired— and the rents she had from them. "And if it isn't, does that mean I should no longer pay it attention? Mind my customers and my accounts?" she replied lightly, keeping in the spirit of his humor. "Nay, Mr. Seaver, but if I were so careless, you would no longer seek my advice."

"I shall be more considerate in the future," he said. "Now, may I ask your opinion on this matter of mine?"

"Please," she said, bringing the rum and a glass for herself, and taking the seat opposite him.

"I have an associate with whom I've exhausted my store of patience."

Anna suddenly regretted having barred the door and dismissing Silas. She'd seen the results of crossing Seaver, and imagined that having once been in his favor, subsequently falling from it would bring even more severe consequences. Worrying he might be referring to her, Anna thought how to protect herself if he should strike.

She smoothed her skirts, reassuring herself of the presence of the knife tucked in her apron. "Patience is but one commodity. Does this fellow have any other use to you?"

"Not any longer. I used him in one or two small bits of... surreptitious work, but ultimately deemed him unreliable. Especially in matters of discretion and drink."

"A lamentable failing, in any enterprise." Anna breathed a little easier. Drinking to excess was not one of her faults, though she reasoned she might not be safe just yet. "Can you redirect his efforts to less sensitive matters?"

"Alas, I've tried, but he's eager for advancement. He imagines my estimation of him is greater than it is, and worse, has ideas too grand for his execution." Seaver sipped at his drink. "He's made an effort to put his nose where it doesn't belong and I don't tolerate prying."

"Ineffective, indiscreet, and a snoop?" Anna sat back, a rare gesture of comfortable familiarity. "I cannot think there is anything for it but you must put distance between him and you, of a final sort, so that he never troubles you again." She remembered how her father broke off with his partner in the tavern, when the two could not come to an agreement. It had taken a good deal of consideration to protect the Queen after that. Soon after, he'd made the deed of the tavern to Anna, and she'd approached the court for legal permission to own and run it.

"You mean to kill him."

It was a relief to be blunt. "Or you find some useful cousin in a faraway location and offer him employment there. Overseas, if possible." She smiled. "And have that cousin deal with your man and his poor character."

"I suppose you are right," he said. "I hate to squander any potential resource, though."

"Thrift is a praiseworthy trait," Anna said.

"Do you ridicule me?" Seaver did not move, but his face went blank and his eyes glittered. Anna went from confusion to fear, and realized again how alone and very vulnerable she was.

She squared her shoulders and sat straight. "I do not. I find thrift a most important quality, so long as its practice does not over-constrain the expansion of commerce. One may become so rapt in collecting small pieces of twine that one forgets the purpose of that twine. No, Mr. Seaver, I do not ridicule you. I only speak the truth."

As she spoke, she saw him relax, and felt the tension leech slowly away, finally leaving her with a last shiver. Shaking off that fear, she was inspired, and a plan formed instantly, flooding her mind.

Daring greatly, she said, "I myself was wishing for such a useful cousin today. I too have an associate—too elevated for a servant, too petty for a confidante, and yet whom I might have called friend—or more—who has conspired against me. Alas, she did not succeed in her attempt, which caused me hurt both physical and economic, but now she is aware I know she betrayed me."

Mr. Seaver raised an eyebrow. "Is her involvement in your affairs of such a nature that she might also need to be sent away...to this obliging cousin?"

Anna shook her head. "It is my great misfortune that she has taken steps to prevent any sudden accident befalling her. There is a letter, she claims, in the safekeeping of a merchant, who will go to the authorities and reveal what she claims to know of my activities...that they do not already know. I have seen a note from his clerk, acknowledging receipt."

"We are beset, Mrs. Hoyt!" Seaver slammed down his glass. "A plague on the inconstancy and unreliability of our people!"

"We are not such terrible employers, are we, Mr. Seaver? For my part, I do not ask anything of others I am not willing to do myself and I have learned the benefits of generosity with regards to loyalty."

"I cannot think we are any worse than many who walk the earth, Mrs. Hoyt."

"But perhaps I have found a way to the solution of both our problems," she said.

"How? Neither of us can afford direct action, or in your case, any at all."

"Then we must not be seen to take any action. Or rather, I must be publicly seen to do nothing at all. More rum, Mr. Seaver?"

He inclined his head, and she poured. "You interest me greatly, Mrs. Hoyt. Tell me, please."

"The difficult part first." Anna paused. "It must be done in the presence of the day watch, and yet, we must act at some remove."

"We must have the law watching, to demonstrate your innocence," Seaver agreed. "That should not be difficult; the watch is ever underfoot around here. And to do the deed?"

"I propose the young man who has been a source of so much trouble to you."

"Hmmm, Daniel Malmon? And how do we do that without raising suspicions? As soon as I propose it, and he does as we ask, he'll be captured and tell the watch everything."

"Two steps, both, again, at a remove. Do you have a man you can trust to do work of...this particular nature?"

"I do."

She outlined the plan to him. "The letter damning me is our largest obstacle," she finished.

"I think you may leave that to me. Can you imitate Clarissa Jones' handwriting?"

"I have not tried, but it shouldn't be difficult to get the trick of it. She has mastered the basics but has not yet developed a characteristic hand. And I have plenty to copy. Why?"

"I shall create a story. You will transcribe it in the nature of her hand and I shall bring it to Marsh's clerk. I shall return it to you, and we shall burn it together."

"You have access to him? Can convince him to give it to you?"

"If you write as I direct you, I can."

Anna thought briefly about the wisdom of allowing Clarissa's letter into Seaver's hands. Could he be in league with Clarissa? He would never bother with something so petty as the girl's blackmailing—or would he? Anna decided Seaver had as much to lose as she did, if she was caught. Anna knew enough of Seaver's secrets to bring him down with her.

It was a good risk. She nodded. "Very well. When shall we execute this plan?"

"We have neither of us any time to spare. But two weeks, at least, so that I may have time to get Malmon acquainted with Clarissa. It must seem as though I am sending him to recruit her for my uses."

That echoed too much of Anna's earlier thought, but she was committed now. She nodded again. "Soon, then."

Over the next weeks, Anna observed the brutish Malmon loitering in the tavern. He stood a good head taller than many of the men there, and his arms and face were bronzed from hard work in the sun, his huge hands knotted from his labor at the shipyards. Once when she served him, Anna saw that crude tattoos marked his hands in geometric patterns—perhaps some souvenir of a voyage to the South Seas. She was careful not to leave every time he and Clarissa were near each other, struggling to keep her actions as regular as possible. They were so stealthy, however, no one but Anna would have known they were conspiring. She noticed every furtive word whispered, and, once or twice, a note passed.

Anna had no doubt they met outside the tavern as well, and once again, the fear that Seaver was crossing her filled her. She fought to put it aside, anything to be rid of Clarissa. She would deal with his perfidy if it appeared. Wariness would have to be enough.

Finally, after much work, Seaver pronounced Anna's efforts at copying Clarissa's handwriting successful. "You have tried something of this art before now?" he asked, scanning the sheets.

Anna smiled a little and shrugged.

"Very good. Are you ready to implement the plan once I have completed my first task?"

She nodded. "I am."

"Good," Seaver said. "I have but to speak to Mr. Marsh's clerk and to station Mr. Daniel Malmon nearby. I've told him to keep an eye out for Clarissa Jones leaving today. And we need to wait for the tavern to fill a bit more, inside and out. Half past twelve, or thereabouts, would be best. We want witnesses. In the room, in the street."

"We are ready, then," she said.

"Excellent. I'm off."

Anna put her hand on his arm. Seaver paused warily. "You're certain Mr. Marsh's clerk will surrender the letter to you?"

"He has much to lose. I'll show him the letter you wrote in Clarissa's hand, accusing him of stealing from Marsh. He'll give me whatever she's left with Marsh, cover up the theft *and* thank me for it!"

"And you are not concerned with…besmirching your own character? Adding your name to this list we've created, of men being blackmailed by Clarissa?"

Seaver gave an abrupt, harsh laugh and left.

Several hours later, Seaver's man gave Anna the signal to begin. All morning, Anna had been in a frenzy of anticipation, her temper out of sorts. Added to the store of anxiety from the past month, she felt as if she moved in a dream. Now that it was time—to lose or win all—Anna was uncertain she could maintain her composure well enough to perform her tasks. Her hands shook, her thoughts were scattered and her stomach rebelled at the thought of food yet ached with hunger. So much relied on the successful execution of many small actions. So much might yet go wrong.

She had arranged that Clarissa would work at the tavern that day, and the girl was now in the kitchen, eating her midday meal. As she watched the other woman, Anna very nearly decided to call a halt to the entire proceeding. She herself had been in the position of sharp dealing with those around her—how was Clarissa any worse? She remembered a moment from their first meeting when the girl had sobbed in gratitude for Anna's help. Surely there was a way to resolve this?

Just she noticed that Clarissa was wearing Anna's favorite ribbon, the girl drained her mug noisily. She held it to Anna without looking at her. "More beer."

Anna stared at her, and, caught up in her own thoughts, thought she'd misheard her. "What?"

"I said, get me more beer." Clarissa looked up and shook the mug.

Automatically falling into the habit of nearly twenty years behind the bar, Anna reached for it. Clarissa let the mug slip through her fingers and fall to the floor, the deep red clay body shattering into a dozen pieces.

"Next time, don't make me ask twice."

Anna's vision narrowed. All doubt, all hesitation, vanished. *She* had earned all she owned, and if she had, once or twice, acted in self-defense, it was no more than that. All was clear to her now.

Anna felt her world settle back into place. She pulled out a knife, very like one Clarissa favored, and cut the bottom of her own right hand. Then gasping two or three times to ready herself, she ran the blade, honed to razor-sharpness, across her chin.

Clarissa was aghast. "Mother of God—!"

Anna screamed sharply, dropped the knife to the floor, and

slammed her fist into the side of Clarissa's head. She felt the sharp pain of Clarissa's teeth tearing her knuckles open. Clarissa's head lolled and she moaned, reaching blindly for Anna.

She punched Clarissa again and again, not caring how much it hurt her hand. When she could think clearly, Anna produced the second note that she had forged in Clarissa's writing and clutched it.

Clarissa was crying now and swinging back, wildly, occasionally catching Anna in the head or shoulders. She shrieked with rage as Anna grabbed her by the back of her collar and hauled her into the main room of the tavern.

"Someone call the watch!" Anna shouted at the doorway. "Where is Hugh Williams?"

She was startled when she saw him stand up from a small table, setting down a mug of beer as he did so. His thinning black hair and beard were carefully trimmed. The watchman was considered a well-made man, even given his lame leg. "I am here, Mrs. Hoyt. What is this disturbance?"

"Thank God, Mr. Williams. This girl brazenly tried to blackmail me with false claims. When I laughed at her impudence, she attacked me!" Not releasing Clarissa's collar, she held up her own bleeding hand, showed her cut chin.

Hugh Williams looked from one to the other. Both were bloody and Clarissa was still struggling. "Both of you must accompany me to the magistrate—"

"I am the party wronged!" Anna protested. "I have a letter here, in her own hand, filled with malicious lies, saying how I sold myself to men and gave short measure in my drink. She demanded I pay her! I will no longer harbor this villainous creature in my house! I want no more of her!"

Clarissa's outraged screams of protest were accompanied by a renewed struggle, and she landed a tremendous blow against Anna's cheek. Seeing this opportunity, Anna let go of her and fell to the ground, wide-eyed and gasping. Clarissa ran into the street, pulling up her skirts, her feet pounding. She stumbled over a cobblestone and might have fallen but for the assistance of Dan Malmon coming out of the alleyway. She clutched his shirt and spoke. He nodded and they fled back the way he'd come, through the peddlers, hawkers and folk about their business, toward the harbor and its confusion.

A crowd had gathered around Anna, and Hugh Williams himself helped her to a nearby stool. After a few more sobs at the cold shock of a damp cloth held to her bruised face, Anna was able to compose herself. "That little bitch had the audacity...did anyone see where she went?"

Williams's assistant had returned from the search, shaking his head and breathing heavily. "I lost them. There was a fracas down by the wharves, and they might have vanished into any number of cellars or houses."

"She had accomplices, that much is certain," Anna said, waving the note she'd forged. "She said she was having me watched, that if I moved against her, she would make certain I suffered for it. She is mad! Claimed I was plotting against her. I, who have done so much for the little wretch!"

As Williams read the note, his face grew increasingly clouded with concern and anger. "I shall put the word out to look for her. Her viciousness is unrivaled."

"She is capable of anything, though she looks as if she had no more guile in her than an infant," Anna confirmed. She let her voice quaver, just a little. "But please...won't you let me know if you should find her? I won't rest easy until I know she's apprehended."

"I will, Mrs. Hoyt." Hugh Williams found Anna's hand and gave it a furtive squeeze, as he helped her up. "Do you need assistance going to your chamber?"

Although she was about to say that she had no intention of leaving so full a taproom, Anna replied, "Yes, please." Acting as if she needed to retire would create more sympathy for her. "Thank you."

They made their way up the stairs, more slowly than necessary. Anna was surprised; Mr. Williams seemed to be overestimating the seriousness of her injury. She was used to this kind of pain from childhood and had endured worse at the hands of Thomas Hoyt, of Griswold, of so many.

Once Anna was settled in her chair, Williams did not immediately take his leave. He was so solicitous and quiet, she grew apprehensive.

"For some time, I have been concerned that you are not fully aware of the true nature of some of the people who frequent your establishment, Anna Hoyt. This unfortunate matter with Clarissa Jones is only the most recent example. Even her name seems false, bespeaking a scurrilous past. I am uneasy for you."

Anna looked up at him sharply, though careful to keep her face expressionless. She had suspected this as well, and her suspicions had only made Clarissa seem even more able. Whatever was the man saying? "Mr. Williams, I thank you for your assistance and your very kind attentions. You know well that I was born and bred in this very place. You yourself were born here. Its people are no strangers to me, nor I to them. Most of those who come here are known to me, friends even."

She shrugged. "Many of our neighbors are unrefined, perhaps, and that is the nature of any port. But there is no harm in them, as you know. It has generally been my experience that these are good folk, and hardworking, as are most of those I've met in my travels."

She paused delicately. "I'm afraid it is when outsiders come in, and become greedy, that things go badly for us all. I took pity on Clarissa, seeing a woman—I will not say *lady*!—trying to make her way in the world, but knowing nothing of her true character."

"Your heart is too tender," Williams said. "And you should guard against the kind of advantage some would take with it." He sighed. "Though I hardly do myself any favor to tell you so, for I am one of them."

Alarm flooded Anna's mind. She fought to make her face soft and inquisitive. Did he somehow know the truth and sought to blackmail Anna himself? She thought of the knife she'd dropped downstairs and the distance to the pistol in the trunk by her bed. "Tell me what you want, Hugh Williams, and if it is within my power, know I will deny an old friend like you nothing."

Nervously, he took a deep breath. "May I see you, under more felicitous circumstances? If it pleases you, I would pay court to you."

Anna froze. This was nothing like what she had anticipated, and more, his expression bespoke a genuine affection that she hardly expected from any man. Her first thought was to put him off, but then she began to wonder if that caution was necessary. The watchman had always been decent to her and had not taken advantage of her position as the owner of the Queen overmuch. More than that, he had listened fairly when other tavern owners or clergy or angry wives had taken up against her.

Perhaps there was something more here, with Hugh Williams.

"Thank you, I...I would be honored," she said, trying to remember how one behaved during courtship. Her life before Thomas Hoyt was only two years past, but a lifetime ago. Perhaps a man of some standing in the community would benefit her. There was none of Thomas's bravado and swagger and nothing of Bram's mercurial passions in Hugh, and that would make life...peaceful, perhaps.

In any case, she knew it was dangerous to be a woman alone. "When would be most convenient for you?"

Later that evening, the tavern closed after an excellent evening. Just enough scandal was good for custom.

A knock at the kitchen door. Anna saw Adam Seaver there, a heavy bundle, carefully tied up, in one hand. She hurried him inside and upstairs, to her chamber.

"Did Marsh's clerk give you the letter?" She wondered whether Seaver would hand it over to her. "Did you bring it with you?"

Seaver placed his bundle on the floor. He reached into his pocket and pulled out a packet of letters, tied up with a red ribbon. Anna barely managed to keep herself from sighing with relief.

"Yes. The surprising thing was, there were several such. Our girl had quite a number of fish on her line. She never let an opportunity pass her by." Seaver dropped the packet onto the desk. There were fragments of red wax flaking off where the seals had been broken. "There's a half dozen or so."

"I am surprised only by her industry in this matter. Where's the one for which I took such pains?"

"On the top."

She took it, read it quickly and threw it into the fire, watching it burn. "Are there any others that concern us? Any associates of ours?"

"No. A few are strangers to me, but the rest…" He shook his head. "None of our friends. Or Mr. Browne's. I gave the forgery you made to Marsh's clerk, who burned it in front of me. He was vastly grateful."

"And what of Clarissa and Dan Malmon?"

"All is well. He spirited her away, and when they later met up with a group of my men as per my direction…well." He glanced at her. "The two kept their appointment with my 'obliging cousin.'"

Anna nodded, a great weight lifted from her. The distress of living with Clarissa's threats hanging over her head was gone. She could breathe freely again, some cuts and bruises a small price to pay. She nudged a fly-away piece of charred paper back to the fire with the tip of her shoe, and when it flew back on a contrary draft, she crushed it to a pile of ash with a twist of her foot.

"And is that parcel anything to do with our activities?"

"It is. Would you care to see it?"

Anna was suspicious of his offer but agreed. Seaver fetched up the bundle, setting it carefully upon the desk. He undid the twine closing a bit of burlap, and then unwrapped a large piece of waxed cloth. As he did, a terrible smell assaulted Anna's nose, spoiled meat, iron and decay. Inside was a bloody mess of hair and skin. There was a little linen bundle, bloodied at one end, and Seaver opened that with difficulty, the linen shredding and raveling as it resisted the stickiness of the drying blood. She saw a hank of hair, long and black. Seaver lifted up the scalp, and Anna could plainly see it had once been Clarissa's, Anna's treasured blue and gold ribbon still tangled up in the girl's hair. Her hand flew to her mouth as he produced what had been Dan Malmon's hand, the unskilled mark of his tattoo still visible above the curling, rotting fingers.

Anna could not conceal her horror. She stepped back, her fist to her mouth. "What have you done, Adam Seaver?"

"I kept my part of the bargain, woman. What did you expect I would do? This was always going to be the inevitable solution to our mutual problem. You knew that, or so I believed you did." He had a dangerous air about him, as if he expected her to protest.

"Yes, of course, but I did not expect you would endanger us both by bringing *this* back to Boston!"

Seaver laughed. "I thought you would require proof. And you should, you know. But if anyone had stopped me, and dared to search my person, either they would have been dead themselves or I would have told them I taken these from some thieves or Indians and was bringing them back here for identification. You are too apt to assume guilt."

"You are correct." Anna's shoulders relaxed as she realized that he had taken no particular risk. She nodded: Another lesson learned, and in time to be useful. "Yes, I understand. And thank you for that courtesy. What will you do with this now?"

"I thought I would take a stroll to the harbor and throw it in. Perhaps you should not accompany me, but if you could provide water for washing after I retie this, and a glass of your excellent rum waiting when I return, I would be grateful."

Anna smiled. "It would be my pleasure, sir."

She poured water into her basin, and after Seaver had reassembled the parcel so that it was tidy, he washed.

Anna quickly glanced through the other letters, noting names, then re-bundled them, tying the string. As Seaver dried his hands, she hurried over to the old cupboard at the side of the chamber, a fantastical and bulky piece cherished by some long-dead and unknown relative, unlocked the top safe and placed the letters there. She locked the door again and put the key back on her new, sturdier chatelaine. She sagged back, filled with relief.

Seaver looked over and raised an eyebrow. Possibly there was a trace of amusement at her action, but Anna had decided that either he'd already taken whatever letters he could use or he would challenge her custodianship of the bundle.

He said nothing.

Anna shrugged. "You never know when such things will become useful. I'll see you out."

Chapter Six: "Tumultuous Company"
October 1746

At first, Anna hardly noticed that Hugh Williams paid any extra attention to her that autumn. He'd been present before, and she'd often encountered the watchman on the way to church. Now, rather than simply tipping his hat, he walked beside her. Sometimes he spoke, sometimes he did not, but after the second week, he saw her to her place before taking his own. As they departed, Mr. Oliver Browne nodded to her, a small smile playing about his lips. Anna realized almost immediately that Mr. Browne must think she was cultivating the watch as part of a scheme.

It was not a bad idea, as Williams was so often about, and she set about probing with innocent questions to see how this might be put to work. While Anna had been very careful to keep some of her business out of their conversations, she began to inquire about what he knew of the dealings of certain persons she considered her allies or her rivals in Boston. Who might be truly well-off or who might be struggling and be open to a bribe. In the guise of asking about his day's work over ale, she learned much, and Williams seemed almost to preen as he told her of brawls and thieves and, often, less helpfully, about his adventures in the King's War against the French and Indians in Canada, where he had been wounded and lamed.

One evening, several weeks after her narrow escape from Clarissa's threats, she invited him to share part of a pork pie with her for dinner, sending the rest home with him. The next day, Hugh appeared in the tavern when she was there and left a basket of oranges for her before slipping away. He also left a note that only contained his initials and hers, intertwined. Anna noted, with some impatience, that she already regretted having accepting his courtship, the turmoil caused by Clarissa's betrayal causing a momentary weakness in spirit. The next week, he kissed her, and after a moment, she kissed him back, unable to think of a reason not to. He was very slow, almost dragging his feet, in his pursuit of her, which puzzled Anna, but she was in no rush either. And so it went, trudging down the all-too familiar road of courtship with its parade of tedious niceties. She soon found a good day was when she had not seen him.

"What do you think of Hugh Williams, Mrs. King?" Anna asked one night as they sat exchanging news.

"I think he is a fine man, Mrs. Hoyt," Mrs. King answered, taking a sip of her rum as she watched out the window. "He has been courteous enough to me, and paid promptly for a bit of mending I did for him."

"Mrs. King, speak freely, please."

Mrs. King sighed and set her glass on the table. She smoothed her apron on her narrow lap as she thought. "I think he's the kind who can do a body a great deal of good, Mrs. Hoyt. I also think you are playing a dangerous game, hoping to keep him and his magistrate friends out of your business, but you've always had a stronger stomach for that kind of risk than me. Don't trifle with him; play him as long as you like, but if you do not think you will marry him one day, never even mention the word. Don't give him any reason to think you're willing."

Anna, deep in concentration, nodded absently.

When Anna said nothing, Mrs. King continued. "Or did you

mean, do I think he's too skinny? But you already know that answer, for you of all people know I prefer a man who is built like a bull."

Anna burst out laughing along with her friend. "Oh, how well do I know! Poor Mr. King, a veritable scarecrow—"

"Now, now, he had other attributes pleasing to a lady. Sometimes to several ladies besides me. But we solved that problem, didn't we, Mrs. Hoyt?"

"Indeed we did, Mrs. King. Indeed we did."

After her discussion with Mrs. King, Anna spent more time on her affairs outside the tavern. Mrs. King acted as Anna's agent; after all, the merchants who favored the fine shirts she made knew her well and were happy to take her increasingly large investments. Anna also made Josiah Ball her proxy in several purchases, running errands and carrying correspondence, and she began the search for another man to act secretly on her behalf, so that none would suspect her actions or her true worth. In this respect, Hugh Williams proved his usefulness once when he repeatedly declared that Mr. Gerrit Van Meter to be a scrupulously honest lawyer. She found this to be true, and began to use his services.

One day, on her way from the wharf to the still, she found Mr. Browne surveying a recently arrived cargo. Rather than admitting her true errand, which was checking a share of a cargo of her own, she said she was speaking with a cooper about an order for more casks. Anna was pleased to have so many pretexts to be on the wharf and felt herself increasingly comfortable navigating her several worlds: that of her tavern, her investments and her work for Mr. Browne. Indeed, she had established herself among one of the first ladies of her congregation, as comfortable and familiar with the fine merchants and professional gentlemen as she had ever been among her sailors and laborers. She had also visited the tavern and the still and the print shop; in every instance, she was greeted with enthusiasm and respect. How much had changed in just a few years! She now felt a surprising confidence.

And so it was with an air of polite curiosity that she heard Mr. Browne's request. "Will you dine with me and a few friends, Thursday next?" he asked.

Anna was about to protest she had too much work for social calls, but then considered that this was business. "Thank you, I would be honored. At what hour?"

"At seven. Good day, Mistress Hoyt."

She made a courtesy. "Mr. Browne."

Three days later, on a brisk October evening, Anna donned her best violet gown and rented a carriage to visit Mr. Browne's home in Medford. If the tides had been with her, a sloop would have been faster, or a horse, but she was determined to arrive in a state of perfect array. The leaves were turning, a blaze of orange and scarlet, the air crisp and refreshing.

When she arrived, all the lights of the house appeared to be lit and there were several horses and carriages already there. Judging by the hilarity that poured forth with the light, Anna concluded that the others had arrived some time before her and wondered why Mr. Browne had asked her so late, for she knew she was not mistaken in the appointed hour.

A Black servant let her in and took her mantle, saying something she couldn't hear over the general riot. A nod of his head, however, showed her where her host stood, in a quieter group, heads bent together, in the corner.

The uproarious scene was something out of Anna's worst nightmares. Men drunken to the point of reeling mobbed the great parlor. Most were laughing at vulgarities, a few fighting, one or two being ill near the fireplace. In addition to the smell of rum and beer and piss—there was a pot slopping over in one corner—there was an odor of what Anna could only describe as "danger." As it filled her nostrils, she actively worked to suppress her urge to flee. It was borne of years of observation and tutelage by her father how to keep a tavern free of riot, especially when dealing with sailors who had been at sea for years, fishermen who strove against nature to feed themselves or the coarse shipyard workers, whose hard livelihoods were as unpredictable as trade itself.

She would have emptied the Queen long before it had reached this state, banishing the instigators of such disorder; her father had spilled blood to prevent it. That this, a gathering at the private home of a wealthy and respected gentleman, should have achieved such proportions of upheaval and incivility was unthinkable to Anna. She would have been better served if she'd showed up in her washing day homespun and stout shoes than silk and embroidered heels for this brawl. She did not know whether to play the duchess or the alewife in this stormy setting; she would have been comfortable in either role had she but some indication of which was appropriate.

Her hopes that the servant would escort her over to Mr. Browne were dashed as he was called away and disappeared into another room, shutting the door behind him. Anna was forced to shove her way through the free-for-all alone, across the parlor and to another fine addition built onto it.

Stepping around a broken punch bowl, its contents sticky and drying on the sherds of porcelain, Anna pushed her way through a knot of men. She wished for Josiah and his cudgel, or at least something more substantial than her fan, which she hid in the pocket beneath her gown, afraid for its fragility. Just as she was wondering whether she'd need to draw her knife from its hiding place, she heard one man ask, "That's never Philip Sommers' girl, is it? Surprised to see any of that lot within a mile of this place."

She turned to see who had asked when a soft hand landed on her bosom. A short, bald gentleman with a bulbous brow and pug-like aspect and bulging eyes stood in front of her.

"Why, that's as soft as a kitten and as white as..." The drunk apparently had no sufficient comparison to complete his statement. His head wobbled tipsily and his gaze was unfocused, but he grinned.

Once she understood what was happening, Anna tilted her head and pressed her hand warmly upon his. As the drunk stepped closer to her, eager to see what his boldness had bought him, she bunched her fist around a handkerchief knotted around some coins and smashed it repeatedly into the side of his head. She released his hand and he stumbled back, clutching his jaw, before he tripped and fell back, hitting his head against the hard floor.

The room went suddenly silent, all eyes upon Anna. A panic welled up in her as she had no desire to be at the center of attention of this rambunctious crowd. Adam Seaver appeared instantly at her side, but she did not take his arm, and left him in her wake as she strode toward Mr. Browne, her head up, her face composed, her spirit offended.

Mr. Browne had been watching her since she'd arrived.

She locked eyes with him, stopping about ten feet away. She dipped a curtsy and said in a loud voice, "I'm afraid I'm late, or else I have the wrong evening, Mr. Browne. I certainly did not mean to intrude upon such a party." She could not make more reference to the state of the company without causing offense to Mr. Browne himself.

"I must apologize, Mrs. Hoyt. Our before-dinner revels got somewhat out of hand. Seaver! Get those who are too insensible to eat out the door. The rest may join us."

Seaver began to haul up Anna's assailant, none too gently.

Mr. Browne smiled. "Please, let me take you into supper."

She inclined her head and took his arm. Somewhere behind her, Anna heard a whisper. "I didn't know the whores would be invited, too? I would have brought my own, for they eat a prodigious amount."

Anna felt her mouth harden. It did not matter if the remark was in earnest or jest. She fought to breathe calmly, so that the panic that boiled inside her would remain invisible.

Whatever the temper of the party outside, the meal was abundant, with the imported exotic touches that many in the island trade preferred: turtle soup, rum punch, venison, all very well-seasoned. Anna's own tentative forays into investing in the West Indies informed her appreciation of these delicacies. She could not understand why he would waste such fine food and risk so much good chinaware on this band of drunks and half-pirates. She sat at Mr. Browne's right hand, as any mannerly company would have expected, but the other guests seemed to take such a traditional honor badly. Again and again, Mr. Browne plied her with questions about her London trip last year, the fine things she saw there and the elevated sorts she knew. Immediately, she understood that he meant to set her apart from the other guests, but why should he go to such lengths to show her respect at the same time he singled her out for the company's whispered comments? There was no need, for she was the only lady, and if such a party was meant to make the guests feel welcome, it had the opposite effect on her.

Quickly, she began to deflect his questions, making less of what she saw, sometimes feigning ignorance of the matter at hand until she believed she appeared silly and addled, not knowing what role he meant her to play nor which would best serve her. She struggled to keep her voice calm and face gentle but was seething within.

At last, brandy was served, and Mr. Browne asked Anna to remain with the men. He welcomed the assembly and dismissed all but a handful, thanking them for attending. When they were gone, the five who were left, with Anna, retired to an upstairs chamber. It was furnished with a table covered with a turkey-work rug, chairs upholstered in leather and some cupboards, all knobs and dark wood, in addition to an excellent modern desk. It was small and comfortable, well-appointed but not in the first ranks of taste, she noted.

"And now to business. There are several new pursuits we ought to take on this quarter, and I have determined how I will distribute the tasks."

The men around Anna caught her breath, and she realized that this was when Browne would disburse the employments that made their livings. She identified one of them as the man who'd laid his hand on her with some dismay; but apart from Seaver and Browne, she knew none of them by name or by character. The darting glances told her that who got what share was by no means predetermined or expected. All was at stake here. That she was included suggested that she might be given the larger role in Mr. Browne's interests that she'd hoped for. Indeed, some of the faces of the five men revealed distaste and anger at her presence, suggesting an insult to their manhood and disruption of their livelihood.

She kept her face pleasantly unreadable but could not help but notice an excited flutter in her belly, a clamminess in her hands. She had proved herself, after all, and was surprised Mr. Browne was generous enough to acknowledge her contributions. And he owed her a great deal for his offenses against her.

"The first, and largest task of leading our enforcement, will be given Mr. Adam Seaver, along with both our new privateering and honest smuggling."

Anna nodded approvingly. She knew how much cheaper it was to buy molasses from cargoes brought through without paying the tariff. Such endeavors were universally approved in New England, as a service and a savings to the locals who produced rum. She also understood now that Seaver must be quite well-off in his own right, to have the care of such a lucrative business. She made a note to inquire discreetly where he lived, so she might ascertain this.

Seaver's face remained impassive, and Mr. Verner, a tall, thin graying man with a scar, actually shrugged. It was to be expected.

"The management of the smuggling south of Boston, and the two cat houses, will go to Mr. Bell. And you may begin our wrecking scheme. Set the first false light off the Graves. If we lure any ships to ground, you may expand from there, farther afield."

A few raised eyebrows at this, and all gazed at the unconscious man, who was clearly Mr. Bell, who had by now lost both his wig, his stock and his coat. Mr. Hammond openly scowled, wishing it for himself. The gentleman was stout, his wig askew, his face cratered by pockmarks, and one piggy little eye was screwed tight and scarred over from some injury. "But that was my idea!" he protested. "The moving light, the team ready to take any wrecked ships that might be drawn in—"

"And you shall be paid ten percent for your idea, Robert Hammond. You shall have the maintenance of our ties at the customs house, plus part of the distribution of whatever Seaver and Bell take based on these relationships. You will share these tasks with Mrs. Hoyt."

Mr. Bell did not rouse from his snoring, which was wet and bubbling with the blood still leaking from his nose where Anna had hit him. Anna was horrified that the man who'd groped her—the man she'd beaten as if she were any common fishwife—would now be her partner. And now she understood: The Queen's Arms would greatly assist in the distribution of both the stolen and gainfully seized goods. The crowds regularly seen there, funneling to and from the waterfront, provided the perfect cover to conceal the true nature of the transactions going on there.

But that was not all of it.

"You had promised me the half share with Bell," Hammond shouted. "Browne, you cannot give what you promised to me to that...that..." His face contorted with disgust, he could only gesture at Anna.

Apparently I have so offended Mr. Hammond with my presence that he cannot even name me. Nay, he cannot name my sex nor look at me, he is so angry.

What on earth can Mr. Browne imagine he will achieve with this?

she wondered. *If he wanted to destroy me, he could have picked a faster way than by creating such disgruntled anger and vitriolic jealousy. But why so much unnecessary turbulence? So much easier to let me go my own way and skim off that. What can he be thinking of?*

"Are you unhappy with the cargo insurance schemes, which has been your area? It's larger than the half shares given to Mr. Bell and Mrs. Hoyt."

Ignoring the warning glances and frustration of his fellows, Hammond pouted, muttering into his wine cup. "I had made very particular plans in anticipation of the scheme, plans I believed you had approved in addition to having indicated I was to have that task. I have sunk money and time into it, bought property. Made bribes, abased myself in company! Why would you play me so falsely?"

There were a few gasps around the table.

Mr. Browne fixed Hammond with an unblinking stare. "I changed my mind, Mr. Hammond. You may have this or you may have nothing, and I shall consider our connection severed."

Mr. Hammond could make no reasonable answer but merely stammered and spluttered in his emotion. "As you will, I shall take it," he spat finally, sitting down.

Mr. Browne waited. A small frown introduced a line in his brow.

"With my thanks, of course," said Mr. Hammond finally, realizing that he'd been too frank about his disappointment and protest. Familiarity was not a trait favored by Mr. Browne. "And my apologies for my outburst. I sometimes become choleric after too many passes of the punch bowl."

Mr. Browne waited the space of ten heartbeats before he inclined his head at last. There was no other acknowledgment of Hammond's apology. "Perhaps, since you have put some effort into the distribution, you would be kind enough to share your information with Bell and Mrs. Hoyt?"

Hammond's face went from pale with his narrow escape back to brick-red. Unable to trust himself speaking, he merely nodded and drank quickly.

And if he had any hope of having smoothed over that little contretemps, Anna thought, *it's gone now. Why disappoint a man, then rob him after? And so publicly? I do not understand Mr. Browne's thinking at all.*

A few trifling matters were quickly dispatched and Browne declared their business completed. A servant helped Mr. Bell to his feet, still insensible, and Anna realized he would likely have no recollection of the meeting. She'd have to tell Bell herself. She wondered if she'd also have to tell him how his face came to be bloodied. Perhaps Browne would—

Anna's thoughts were interrupted as Mr. Hammond stormed from the room. The others followed, not inclined to do more than nod to her or feign conversation to better avoid speaking to her.

Anna spoke loudly and pointedly to her host. "My thanks, Mr. Browne, for an excellent meal and lively company. I look forward to our business together."

"Mrs. Hoyt," he replied, his round face red and sweating from so much entertainment. "I'm so pleased with our new arrangements."

Nothing about the insulting party she was exposed to before dinner. Not a word about the disastrous announcement, not a word about Mr. Bell's behavior and Mr. Hammond's response to her. As Browne handed her into her carriage, it was exactly as if they were old acquaintances after a successful first meeting on more intimate terms, his demeanor polite but reserved.

She left, hardly knowing whether she'd succeeded in convincing Mr. Browne that she'd be a steady business partner, unperturbed by whatever unforeseen troubles might appear on the horizon. It was then that Anna felt the pain in her hand for the first time. She'd hit Bell very hard but had not sensed that until now. She tried to uncurl her hand and touched at the skin gingerly through her mesh mitt. There'd be bruising, she knew, but the skin was only abraded and there was not, as she feared, any bone break. It would take a poultice of mullein to mend it. She could hardly remember how she had eaten normally. The aching was such that it must have been pushed to the far corners of her mind, because she could not see how else she might have ignored it save for the devouring wrath she experienced.

Test her, would Browne? Is that what this evening had been? When she'd become the sole proprietor of the Queen, and used to far rougher crowds than this for years? When the world knew how she was abused by Thomas Hoyt and yet carried herself without any show of hurt or trace of emotion, better than anyone could have? More than that, she'd managed Mr. Browne's errands, at home and abroad, to everyone's satisfaction and her own profit—and still he saw fit to test her?

Or what if it was more than that? She'd seen the reactions of the men she dined with and heard the muttering. Perhaps he meant to set them against each other, to his own benefit, or see which of them was capable of working with *her*. Or how they would compete against her. She did not like the idea that he would behave so cavalierly with his avowed partners, playing loosely with their lives and fortunes when they already risked so much for their collective business. And she did not like to think of the complications of so many new potential partners who might also be enemies. It was a great deal to ponder, adding to her already sizable burdens. She must learn everything she could about each man.

Anna's mood fed a longing for violence. Perhaps Mr. Browne would discover that he was not the only one capable of pitting one man against another.

As the carriage swayed and bumped along the road back to Boston, Anna cradled her hurt hand and swore that if she ever had the chance, she would pay back Mr. Oliver Browne for his insult, as well for his impudence, profligacy and carelessness. His earlier insults, and for keeping Bram from her. For weren't they all struggling survivors in the same ship's boat, working together for their salvation, and he fooling with their precarious state?

It was very late when Anna arrived home, feeling as wrung out as an old rag, and downhearted at the disastrous evening. She had only put her key to the latch when she heard a cry.

"Anna, whatever are you doing abroad at such an hour?"

Hugh Williams was on his rounds. She'd noticed that he'd started walking past the Queen more regularly in hopes of meeting her. She sighed. One more thing.

"You work so hard, my dear. I worry you exhaust yourself."

He put his hand on hers, and Anna was briefly grateful. So far from treating her with rudeness and hostility, someone was showing concern. There was no spark of desire, as there had been with Bram or Thomas, but the comfort was welcome. She leaned her head on his shoulder.

A rush of uneasiness and obligation overtaking her was discomforting in the extreme, but she lingered in his embrace. "It's...I'm very tired. Only, I've had a disagreement with Mr. Hammond about the price of his molasses, and I don't know what to do."

"Don't worry about him now, sweet."

Anna sighed. "If I knew his character better, I would know better how to deal with him, but he is averse to any civil discourse with me."

"He is notoriously biased against your sex," Hugh admitted. "If you promise me you'll retire immediately, I will promise you to tell you what I know of him. *Tomorrow.*"

"Thank you, my friend," Anna said. "You are ever taking care of me." Realizing she must express some gratitude for this, she took his hand and led him inside, locking the door behind them.

The next morning, Williams long gone, Anna dressed for the day. She made inquiries about all the gentlemen at the meeting, including where Mr. Seaver lived, which she was surprised to find was in a quiet neighborhood near the beacon hill, not far from the commons. She learned which establishments Mr. Bell frequented and the pattern of his daily concerns. She noted that he was frequently in taverns, finer than the Queen, and among fashionable people. She followed discreetly and feigned surprise when she happened upon him at just such a place that afternoon. Anna noted that the public room was as neat as a pin, an air of orderliness pervading the place.

She approached him as he sat in a corner, away from the main body of the customers. "Mr. Bell, I would ask a few moments of your time."

"Yes?" His watery-eyed look of puzzlement gave Anna hope. He did not remember her. And when he was not completely besotted, he seemed much more a gentleman, his wig diminishing the appearance of his large forehead and focusing his eyes.

"Mr. Browne's dinner, last week? He said that we were to share in...certain efforts. Pertaining to the...management of oppressive levies."

His face cleared, and he rubbed at his jaw; a bruise shone around a bandage there. "So you're the one."

Anna was determined she'd not be the first to bring up his drunken groping and her response. "I am."

"I'm still eating pap," he said. "My wife makes one bowl for the baby, and another for me." He reached for a decanter, shaking it meaningfully. "Still, *this* helps, and I'm grateful for it. Will you?"

He signaled for another glass without waiting for her answer.

"Thank you." Still she clenched her teeth, refusing to let an apology or explanation out. It was on him; she'd only responded as any lady—any woman—might, and the more reproach for those around her for not coming to her aid. It was a new thought to her: She had never traveled much in circles where the notion of a gentleman might come to her aid, and it was her reputation and that of the Queen's Arms that generally kept her from insult. She'd never expected friends or family to come to her aid—save Prudence King—but in the service of keeping the tavern open, which was the whole focus of their lives.

"Yes, Hammond told me how things are." He cackled at the other man's discomfiture. "Still spitting over Browne's decision. And most unwisely, too, to my mind."

Anna only nodded.

"And he reminded me of how you and I were first acquainted that evening."

Anna said nothing. She forced herself to keep her clasped hands relaxed, not to show that every moment she expected violence from him. She put the small blade she had concealed in her mitt out of her mind save to note its presence.

"Well, now I know several things, having no memory of the evening in question. You don't take nonsense and won't stand for an insult. You hold your ground and hit hard enough to loosen a man's tooth and rattle his brain in his skull. And Browne had you there for a reason, so you must have other qualities in addition to those I've listed. I hope you will put my former churlishness from your mind and we shall concentrate on the matter at hand."

It was no apology, but it was sufficient. A practical man. "I should be very happy to, Mr. Bell. How shall we proceed?"

"What are your thoughts?" He turned his glass around in place.

Anna saw that this was not courtesy, but a desire to keep his own thoughts secret. He was still unsure about her. "Is there any value to speaking to Mr. Hammond about his preparations? Does he have anything useful in place?"

"That was the other thing we discussed yesterday. He wants fifty pounds to give us his information."

"Too much," Anna said instantly. "By far."

"Why do you think so?"

"It's his first offer, for one thing. For another, do you believe what he might share with us, for a price, is worth that much?"

Bell shrugged. "I doubt it. But I think we must give him something, otherwise he is capable of sabotaging us. He is a creature of pure spite."

That coincided with Anna's assessment. "What are his strengths? For he must have some talents, to be...at dinner at Mr. Browne's?"

"He has a kind of cunning. And he has good connections at the customs houses here and in Salem. Not exclusive, not anything like it, but he has put in his time and he has a solid reputation. He's a hostess without skirts, and something in his unctuous manner puts officials at ease."

Anna nodded. "So a show of good faith would be necessary."

"I think so."

"Then we should pay him a good portion, though not all he asks, neither. Just a fraction below his next counteroffer. We may want him later."

"Very good. Shall I start?"

"We both shall. It's better he understand we are all partners from the start," Anna said. *And better you understand it, too*, she thought. "If you will arrange a meeting, I will be there. And when we have an agreement, written out, mind you, I shall pay half."

"Then we are agreed. Shall we say next week?"

"Yes. At the Queen? After it closes?"

"If you like."

Concluding her business, Anna returned to the Queen to find a new crisis borne of her good luck in the marketplace. The cellars of the tavern were filled to overbrimming with her stock of new-made liquor and beer, and more space was needed. She had a share of a warehouse, but she could not take possession of the space for another month. She needed space for a new shipment, and quickly. She sent a note to Mr. Van Meter to inquire about building a warehouse of her own, or buying one, but realized she'd have to find more room in her already overflowing tavern.

The cellar immediately under the kitchen and seating area was devoted to the immediate storage of ale and spirits and winter vegetables. She thought about the one beneath what was now the tavern's public area, and sighed. It was full of rubbish and lumber from Thomas Hoyt's family. He had never let her down there while he was alive, for it held all the things from the house he'd inherited from his parents before Anna expanded the Queen, turning their shop into the other half of the tavern. And in the year since his death, Anna had much more pressing matters on her mind than clearing and making the repairs it badly needed.

Making certain her people were well employed in their appointed tasks, she took a deep breath and struggling mightily, heaved open the trapdoor that led into the second basement. A damp foulness, equal parts rot and spoiled food assailed her. The indignant squeak of rats too long left to their own ways filled her ears as they fled the light of her lantern. Anna knew well enough not to go into a cellar without a stout stick and laid about, catching a few of them upside the head. She kicked these corpses aside and carried on until she had taught the rest enough caution to avoid her.

No wonder the place had been teeming with vermin: The first three sacks Anna opened were filled with food long spoiled. It was no longer the smell turning Anna's stomach; it was the shameful waste. She saw the remnants of a sacking label, dated many years ago, and with a shiver, she realized the truth. This was food hoarded by Thomas

Hoyt's mother, long after the privation of her youth and the uncertainty during the epidemic had passed. And because it had belonged to his mother, Thomas hadn't had the heart to throw the food out after her death.

A quick survey showed one third of the room was filled with that kind of rubbish. Anna suppressed an urge to light the whole of it on fire where it sat, but her better sense prevailed and soon her stomach stopped churning. She inspected the rest. One side was old furniture and other lumber, badly mildewed, and no good for anything but burning. Two small chests were stacked before an ancient table with a badly mended broken leg.

The smaller of the two chests was locked, but two hard blows with a rock broke the hinges. Underneath the wood was a small cache of silver and gold coins.

The other chest opened easily enough and held a pile of rotting textiles. Anna frowned, until she moved it. Below the table, she could see a hole. With an effort she moved the table and found a small doorway, poorly boarded up. She could smell damp and rot, and her light could not penetrate the shadows beyond.

A tunnel in the basement could only lead downhill, to the waterfront, possibly one of the warehouses there.

Anna's mind was awhirl with questions, but she could no longer spend another moment in the filthy pit. She scrabbled her way up, closed it tight, and went straight to her chamber to change her clothing. A quick drink of rum and she struggled to collect her thoughts.

The gold and silver... If Thomas had known about it, he would have spent it instantly; this had been untouched for years long before their marriage. Where had it come from? Such a prize could only have been gotten as the result of some mischief. And the tunnel...

A tunnel must have been built long ago, at the first construction of the houses there. Houses that had been built by...whom? Thomas's parents? Grandparents?

It might be salvageable. How invaluable a tunnel might be to her, a concealed way to move goods from the harbor to the Queen? Such a thing was perfect for smuggling, and ideal for an escape. Where did it lead?

She summoned Josiah and told him what she'd found.

"Had you any idea?"

"None," Josiah said after a moment. "Would have told you."

"How was it that Thomas didn't know about it?" She told him about the cache of coins.

"Would you have trusted him with such a secret?"

Anna shook her head. Of course not.

"Always been rumors about smuggling," Josiah said. "But everyone talks up how tough they are, how smart. Never heard any of them from the Hoyts."

That settled it for Anna. Josiah owed her family everything and made his loyalty to them well known. He was part and parcel of the Queen's Arms.

Anna made a decision. "We'll say we will do the cleaning and repair work at night, to avoid the noxious miasmas of the rubbish and avoid disturbing the patrons. As far as anyone will know, we are trying to improve the cellar for storage. And that's nothing more than the truth."

He nodded and left without a word.

It took four long nights of work to clean the place. Things might have gone more quickly had Anna hired skilled workers or used the other servants, but she wanted the secret to go no further. Josiah had proved many times he was incorruptible.

She was tired but exultant when she readied herself for the meeting with Bell and Hammond two days hence. If she could navigate her way through the treacherous waters of Mr. Browne's company, so many profitable things were just within her grasp.

Bell's mouth had healed somewhat, and he was sober and could speak, so the meeting was already improved over their first encounter. But all through the evening, even when she spoke, Hammond would not look at her, keeping his bad eye to her, his porcine face creased in disapproval. Even when he responded to some point or other she raised, he looked at Bell or else seemed to speak to the air. Anna tried touching his hand, to see if that would elicit some warmth or civility in his manner, but he drew his chubby hand away abruptly and continued to speak as if nothing had happened. Only the growing rapidness with which he spoke and a fleeting frown indicated his irritation.

After that, Anna refrained from trying to speak to Hammond, and gave up looking straight into his face. Instead, she kept her remarks addressed to Mr. Bell and spoke to the side of Mr. Hammond's face, the candlelight casting devilish shadows in the draft. Inside, her guts were a-roil, trying to discern how best to address this imbalance, and his insultingly obvious disdain.

I must show myself cooperative in this. Even if there would never be any semblance of cordiality between her and Hammond, Anna was determined to show Bell it was through no fault of hers.

"Mr. Hammond," she said as their meeting concluded. "You will remember that Mr. Browne himself decided that I should work with

Mr. Bell, will you not? At our next meeting, I beg you to include me in your conversation."

There was silence for so long, Anna started again. "If we are to be—"

"Mrs. Hoyt." Only now did he look anywhere near Anna's eyes but did not meet her gaze. "Our association is at an end. Mr. Browne has made his choices. I have often failed to understand his reasoning, but to this day, they have made many of us wealthy, and so I trust him. But this is a step too far and I cannot for the life of me fathom his interest in allowing...a...a...person such as yourself in our company. I think...I think him unwise in the extreme. The business we had, here, today, being transacted, we need see each other no more."

He nodded. "Bell."

With that, he clapped on his hat and slammed the door behind him so that Anna imagined she could hear the ancient building rattle from the impact. Indeed, a bit of dust and rotten wood sifted down between the planks of the chamber floor into a little pile by their feet.

A silent moment passed. "He's right," Mr. Bell said. "Our business is done, for now. You'll never get any more than that from him, so be glad we're rid of him for the nonce."

Anna nodded, shrugging a little. "Will you have another drink?"

"I will."

Anna observed very quickly that Mr. Bell was the sort who had a wonderful capacity to consume liquor, unmatched by a similar gift to hold it. She had a growing suspicion that this was exacerbated at moments of unease or agitation. She preferred someone steadier in temperament as a partner, but this new situation had her out of her depth in many ways.

Shortly thereafter, Anna met Mr. Browne at Warren's, a fashionable tavern among the better off. The request to meet, his. Anna was acutely aware of how vast a difference there was between this place and the Queen. A warm glow of satisfaction filled her. She'd never made more money at the tavern than she was making now, and far more than her father ever had. Left to her own instincts, Anna had contrived precisely the correct ambiance for her clientele. Anything rougher, and she'd get the kind of dregs found at the Ship Tavern; anything finer, and she'd drive her sailors and wharf workers away. Her customers weren't too poor and weren't at all rich, and many made livings in a variety of shadowy—nearly legal—trades. Her understanding of all this pleased her greatly.

"How goes it, Mrs. Hoyt?" Mr. Browne asked after greeting her. "Smoothly, I hope? No hitches in our plans? They go forward in a day or two with your partners, correct? The bribe will go to the customs agent, as we expect?"

Anna decided it was better to be frank, shifting the blame from herself should things go wrong because of her partners' idiosyncrasies. "Well, you saw the contretemps at your dinner?"

Mr. Browne frowned sternly.

"My partners, well..." Encouraged, she continued. "Mr. Browne, I consider you a friend, ever more dear to me. You did not see the incident. I'm not sure we can work together as you desire, much less in friendship."

A small shrug from Browne. "It is the way of such things: He has precedence in my circle of business connections and has the benefit of his long standing there to grant him certain...leeway. Do not take it so hard, Mrs. Hoyt, it is nothing, in the wider scheme of things. It is not so great a matter, after all, and I hope you will ignore what was clearly a gesture of admiration."

Her face cleared. "Oh, that with Mr. Bell? No, that's all smoothed over. You misunderstand me. I must say, Mr. Hammond resists the idea of working with me." She saw he looked puzzled. "Because I am a lady."

The sternness returned, five times as menacing as before. "I hope before too long, you will be as firm friends as I could wish."

Anna was silent too long.

"Mrs. Hoyt, I hope we understand each other. This is my decision. If you cannot find that you can set this aside and free up your good feeling toward Mr. Hammond, I shall take it very poorly indeed."

"Of course, Mr. Browne." With a sinking feeling, Anna realized she'd taken Mr. Browne's inquiry for genuine curiosity. He did not want to hear about petty grievances, as he supposed them. He wanted to know all was well. It was up to her to make it right.

Her response had come too quickly, too dismissively. Mr. Browne's good humor had entirely vanished.

"Put it aside, Anna. Should I find you had any unpleasant response to Mr. Hammond's supposed slights, I would not hesitate in taking up his side. We must all work together and mend our personal differences."

"Yes, Mr. Browne." Any thought that she might share the news about her tunnels, and the work she and Josiah had put into shoring them up evaporated.

He rose and put on his hat. "I don't wish to hear anything more save the successful conclusion of the affair. Am I understood?"

"Yes, Mr. Browne." He was treating her like a naughty servant.

He saw her discomfort and the vestiges of some humor played about his lips. He wagged a finger playfully at her. "If you cannot succeed in this, I cannot believe you fit for better things, Mrs. Hoyt. Don't make me doubt my previous confidence in you."

Previous. "Yes, Mr. Browne." Chastened and suppressing her anger, Anna left quickly thereafter. She considered this rebuke one more grievance on the wrong side of his page in her ledger, outnumbering the "good" he offered her. She consoled herself by trying to think how she might trip up Mr. Browne.

When next Hugh Williams called later that afternoon, Anna was at her books. Her maid led him in despite Anna's request to be left alone. Lizzy compounded her error by smiling shyly at Anna as she led Williams to the chamber.

"Will you come out to see the market with me, Anna sweet?"

"I cannot," she answered absently as she slid the accounts for her illicit molasses purchases under another sheet. "Tomorrow I must view a piece of land outside of town. My friend Mrs. King wishes to examine it with an eye to purchase for her old age but does not trust her judgment alone." It was Anna's land, and she was already building a farmstead there; she and Mrs. King often talked about retiring there, when the weather was too warm.

"Surely she is not so old?" he said.

"Indeed," Anna said. "She is five years older than me, no more. But she is cautious and prefers to plan against the day."

"But that is so much better!" he cried. "With your permission, I would be happy to accompany you. Perhaps if you can furnish a basket of victuals, I will provide the cider?"

"I have cider if you wish it," she replied with a forced smile.

"But I do not invite myself along, only to have you assume all the burden of our entertainment. Let me...no, I have an idea. I shall meet you here tomorrow, at what o'clock?"

"Shall we say ten? That will ensure I have enough time to finish my work here and give us enough time to get there and return by night."

"Excellent! Until then." He pressed her hand with a warm smile and left.

"Will you be preparing something special for him?" Lizzy said as Anna went to fetch a glass of beer.

"Preparing? What?" Anna had forgotten all but her accounts for the moment.

"For your lunch. You've given him pie and then your stewed chicken last week. I'm sure you want to show off your other talents?"

The glass slipped from Anna's hand and hit the floor with a tinkling crash. Waving off the girl's cry of dismay, she stared at the mess for a moment, then mechanically went to find a broom.

Anna had fed Hugh the pie because she hated waste and sent the rest home with him as he seemed not to mind that it was already a day old. The stew was to repay him back for all the little trinkets, posies and bits of rubbish he was always bringing her, like a mangy dog offering its favorite bone. Anna disliked being indebted to anyone.

She sighed. She didn't want to make him a meal. Any meal, really. "I suppose I should."

"There's a nice bit of mutton in the larder?" Lizzy offered, all suppressed excitement.

"Very good," Anna said absently, sweeping up the broken shards of glass. "Please see to it."

It took her several tries to collect up all the fragments—her broom seemed to be hexed and splinters of glass leapt away, propelled by the straws across the uneven wooden floor. Anna disposed of the glass in the privy, scattering the searching chickens in the yard, and dusting off her hands, climbed to her chamber. The room was too small to contain her quick steps, but she didn't dare go outside to clear her mind of its riotous thoughts. She might encounter Hugh again, ever loitering about the tavern. She felt safer here, though sickeningly confined, too.

Her shaking subsided with pacing. She didn't like this developing attachment with Hugh, didn't want to be subject to his orders, his whims or even his affection. She didn't want to be bothered with his constant attentions. He was thoroughly unlike Thomas Hoyt or Bram Munroe; and that was enough to give her pause. He would surely continue to press her on marriage, just as he had after the first time they'd coupled. He was just the milk-faced mooning sort to assume that her sleeping with him implied assent to wed.

More than that, she didn't want to lose the tavern, and while the law might be on her side, society would take the part of any new husband she had. She didn't want to give up her businesses elsewhere, neither, and she wondered for a moment what had possessed her to let him court her. Was it the tumult after the incident with Clarissa that left her so unsettled? Even after spending so much time in his company, she couldn't fathom his intentions, and though she could not sense any immediate threat from him; at the least, he was the law. The law was always a threat. He was a man. There was always a price.

Had she accepted him merely out of habit? A young widow

should be eager to marry again, society knew that—there were so many jests about the unbridled lustiness of a widow—but so far, she'd heard none of them directed toward herself. Was it security? With a laugh, she acknowledged that it had been at the back of her mind, but it was a foolish and persistent relic of her girlish ambitions and fears.

At the moment, she had no need of a man at her table, in her bed, her house. In her life.

She would put an end to it. Tomorrow; she'd break off with him after her business with Bell and Hammond was completed.

The next day, she went to meet Mr. Bell so that they might visit the customs officer, Mr. Abbot, together.

She set out confidently but a growing worry gnawed at her when it took repeated banging on the door to gain entrance to Mr. Bell's house.

A surly maidservant answered. "What?"

"I'm looking for Mr. Bell," Anna said.

"He ain't well, is he?"

"But we have an appointment—"

"Well, you and that other gentleman, too, only he got here first. There was a terrible row, and now the master's unconscious drunk and there's no rousing him. Come back tomorrow."

Before Anna could respond, the maid slammed the door.

Anna tried to quell the panic that began to eat away at her resolve. Bell was an unreliable sot; she would still make the bribe in time on Mr. Browne's behalf. She had the information from Mr. Hammond and the notes against tobacco, cotton and rum as well as coin; all she had to do was convince Mr. Abbott the customs officer that she was a trustworthy messenger.

Once she'd arrived at the house of the customs officer, however, worse things waited. Mr. Abbott, white-haired and florid, sat behind a desk and heard her case. His leg was resting on another chair, a crusted bandage around it, and his face was puckered with pain.

He glanced at the pile of notes and coins from England, France, Spain and Portugal Anna placed before him and sipped his wine.

"It's not enough," he said. "Your colleagues knew this, and yet you bring me too little."

"But it is exactly the correct amount," she said. "I have it on the best authority, as I come, from our mutual friend, Mr. Browne, as advised by Mr. Hammond." Was this an attempt to enhance the bribe because Mr. Bell was absent? Suddenly, her stomach filling with icy dread, she knew this was some scheme of Hammond's.

"It was," Mr. Abbott said. "Now, last week, I've had news of the boss's death back in England. All new arrangements must wait upon approval from the *new* boss. It was always Hammond's job to facilitate this arrangement. He told me just last week that it was now up to you and Bell. He might have told you as well and then Mr. Browne could have made communication with the boss, Mr. Grenville."

"But it is not a new arrangement, is it?" Anna asked desperately. "It is exactly the same as before."

"But I don't know you, do I?" Abbott said. "You could be anyone. I need the go-ahead, and it has to come from himself over the pond."

It did not matter that Mr. Hammond had information that he refused to share. all Anna knew was that Browne would blame her if they lost their preferential treatment and occasional blind eye at the custom's house.

"Mr. Hammond had not informed me of your associate's death,"

Anna said, struggling to keep her voice calm. "May I have more time to consult with Mr. Browne?"

"Take all the time you want, madam; it matters not one whit to me. I've been told to wait until I hear from the boss, and the sooner you get his assent, the quicker you'll be back in business. I will tell you, you're the first one here, so no others know of this opening." He glanced at the pile of notes and letters of credit. "And it will stay that way, if you leave that for me."

"Yes, take it. I'll inform Mr. Browne, and you will get your letter of on his behalf from—Mr. Grenville, was it?—as quickly as may be done."

Anna excused herself.

She all but ran to Mr. Hammond's house, her heels clicking hard against the cobbles. "How could you fail to inform me of this?" she said upon entrance. "It is crucial to all our plans! Yours as well—you will suffer the loss of your percentage if the agreement goes to someone else!"

Now he looked at her with his one eye. "Did I not tell you? My dear Mrs. Hoyt, I was quite certain I did."

"I haven't seen you for weeks! Can you hate me so much that you would endanger your profits and Mr. Browne's operation?"

"Perhaps you should speak to Mr. Browne again. Tell him *again* how I've wronged you. After you chiseled me out of a goodly sum at that talk we had at your nasty tavern. And I know for a fact that Bell skimmed some of that off my rightful fee."

Now she knew that Mr. Browne had mentioned her complaint, but not her capitulation to his wish that she work with Hammond. "You know I cannot. This is on me alone. Mr. Bell...could not be present."

"Too nervy, was he?" Hammond snorted. "He does that, doesn't he? Bell cracks under pressure. Gets off his head. Not the first time, alas."

"Your friend, your partner!" Anna cried. "You'd cross him, as well?"

He shrugged. "I told him, he forgot. Now, I believe you have some choices to make. If you will excuse me..."

Mr. Hammond left her standing in the parlor, trembling, her mind racing. How could her world have become so upended? She had thought to work with these gentlemen as partners, but they were nothing more than vipers, fighting in a sack.

After a moment, she distantly heard a door slam. And another open. A soft whisper of skirts on the staircase. Anna looked up and saw the lady of the house. Short, slight of stature, with a pursed mouth and eyes as hard as little pebbles.

"Will you take tea with me, Mrs. Hoyt? I have it ready to be served."

So flummoxed by her conversation with Mr. Hammond and not having the faintest idea of what she should do next, Anna fell back on social habit. She nodded. "Yes, thank you. Tea would be...very welcome. You're Mrs. Hammond?" she asked mechanically.

"I am," came the reply, and nothing more, until both were served.

"Here, now," Mrs. Hammond said after the first sip. "You're Mary Sommers' girl, aren't you?"

"Yes." Anna looked up from her ruminations, curious. The tea had scalded her fingertips through the fine porcelain cup, bringing her back to her present company. She had not heard her mother's name in some time, and this was the second unexpected question in ten minutes.

"I heard you might be by today, and my mister had a nasty look about him." She nodded to the tea, and Anna inclined her head in thanks. "My mum was tight with yours, years ago. She used to say how hard yours worked at the tavern and her many other demands, what with family and all."

Anna had no idea what the woman could mean. "Yes, Ma worked hard all the days of her life. I never heard rumor of your mother ever letting moss grow on her, either."

Mrs. Hammond nodded. "She was on the move from sunup until well past dark. When...more particular...folks were abed."

Anna heard an archness in the last sentence she did not like. "Indeed."

"In fact, your Ma was known to help folks a time or two, when others mightn't."

"She was a good neighbor," Anna said, determined for the other woman to make herself plain without asking.

"And my Ma used to say, 'Charlotte, don't you take nothing off a plate or a cup from Mary Sommers unless you seen her eat or drink it yourself. And maybe not then.' And I never did."

"Well, we were all taught to wait on our elders before eating," Anna said, intentionally ignoring the last few words.

"Mrs. Hoyt, I think you may have some of your mother's capacity for...herbal ministration. I've asked you here to get your help."

"I'm sorry, but...what help is that?"

"I have a rat problem. He's a pest in the house and out, and I'd like to be rid of him. I think you would, too."

"You know the rat is a male?"

"You have no more reason to be fond of this rat than I do." Mrs. Hammond stood and went to the portrait of her husband, holding Anna's gaze. "I know your ma had a family recipe, worked better than anything on rats, with the least amount of interest raised in anyone else. I want it."

"For...rats."

"For rats. Big, horrible ones."

Anna stirred her tea a while longer, then set the spoon aside. "A trap is often very useful, but you want to bait it properly. Food or drink, strong smelling and strong tasting, is best to conceal the odor then the taste so that it's all taken in."

"What if I wanted to make extra sure, say, that he didn't get out of the trap? This one's wily and eluded me a time or two before."

"It's been a long time," Anna said. "I do not know if I still have that recipe." She took another sip of tea.

"If you did, I would be very grateful."

"There's one more thing." Anna paused to make sure her veiled meaning was as clear to the other woman. "Rats...accumulate papers of every sort to nest in. You'd want to make sure those were gone, too, else other, larger rats would take the opportunity to seize an abandoned...asset like that. I'd be happy to remove those as well. In fact, I'd insist on it."

The delight could hardly be brighter in Mrs. Hammond's eyes. "Done. I don't want his filthy account books and papers—" The woman caught herself. "Or anything else the rat might have accumulated."

"Very well. Give me one of your wine bottles—the ones with your seal? If I can find the recipe, I'll mix it up, and send it back to you in that. Wait a week before using the concoction. It sets up best that way." She set her cup down. "Is there anything else I can do for you?"

"Not at all, beyond forgetting we ever met and ever drank tea and ever discussed rats. And thanks again."

Anna's nerves calmed with the excellent tea. Her mind restored to this turn of practical, household things, she took her leave. If the position was open until someone got word to the new man in Plymouth, then she would get there first.

She went from there directly to her ship's master, the only one who knew she was the majority owner of the *Audacious*. "When's the next tide? I need to get to Plymouth."

"Tomorrow morning. But we haven't finished loading and will wait a day."

"You're leaving on tomorrow's tide. A bonus if you finish loading, but I must be to England with all the speed we have."

Familiar with her determination in such things and her understanding of their business, he inclined his head. She went to the Queen's Arms, and out of sight of anyone there, produced the wine bottle and mixed the poison. She sealed it carefully and sent Lizzy with it to Mrs. Hammond's house with Anna's compliments.

There are no rules among these villains, either, Anna thought. *I am on my own in this, where I expected a cooperative spirit. So, having no regard for me, I shall have none for them, and the devil take the lot of them.*

She then went to her bankers and had each of them draw up several drafts. By now, they were not surprised to see how active Anna was in trade. Surprised at how much her investments—in cargoes, land and room rents, whiskey and her other businesses—had raised, Anna also took a significant quantity of gold. Bribes and who knew what made such a necessity.

Finally, she went to Mr. Browne's house in town, arriving flushed and sweating.

"Mr. Browne." She hastily explained what had happened, watching Browne's face grow nearly purple with anger.

"You are very bold, to come here to tell me of your failure. Do you have any idea what this will do to our various endeavors?"

"But Mr. Hammond—"

"Damn your eyes, I told you to work with him!"

"Mr. Browne—"

"What do you plan to do? You've jeopardized every part of our work! I was a fool to have trusted you at all, but one does not learn to swim without being thrown into the water!" The skin at the roots of his white hair was now so dark, Anna thought he might have a stroke. "Others have worked with Hammond, we all have our little foibles—"

Anna slammed her fist upon the table. "Mr. Browne! Will you hear me?"

His astonishment at her interruption could not have been more pronounced. It was as if someone had dashed him with cold water, and Anna wondered if she hadn't seen a fleeting fear in his eyes.

She took a deep breath. "Mr. Abbott at the customs house demands a letter from his patron in England. I will leave on the dawn tide and see to it myself. No letter will travel more quickly, and he has assured me that the bribe I gave him will be enough to buy us some time in this. I will get our rights to bribe him—exclusively—secured!"

Browne was breathing deeply, his violent emotions taking a toll on him. He sat up with a groan—gout was troubling him again—and leaned forward, his voice a quiet growl. "You had better do as you say, or you will make an enemy of me. And you do not want that."

Anna almost left, she'd had enough threats. But something made her stand her ground. "I went to England on your behalf before and was an outstanding success. I will do the same for you again."

Browne leaned back, thinking.

"I will create more connections for you there and expand on what I may learn from Abbott's patron there. You know I can do this."

"Go," Browne said finally. "And come back prepared to dazzle me with my new fortune. Anna Hoyt, you may think to run, but you must not. For if you do not do as you say, I shall hunt you down after I burn everything dear to you here at home. Do not fail me again."

Anna nodded and quickly left.

As she descended the stairs to the street, she saw Adam Seaver there, deep in thought, a frown on his face.

"Mr. Seaver, I am very glad to see you."

"I also hoped to visit you later, hoping you would give me advice."

She shook her head. "I am happy to do so, but I am in dreadful haste. The customs house is in jeopardy."

He could not have been more shocked. "Tell me."

As she spoke, the creases in his weathered brow deepened to match his frown. "What about Hammond?" he asked. "Shall I visit him? Explain the error in his actions?"

"Only if you do not hear it is...no longer necessary...after two or three weeks," she answered, giving him a significant look, recalling her conversation with Mrs. Hammond.

He raised an eyebrow, then nodded.

She placed her hand on his with a kind of gratitude. "And what of that advice you hope to gain from me?"

He glanced at her, then shook his head. "It's nothing in the face of your problems."

"I have only a little time, but what there is, is yours, my friend."

"Too complicated to discuss briefly, and... I already know the solution, I suspect. I believe it was my intent in coming here that made my plans take final shape." He stood, fashioned a sort of grin, his dentition sorry and his demeanor grim.

Anna knew he was lying, but there was no malice toward her in his eyes. "As you like, but I am as close as the nearest ship." She smiled ruefully.

"And but several weeks on the stormy seas," he agreed, returning her sentiment.

"Thank you, Mr. Seaver."

He kissed her hand, pressing it, and immediately continued on his way to Browne's. Anna continued home.

While Anna was in the midst of organizing the daily tasks for the servants and packing, Hugh Williams arrived.

"You are leaving? You never met me for our trip to the country! Why must you go now?" he cried. "Surely this is something that can wait. Why such immediacy?"

"It can't wait. I have had news from my distant cousin who is dying. He has asked for me, and I must make haste." Anna selected several more gowns, packed them in her trunk, then returned the rest to her chest. She found her satchel, added a few packets of herbs and then, on top, her large family Bible. She had debated making the fictitious cousin "she," which would imply more sentiment, or "he," adding a

perceived authority. "My apologies, but the next ship is tomorrow."
She called Josiah to move the trunks down to the kitchen.

"If you cannot stay, and I cannot go, will you at least give me some
hope that I would have good reason to look forward to your return? I
love you, Anna, I would not have you leave without securing your
agreement to marry me. When shall we marry, sweetheart? Name the
day!"

Anna froze, her mind racing, a heat rising through her face, flooding her limbs. "I told you I do not like to think of such things."

"Better still!" Hugh spoke, not hearing Anna at all. "Tarry until
we are married and I will...I will go with you!"

The idea gave her chills.

"Anna?" Hugh's insistence broke through her panic.

"I will be home before you have time to miss me, Hugh." Smiling,
she reached out and took his hand, kissing him passionately as she
could.

Several hours later, dressed for traveling, Anna closed the last of
the small cases containing her papers and her jewels, closing the door
behind her.

"If he has not waked by dawn," she said to the maid, who was
rubbing her eyes, "wake him then. He'll prefer to leave unseen."

"Yes, madam." She paused, blushing, then followed Anna downstairs. "It is kindness to leave while he sleeps, madam," she said, greatly
emboldened. "A few more hours of peace, it gives him."

Anna nodded absently. "In difficult times, kindness is important."

Chapter Seven: "A Gentleman's Education"
November 1746-August 1747

While the voyage over was as smooth as glass, with no sign of the turbulent weather that came with early winter, the exhaustion and worry of the week immediately preceding it took a toll on Anna. She felt monstrously ill, and seemed only to grow worse as the days slipped by. She had no idea what she would do once she arrived in England, but was acutely aware that everything depended upon her actions, and there was no alternative but to go, make a hasty evaluation and act as soon as she could. Imagination was her enemy, as she contemplated every plan she might follow with no more information than the name "Grenville." Worry preyed upon her, and she stopped eating. Sleep eluded her and she grew weak and ill. By the time they reached Plymouth, Anna was barely sensible. When the captain came to speak with her on landing, Anna desperately clasped the letter from Boston customs officer like a talisman and could only respond with, "I must find Mr. Grenville. Mr. Grenville."

Finally, Anna lost consciousness entirely.

Sometime later, she was jostled by a violent motion. She imagined that she was in a carriage with excellent appointments, traveling on a dreadful road. Struggling, she clutched at the strap and pulled herself up to the window. Lightning bolts flashed and thunder seemed to be right on top of her. Her stomach lurched as she beheld a nightmare landscape, a hilly, rocky waste devoid of humanity or any mark of civilization.

At first she'd thought herself in some variety of hell, for there was naught but stone and wind-beaten grass lashed with rain eerily illuminated by lightning. The thunder seemed to press the sky closer to the ground, echoing and reverberating against the rocks strewn upon the ground with as little care as if a child had scattered them like marbles. Having spent her life in the heart of cities, Anna cowered, pulling her hood over her eyes and turning into the upholstery, letting herself slip away from the misery.

Anna awoke in a room of the highest quality, with oak wainscoting, pretty old landscapes and nicely dressed windows. Her shift was soaked with sweat and her stomach roiled. A lightness in her head signaled that she was not entirely well; she felt too weak to walk. She could no longer hear the sounds of the city, the waterfront or anything she had expected from the port at Plymouth. She recalled the wilderness she'd seen in her nightmare and understood she hadn't been dreaming. The light outside her window spoke of mild weather and late morning.

She slept again and woke at dark. A candle was lit, and a tray of food was set out for her. Anna rose, found she could walk and was delighted to discover she had an appetite. She ate with gusto and felt so well that she dressed herself. She followed the candles in sconces down the hallway to a fine, carved stairway. The house was much more ancient than she first expected, given the spaciousness of her chamber. Some rooms were regular in shape, airy and decorated in the modern fashion; other rooms had lower ceilings and diamond-paned windows that reminded Anna of the Queen's Arms.

Descending, she was greeted by a maid who showed her into a fine library, filled with ancient, leather-bound volumes that perfumed the room with the pleasing scents of well-maintained antiquity and wealth long-accumulated. More modern books were lined up, as if for inspection, on a long table, and Anna could not determine the particular interests of the owner, for they covered every topic under the sun. Framed maps and small paintings filled walls without shelves, but two magnificent portraits hung on either side of the doorway.

Anna stared at the portraits, assuming by their place of honor in the house that she must be looking at her host and hostess. The gentleman was some sort of scholar, she imagined, based on the immense number of books on the shelves, and the well-made, ascetic appearance of the portrait. Tall, thin, but of excellent proportions, imposing in appearance, a head full of thick, black hair and appraising eyes. The lady appeared to be almost as tall as he and stouter, with a pleasing roundness that suggested the best of health. Their old-fashioned clothing suggested that the pictures had been painted decades ago.

A creak of the floorboards caused Anna to turn around. A footman pushed a wheeled chair bearing an elderly man. It was the gentleman in the painting, but much reduced in stature, and the skin of his aged hands and cheeks were darkly spotted,

"We cut a fine figure, once, my Dorcas and I." His voice creaked almost as much as his chair, an instrument worn by constant use over the years. "Now she is dead, and I rattle around in this house, prey to every draft and breeze and at the brutish mercies of young Eliot here." He jerked his head, and the footman moved him to the center of the room, closest to the fire, and left. The gentleman bowed to Anna and she curtsied in reply.

"I am John, Lord Grenville. I hope you are feeling better?"

"I am, thank you, sir—my lord. And thank you for your hospitality. I fear I have been a terrible imposition on you."

He waved his hand in a gesture that instantly communicated Anna was not to trouble herself. "A trifle, a pleasure, please. I understand you had business with my son, the Honorable Jeremy Grenville?"

"Yes. I had hoped to find him in Plymouth, but then I fell ill..."

"He is deceased."

"I am very sorry to hear it!" Anna cried, realizing that Jeremy Grenville was the "old boss" mentioned by the customs man in Salem. "I had the most pressing of business with him. Was it very recently?"

"Carried away five months ago."

"My condolences. I will confess to being somewhat at a loss, then, how I arrived here, and as to how I should proceed next."

"Your business with my son?"

"A trading opportunity."

At this, the old man slapped his leg and let out a cackle that was unlordly in the extreme. "You mean he was the one fixing the accounts in Boston, with Mr. Ezekiel Abbott, and you're coming to discuss it? How very enterprising of you, mistress!"

Anna said nothing, smiling a smile that might mean "yes" or "I don't understand your meaning." "I come on the behalf of Mr. Oliver Browne." There was no need to tell him of her part in this.

"Never heard of him." Again, Lord Grenville waved dismissively. "But I can help you in your task. That boy learned his tricks at my knee. Alas, his idiot brother, my other son, is a pious prig, who claims he wants no part of that particular venture. There's no use in having a position if you don't make the most of it. The fool, he would jeopardize *our* livelihood and *his* inheritance! We shall work things out for you, my talented ambassadress."

"How did I come to be here, sir?"

Lord Grenville sat back in his chair. "I happened to be in Plymouth three days ago on business and heard that your captain was seeking 'Mr. Grenville.' I determined I must help a lady, so brave as to travel on her own, with no companion. I was also interested to know of your situation with my son—whatever form that might take. I hope you will forgive my presumption in bringing you so far from your objective."

Anna bowed. "There is nothing to forgive, sir, and I am in your debt for any help you might give me."

"We shall speak in the morning. You are so much restored that I predict a day or two more will see you entirely well." After that, Lord Grenville made his apologies and, after calling his man, retired for the evening. Anna felt herself at the edge of fatigue, and returning to her room, fell into a sound sleep.

The next morning, Anna sat in the garden, enjoying the warmth of the November sunlight. So different from the heat of her fever, the fall chilliness of the country air was delicious. In the shelter of the tall hedge, the wind was bated, and it was exactly like being in a room outdoors. The maze was intricately crafted, impeccably maintained, and like the rest of the estate, seemed to have emerged from the rocks and earth, a natural feature. If she had to be out of doors in the country, then the first room in the maze was an admirable refuge.

She could not identify the age of the house, for it was unlike anything she'd ever seen before. Where it was ancient and uneven, wings had been added to give it a sense of symmetry.

She was almost dozing off as she counted the windows, when the squeak of Lord Grenville's wheeled chair roused her. She rearranged her shawl and blanket carefully, and tucked a strand of hair behind her ear.

"Ah, it is exactly as I predicted," his lordship said. "There are apples in your cheeks once more."

"Good morning." She inclined her head. "Your gardens are lovely." And they were, pleasing in their symmetry and good order, even if late autumn had left everything brown and dull.

"You should see it at its full glory: the pruning seems hard—nothing but sticks and thorns to be seen now!—but yields such blooms come the spring."

He waved his hand and his servant departed. A long piece of string trailed behind the man, one end tied to his wrist, the other to the arm of the chair. When the line went nearly taut, with a low swinging arc, Lord Grenville turned back to Anna.

"I detest having to ring outside. This allows me privacy, with the knowledge that my man is not too far from me and I shall not be stranded."

Anna was intrigued that, for the right price, a man would allow himself to be placed on a leash. Every part of her rebelled at every restriction placed upon her, and the idea of voluntarily assuming actual physical restraint made her ill. Anna could not deny its utility, however.

"Why should we need privacy?" Anna flirted prettily. "And here, of all places?"

Lord Grenville frowned briefly. "I have had a messenger from my son; the ridiculous puppy declares he will not take any part in the trade, since it is 'tainted,' as he says, with corruption. But he's happy enough to have it pay for his opulent life in the country! He does not deign to sully himself with what he calls 'filthy commerce,' even when it is *not* oiled with the efficiency of bribes. He knows nothing of the world, despite all my..."

He trailed off, coughing a little.

"Does he write anything that may give me a way to...effectively communicate my friend's needs and proposal to him?" Anna asked.

Lord Grenville hesitated, then fished a letter from his pocket, and with an effort, read it. "'To further compound the affront you offer me, my lord, you suggest a 'lady' has expressed interest in these dealings. Such an offense against nature can only underscore the degrading nature of the project you'd have me undertake. No, no, keep your she-pirate and your villainous crew on the wharves of all the lands—I shall, with regret, ensure the honorable deputy I've hired to take my place in Plymouth to ignore your offer.'"

Grenville glanced at Anna, assessing what she might say in response.

Anna, having heard far worse from more studied adversaries, ignored the words. "And what about the estate? Surely he'll need the money to support his farms in bad years?"

"He will, but he doesn't understand that yet. I have done all I can, and I will be dead soon, so what do I care what happens? My son will either spend the money wisely and maintain our people and his own comfortable life, or he will go ahead with his nonsense and lose it all. I'd prefer he lost it at cards!"

Anna was horrified. Her father and his partner had come into possession of the Queen over a card game, when the stakes had gotten so high that the other player put the tavern on the table.

"But. I may do as I like now, even more than I have at any other time of my life. I care not. Nothing more can happen to me, as I have had more than my share of life, and with it, ill-health, and disappointment, and bereavement."

Anna marveled at the sureness with which the gentleman spoke. It was with an authority she had never heard before, no, not even from Mr. Earle in London, and certainly not from Mr. Oliver Browne. With Browne, it was all secrets and subterfuge and scurrying and violence, like rats fighting over a spill of grain. Before she could stop herself, she said, "Teach me what your boy will not learn!"

As soon as she said it, she flushed, waiting for his laughter. Instead, there was neither mocking nor displeasure. A small crease in his brow and tilt of his head told Anna all: Lord Grenville was intrigued. Anna was too polite to stare, but she could not suppress a startled look at this unexpected response to her outburst.

"Oh my." He paused a moment, examining Anna with sharp eyes. "If you have come so far to engage at this level, you must be quite advanced among all your sex in these matters. And outstrip quite a few gentlemen, too, I think. I have lost one son to the French pox, and another is a simpering ass. You are clever and resourceful, no doubt, to find your way here, to resolve these issues to your satisfaction. And you are very beautiful. It has been too long since I had such an ornamental creature about. It would be an engaging pastime, would it not, for me to teach you what I know?"

"And what can I give, in return?" Anna said, business-like. She was curious, but not hopeful: Lessons never came without a price.

"I don't know, yet. Perhaps it is just to fox my smug son, who believes he will now reform all my badness *and* inherit the estate. A lesson in humility is needed. It will vex him no end that I spend what he perceives as his inheritance on foolish fancies. But I think purely for the entertainment, I would undertake this. Are you willing? At least, I shall immediately introduce you to my man at the port—he may be my son's 'deputy,' but he answers to me— and with my backing and protection...who knows what we might achieve together?"

Anna had nothing to lose. She needed Grenville to vouch for her to the customs officer in Boston, and this gentleman, who was obviously affluent and skilled, was offering her not only that, but connections on this side of the ocean as well, exactly as she'd promised to Mr. Browne. Somehow, she had no fear that he would turn her over to the authorities.

"I am willing, sir, and please accept my thanks." She'd write to Browne that night, relieved at last, to have news that would please him.

"Excellent." He tugged on the string and Eliot eventually appeared, gathering up the thread of yard as he came, his nose blue and dripping from standing still in the wind. At a gesture, he wheeled Lord Grenville around, then waited for Anna to join them. "I shall do it. I've seen too many scorn what you ask for, and too many reluctant to heed my counsel, as proven as it is. This will be vastly amusing."

That evening, after dinner, they spent an hour in discussion, Lord Grenville determining what Anna knew and didn't know. Many of the questions she didn't understand because of the language he used. But then, when he clarified, she found in fact she had some experience in certain matters he raised after all.

"A rough-cut gem, but worthy of refinement and polish," he concluded at last, ringing for a servant. "Come, we have much to do. Fortunately for us, we can start immediately." He gave her a stack of books to read before bed, and when he could not see her, Anna pulled a face. She was no scholar, and surely, neither Mr. Browne nor Mr. Seaver were either. How would moldy books help advance her cause? Suddenly, her recent optimism vanished, and she repeatedly tried to calculate the travel time to see how soon her letter to Browne might make it to Boston.

Her letter dispatched, Anna felt able to take advantage of Lord Grenville's offer, but she found it difficult: asking questions had always suggested ignorance—dangerous to admit—or prying, which invited rebuke. At table the next evening, soup was served. Anna took careful note of the vessels and utensils used to serve. They were nearly a century behind the most recent fashion.

"You're thinking about something," Grenville said. "Ask me. I have consented to tell you all I know."

"Why is your service so old?" Anna blurted before she could turn coward. "It is hardly fashionable." Her mind drifted toward the elegant gathering at Mr. Earle's London home, its new and brilliant porcelain.

"Because it was fashionable when it was first introduced in previous generations. You will notice it has our coat of arms. Flashy new things are for the nouveau riche, jumped-up sorts like merchants. The fact that my family has had this for generations demonstrates power and pedigree, even though some of the plates have been replaced and the cups' rims are chipped. The next lord may replace them with more modish, but I doubt it. This china reinforces what my title and my house, with its lands and responsibilities, tell you: I come from an ancient lineage, and powerful."

"So why does not everyone buy the old castoffs to pretend to that stature?"

"Because that is an old trick and only the unwise use it when every servant may wear the castoffs of their masters. You must ask yourself: Do they have the manners that are learned at the knee in the use of such goods? Are they gently born, but come down on hard times, or are they wearing borrowed feathers, with none of the awareness of *how* to wear them? Dishes and clothes are cheap to buy; houses and titles are not. Detect the bearing of those around you and extrapolate from their habiliments and equipments to refine your assessment of them."

This led to a longer discussion on the worth of old objects and new dress, which eventually chafed at Lord Grenville. "Anyone can learn this from observation, and as a lady who has seen something of the world, you are a step ahead of most. I will find you the correct book or some scoundrel of a dancing master to teach you these trifles. Let me move to more important things. Why do you think my chair squeaks?"

Anna had never had much time for riddles. She frowned, wondering if the old man was in his right mind.

Grenville rapped his spoon on the table, the noise echoing through the hall and startling Anna. "I have money enough for the best, and for repairs. And yet it makes a dreadful noise. Why do I allow that?"

"I cannot tell you."

"Sometimes I want people to know I approach. I want them, just before I enter a room, to feel a moment of anger or fear or desperation. I want them without their equilibrium when I go to conduct my affairs with them."

Anna considered this. "And does it not also give them warning? Time to prepare themselves, marshal arguments, adjust their person?"

He nodded, his annoyance abating. She understood. "I have several chairs, two much quieter than this. What you most need to learn is strategy, when to use the correct chair to achieve your goals, so to speak. You must learn how to size up an opponent, learn his fears, weaknesses, desires and learn to play them off each other. You have made a good start, if all you told me is true, but now you need refinement of your skills. After dinner, please join me in my study."

"Yes?" Anna's heart sank. He had already given her a stack of books, and while she had started to read them with good will, she had quickly found herself put off. What had Greeks and Romans, long dead, to do with her? Anna had already tired of reading, but was willing to do whatever Grenville asked her more than ever.

"You are going to learn a game."

As he set out the chessboard and its pieces, Grenville explained, "Each of these moves in a prescribed fashion. So it is with many people, who are set in their habits, relying only on that which has served them successfully in the past. Some pieces have more liberty in their movements than others, but any may take the king. Remember that. This is a game of opportunities, of possibilities."

After he explained the movement of each piece, he said, "It is also an opportunity to observe someone in the most intimate of circumstances: while they are in thought. You must learn to play the player, not the board. Study his habits and inclinations. Does he wish to hold back, then spring a trap? Does he rush ahead and attack, not considering strategy?"

Lord Grenville cocked his head. "The same might also be said for cards."

Anna had an ingrained horror of cards and the debts that gambling occurred. It had been over cards that her father and his partner had come to own the Queen's Arms, in payment of a debt. Even though the tavern had come through gambling, Philip Sommers had said it could just as easily be lost the same way.

But his lordship was offering her yet another weapon for her arsenal, and she would pay attention.

Oblivious of Anna's thoughts, Grenville continued. "Do you know piquet? Whist? I shall teach you those as well. There are many things to be read in any player's face, and habits, acted out unthinkingly that may betray his intent."

It was this discussion that made Anna think of Mr. Browne. She described his behavior, in setting his people against each other in such an unfathomable way. Lord Grenville took only a moment before responding.

"I see no utility in that trifling of his," he declared. "Yes, balance out one man against another so that each does his best, or use one's character as a goad or prod to the other. But there is no strategy in this wanton carelessness; I can predict no good result from engendering this destructive atmosphere. It is but a temporary satisfaction of Mr. Browne's own sense of power. The man is a dangerous child, capable of commanding the feelings of those around him, but also ignorant and petty. He is fearful, which is why he sets you against each other."

This was Anna's own estimation of Browne, and she marveled that she'd had the same assessment as such an elevated gentleman. She saw the acuity of Lord Grenville's observations immediately, and swore to take this as a lesson. In a moment, he had evaluated Browne's character, itemized the reasons for it being wanting, and dismissed him. He was able to articulate why something was wrong, not just sense it. She knew she had done well to enlist his lordship's aid, as her instinct suggested.

That night, she wrote to Browne again, reassuring him that a letter to Mr. Abbott would arrive soon from Grenville's man in the port, and that all should resolve itself in their favor, hardly caring about the fact that the other letter had left that morning. One never knew what fate might befall a ship. She reiterated that she had secured the good-will of the custom officer's employer, and that the officer had been informed that Mrs. Hoyt and her associates would have every courtesy extended to them. As soon as that was accomplished, she felt an eager-ness to take up her prescribed reading. Idleness had never appealed to her.

The next morning, Lord Grenville asked, "What papers do you take?"

"I read what is left behind in my tavern and attend what is read in church," Anna replied. "Most often the *News-Letter*. More important-ly, I am made of what happens in town by those directly involved." She said this a little proudly. "The heart of any tavern is filled with news."

Grenville tutted. "You must look at whatever comes by you as a source of information, inspiration and opportunity. I recommend the local, regional and international papers—whatever you can find, whatever you can afford. You'll find making a study of them over a meal soon becomes habit and can do much to broaden your understanding."

Anna shook her head. "Much is mere opinion or worse, speculation. Things long past, it takes so long to be communicated, and trifles of personality and advertisement. It is of slight import."

But Grenville was adamant. "No. The news will tell you much about the people around you, their states, their finances, their politics, their prejudices and inclinations. You must treat all information as gold."

Slowly, Anna nodded. Having learned what to look for in an opponent in chess and cards, this notion of information was something she hadn't considered.

"Keeping current with news and public opinions is vital." He thought a moment. "Do you have any French? Latin? German?"

Anna repeated a few phrases she'd learned in communicating with the sailors who'd come into port. Lord Grenville's ears went quite pink. "Yes, well, your accent is very good, if common, but I must urge you never to use such phrases in polite company. You have an excellent ear, so I will prepare a primer of phrases useful in society and of a less...bawdy nature."

He also learned that while Anna might shy from the ancient writers and abhorred poetry, she devoured plays like a starving man at a banquet. "These are real, like chess, or cards," she said.

When Grenville admitted his lack of comprehension, she explained. "Philosophy is entirely abstraction and flummery, men theorizing and arguing over nothing but air. Religious arguments are the same." She remembered her hollow feelings in the church at Eastham before she saw Bram. Recalled that her father had instructed her how generations before him would open the Bible, to let God guide them to the passage they most needed in the moment. She now understood that while her father had done the same and taught her to do so, he used the verse he happened upon to justify what he already wanted to do.

Her mind raced with so many thoughts, and she continued. "Chess is about life and death, wealth and station and poverty and how to survive. Cards are about finding a player's weaknesses and how to exploit them. That is real. And plays show what happens when characters interact: they are instructive examples. If Juliet had not the stomach to make the more powerful, political choice, then she should have been more careful in her letters. She and Romeo would not have died. If Lady MacBeth had been more resolute, she would have been able to save her husband and the crown. The play is a caution against weakness of purpose."

"Very well," Grenville said. "Perhaps not exactly as the playwright—or I—intended, but it will do. Read the plays and novels, search out the names and places and words you do not know. Soon you will have a solid grounding in the rudiments with very little effort. A good reference library and a little wit are an adequate substitution for a formal education."

Christmas passed as a blur: There were parties and socializing and Grenville made sure Anna had been introduced to the influential merchants in that town during the festivities. He made a point of questioning Anna after each one. He described the sort of business transactions that might be initiated at such events, how to address every sort of person and the best ways to impress.

He explained the fine line between being intriguing and being a scandal. "You must always stop shy of taking the final step. You must always seem to be above reproach and notice. Any publicity, and therefore, bad news, will be doubled or trebled should a lady be involved. Conversely, that may also work for you, as there is universal disinclination to suspect a lady of any action...not usually associated with ladies. That is a great advantage for you."

She recalled what she'd learned from her first visit to London from the drunken dressmaker and from interacting with Mr. Earle's associates.

While she was grateful for this tutelage, Anna grew frantic for news from home. Every day she'd write letters to her people in Boston, giving them directions and guidance. Anna sent simple instructions to Josiah Ball about the tavern's maintenance, and, in secret, to continue shoring up the tunnel and inquire, ever so carefully, who might own the property at the other end of the tunnel. And every day she hoped would be the one that brought word from Mr. Browne, even as she knew her letter might only have just reached him.

At long last, just eight weeks after her first letter, she heard from him in January. At first it was merely a curt note, barely enough to acknowledge he'd received the information she was so good as to convey to him in her first letters. But she wrote every week about how she was acting on his behalf, making introductions with useful people. His replies grew longer and more informative. Browne began to take an active part in corresponding with the merchants she had been introduced to in Plymouth and ports along the coast and in Ireland.

Anna drove herself, frantic to appease Browne and make the most of her situation.

She worked to better understand business from this side of the ocean at a larger scale than she'd ever dreamed. Advised by Grenville, she contrived to establish her own trade apart from Browne's. Anna built her investments carefully, using what she'd earned from her earlier enterprises in the distillery and land. Most of her acquisitions were made on Browne's behalf, at his instructions, but she reserved a few plums for herself.

As she had started with a good sum of capital from her own work and from the gold for bribes she'd not needed to pay in England, Anna was surprised just how quickly her investments multiplied. It occurred to her that it was easy to become rich, if one had a little knowledge and money to spare. But in her world, "spare" time, information and money were almost impossible to come by in the first place.

She learned the value in having a diverse range of investments and hung upon Grenville's every word on the subject. She began to correspond with builders to design a new house for herself, to be built in a fashionable part of town. It was as much a ruse to disguise her affluence—this new house seeming to be an expression of over-ambitious display that would eat all of the profits from the still and the Queen—as it was to expand her holdings.

She enlisted Mrs. King's help in expanding her holdings in Boston, including more farming property purchased outside the city. Despite her friend's initial refusal, Anna made half of those properties over to Mrs. King herself. She also took care to invest some money on Mrs. King's behalf, so that her friend might also profit abroad. The women had always shared jointly in their defeats and their successes; it was, after all, Mrs. King who had pointed out that Thomas Hoyt had inherited his parent's shop next to the Queen's Arms. Anna had little use for Thomas, who was a constant bother, until she understood the utility of this fact. Anna set her cap for Thomas with that in mind, and eventually, that acquisition allowed Anna to expand the tavern and improve her trade.

Likewise, Anna had early on observed the excellence of the work Mrs. King did for the local tailor and encouraged her friend to set up shop for herself, producing fine work for better money. Anna managed to "procure" a sizable amount of fashionable and costly cloth to establish Mrs. King as an independent tailor.

Anna smiled at the memory and made a note to send Mrs. King another lot of expensive cloth and prints of the latest fashions in honor of that first bundle of silk that Anna had "found" for her. It was a show of moderate prosperity to conceal the wealth of both women.

Each night, Lord Grenville and Anna played chess and he described a book or a philosopher, noting how Anna was much quicker in conversation than in study. She began to understand much more, with every lesson, and most nights had to make a list of questions that had been generated by her reading and their talks. She realized that an education not only meant accumulating knowledge but a reordering of her thoughts.

Once Anna's fortune had reached a level of that of the richest merchants in Boston, Grenville advised her on how to buy shares in the ships themselves or build her own. She learned to pay attention to war as a source of income in some areas as much as a threat to trade in others. He instructed her that it was wise to have savings in many places, so that if a threat came, she might leave one place and continue in another. Anna began to seek out opportunities in London, Paris and

New York.

As readily as she accepted all this, he was astonished at her balking at the trade in human flesh.

"It makes no sense! If everything that we love and find useful is so often the result of the labor of slaves, items that you yourself already trade—and happily—then what is the point of caviling at this further step? You do yourself an injustice to overlook such a profitable commodity, and I know you are no Quaker."

Anna was silent. She recalled a moment from many years ago, when her father had cursed the Black man tardy in delivering a pork shoulder, calling him "ape" and "brute." She'd laughed, and later described the incident to Prudence King. Prudence—then Prudence Potter—had frowned, and left without saying a word, staying away for a day or two, which was much against their habit. When she returned, Anna begged to know the matter. "We are friends, are we not? Why do you stay away?"

Prudence Potter's face was grave. "We *are* friends, so I will tell you. You don't know who that man was. He might have been my cousin, for all you know."

"But you have nothing to do with that sort!"

"Anna Sommers, you listen to me well, or we will never meet again, despite all we have meant to each other. My parents' parents' parents were in just the same condition at that man your father mocked, but they were eventually able to buy their way out to freedom, be their own people. You live here, as I do, near Copp's hill, where there are any number of folk who look like me. Some are free, some are slave and some are bound servants. They are Black or Indian or a mix of both, and white, too. But if we leave this neighborhood, we are marked by our skin, and farther afield, fewer than two in a hundred look like us. Even after generations, me and mine must be careful how we go, if we leave these few streets. Anyone may take offense at our presence, or try and cheat us, and it is all but certain, if a case comes to a court, the one that looks like me will be found in the wrong against someone who looks like you. It's too easy to find oneself sentenced and put into the service of a white man for any infraction, and then...too easy for a magistrate to forget that you were once a free man and keep you on in forced servitude. We live our lives on the edge of a knife and must seem neither to be a burden—a sure way to be put into service— or too rich, which would cause jealousy and scheming. So if I ever hear you speak so slightly again, we will no longer be friends, and that would grieve me, Anna, as I love you dearly as a sister."

Something in her friend's eyes made Anna understand that this was no trivial matter. "Prudence, I have the same great affection for you. I understand what you have said to me. I am sorry. I will endeavor to do better in the future."

The memory was as fresh in that fine library as it was the day it was made. "I will not deal in that trade," Anna said firmly. As much as she owed John Grenville, she and Prudence King owed each other their lives. "That is a line I will not cross."

Grenville muttered about lost opportunities but did not mention it again.

Most wonderful was that Lord Grenville let her sit nearby when he worked with his lawyers, so that she might learn their tricks and how he employed them. It was in this way she got to know Mr. Deering the elder, who was particularly diligent on behalf of Lord Grenville's affairs, and Mr. Deering the younger, his son and a quick and able assistant. The younger Mr. Deering, a well-made, very courteous and nicely powdered gentleman took it upon himself to explain whatever Anna did not comprehend. This way, by careful observation and questioning, she learned how to use the law to further her interests in ways she never knew existed. "General rules are for friends, but laws are for your enemies," Grenville elaborated after one meeting, and it seemed to Anna there was a great deal of sense in this.

All the while, Anna knew that even though Mr. Browne was placated by her securing the good will of the Plymouth customs officer, he showed no sign of suggesting she return to Boston. She began to hint that she should come home. She did not like being away from the Queen, and she felt safer when she could evaluate Mr. Browne's temper directly.

Each time, however, Browne asked her to remain, to see to this or that trifle, or find a source of some commodity or other. That put Anna on her guard, and she wondered why he did not come himself or send another one of his more favored lieutenants. All the while she knew that he still had designs on the Queen, and her desire to go home grew. She trusted him less than ever, despite the wealth she'd brought him.

By March, she began to feel nearly as unwell as she had during her voyage over. She did not speak of this to Grenville, but she donned her plainest travel clothing and went into Plymouth one day. Making inquiries at several taverns, she found a lady serving ale and asked her for directions to a good herbwife. "For I do not trust doctors and physicians, always poking at me as if I were a piece of fish at market, and have no money for them anyway."

The midwife, who lived on the outskirts of the town, examined

Anna briskly with knowing assurance. "When was the last time you had your courses?"

Anna shook her head. "Not since the beginning of October." It was now the beginning of March. "But it does not signify anything; they have always been erratic. The physician who saw me said I could not bear children."

"Well, that's far from the first doctor I've proved wrong! You'll be welcoming a little stranger in four months, and I'd lay any wager you like on that."

As soon as the woman pronounced it, Anna knew it to be true. The extreme and erratic hunger, the changes of humor, the queasiness, all the same as the time early in her marriage when she expected her first child, only to lose it. Thomas Hoyt had been alternately loudly distressed and quietly, dangerously angry, blaming her for the loss and secretly worried she knew that it reflected poorly upon him. She'd never caught a child with Bram or the others, and now understood she'd have to be more careful.

"How welcome will this baby be?" the midwife asked. Her back was turned to Anna as she put away the tools of her trade. "Will its father be pleased?"

Anna understood the question for what it was: an offer. But it brought a flood of other thoughts: The child was Hugh Williams's getting. She reasoned that, with a few miscalculations and fibs, it was also possible to lay it at Grenville's doorstep, should they become intimate. He was old, but he was a man, after all, and vanity and conceit never aged. It might be useful to keep the baby, too, as a precaution against Browne's wrath, but she rejected the notion instantly: Browne was no sentimental creature to let a pregnant woman escape his anger.

"I am not certain he will be pleased," Anna replied, "as we have recently suffered some setbacks. But men are fickle creatures, as likely as not to spend money on luxuries the instant after declaring we must be frugal. Who can tell?"

"Well, don't leave it too long before telling him. Men don't like surprises."

Anna scoffed. "Does any one of us?" Then she promised that she would be in communication with her shortly, never telling the midwife she had her own knowledge of the herbs that would do the job should she deem it necessary. She pressed a coin into her hand, large enough to buy services and silence, and with a nod, the midwife saw her out.

She was now happy enough to remain in England a little longer, to plan her next steps. She told no one about her pregnancy.

In a discussion about declaring one's own character in public, Anna told Grenville of her response to John Griswold's affront to her by his burning his tavern, with him in it, and how she had instigated her network of spies in the market and elsewhere.

Grenville's face never changed, but his eyes darkened. "And what if you cannot kill or threaten? You must take that lesson and adapt it to every situation. It is all about suiting the dance to your partner, Anna."

"How exhausting," Anna said. She was tired and increasingly uncomfortable in her pregnancy. "How can I ever achieve anything if I am always planning, scheming, investigating?"

Lord Grenville became very angry now, and he drew himself up with that silent stiffness that signified strong emotion among his kind. Anna imagined that if he could walk, he would be pacing, the strength of his emotion too great to be borne sitting. "Life *is* exhausting! There is no other choice, unless you choose to be a sheep. Then you might confine your interests, take what is given you, and then, after one year or two or ten, be taken from your safe meadow and slaughtered."

He relented, remembering himself. "My pardon, Anna. It is not fair of me; you are receiving this instruction later in your life than others do, sons, seldom daughters, who get it at their father's knee. That you require it now is testimony both to your cunning and wit, for others cannot see their own shortcomings and ask for assistance in mending them. If anyone can succeed in what you seek, it is you."

"And what is it I seek?" Hearing what she said, Anna caught herself, and laughed. "I mean...what is it you think I intend? I have always thought of finding the means to make my way in a world that cares nothing for me."

"Excellent! That is exactly correct. No, the world was not made for those like you. You must always ask for what you want, for even if you never speak those words to a soul, you must be able articulate what it is that you desire so that you will always be able to identify possible means to achieve that. If you cannot envision and express what you want, avenues will be closed to you that otherwise might afford you a viable route to what you desire."

Not long after that, studying *Hamlet,* Anna was struck by a thought so profound, she stood suddenly. She sat just as suddenly and was so overwhelmed, it took her several moments to compose her thoughts.

"It has always been thus, hasn't it, my lord?" She was trembling.

"My dear?"

"Old King Hamlet was killed by Claudius, and Claudius was murdered by Prince Hamlet, and Hamlet himself killed by Laertes. Greece rose and was destroyed by Persia, which was in turn conquered by the Mohammedans. Rome rose in Greece's stead, and flourished, then was downthrown by barbarian Ostrogoats—"

"Ostrogoths," Grenville corrected. "Go on."

Anna could barely slow the tumble of ideas. "...and England rises still in power, but there have been people here farming for seventeen hundred years, and all that time, they've been overrun time and again, kingdoms emerging and warring, and the land and people shaped by them with each turn of history. There is...no ultimate perfection. There is only a cycle of rising and falling; one starts bright, and then falls away, wasting as another rises."

Old Grenville's eyes glittered, and he was barely able to suppress some extreme emotion. "And what conclusion do your draw from that?"

"This...is all there is. Fortunes rise and fall, as do governments." She took a great breath. "There has never been any assurance, no safety, no security. Money helps, and connections are useful, but both of these might fail, and even rank, or prestige, or name does not promise anything at all."

Hook Miller had something like this, before. *I have seen things as bad as they could be, and I have survived,* Anna thought. *I mean to survive, and... now I know how. I have won.*

Anna sat in stunned silence, so many things being answered for her at once. It was as if one thread, being unraveled from a piece of cloth, led to another and another, until the cloth as she knew it no longer existed.

But now she had the threads to weave cloth of her own making.

Lord Grenville, had he been younger, might have turned a caper. He clapped, happily, then rang his bell so hard, that Eliot came running, thinking something calamitous had transpired. "Paper, pen, ink, and wax, if you please, Eliot, and find a footman to take this note," the old man said. "Then fetch me the most ancient claret in the cellars—I will toast this most singular, this nonpareil of women! Quickly, boy, I may not survive such an overwhelming joy for long!"

Grenville scribbled rapidly and applied his ring to the wax of the melting taper.

"My dearest Mrs. Hoyt, you have done the unthinkable! You have given me a reason to hope for the future. When such a mind exists, is there not hope for us all? You have the right of it, in less than a half year. Not so many youths at Oxford and Cambridge arrive at such a conclusion, so quickly! Anna, you have made me so happy, and given me so much diversion, I am determined to reward you."

He handed the hastily scribbled note, now sealed, to his footman. "Bring this to my agent in Plymouth, immediately. And send for the Deerings; I shall see them tomorrow."

He settled a large sum of money on Anna in an annuity, so greatly did she please him. Even if every one of her mercantile schemes failed, this would keep her in fine style for the rest of her life. And Browne knew nothing of it.

Several weeks later, Lord Grenville asked Anna to accompany him on a long day's journey. "You must pack what is necessary in case the weather forces us to remain overnight."

"Happily, but may I ask: Where are we going?"

Grenville shook his head, his eyes not meeting hers. "I think I shall keep that secret, for now."

She was able to conceal her growing belly under her skirts, but Anna always felt tired. It wasn't long after she had seated herself in the carriage, having had the maid pack a small trunk and donned her traveling clothes, that she fell asleep.

When she woke from her drowsing, the sun was at its zenith and the air no longer had the freshness of the Grenville estate. She smelled cold stone and a brackishness on the wind that howled outside, buffeting the carriage. The same void that possessed her in this same carriage, just six months before, assaulted her, and she resisted the urge to throw herself to the floor of the carriage. She did press herself into the upholstery, as if by making herself smaller and more compact, she might diminish the terrible sensation of...unconfined space. The sky was so vast it gave her vertigo, even when weeks of being at sea had not similarly afflicted her.

Grenville turned from the view outside, glanced at her abjectness, and turned away again.

"My lord Grenville." Anna's voice trembled and cracked with fear. "If you had any idea how this place terrifies me, you would never have taken me here!"

Still giving her his back, he said, "Indeed, I was made to understand by my people the exact degree of your fear."

"Then, my lord, you are cruel to subject me to this!" There was barely room inside of Anna's panicked mind to suggest that he might be taking her away to this remote place to kill her.

"You fear this place—what is its nature?"

"It is a desert, a wilderness—barren, no trace of taming or improvement of any kind," she sputtered, as if saying the words trebled the fearfulness of the place. "There is nothing safe or useful here."

The carriage, which had been slowly winding its way up a hill, finally stopped. The servants helped Grenville to his chair, making short work of it through years of practice. Then he insisted Anna join him.

Anna forced herself to get out, but she could not help but feel betrayed. She clutched at the back of his chair for support. The altitude, the expanse of the vista, the bare, rocky wilderness around her made Anna imagine she might be picked up by the wind and flung out into the vast space.

Grenville's manner was of a parent urging a child to some small bravery. "Come now, you can see, just a few miles hence, the harbor and the thriving businesses there. But no one cares for the land, here, for miles around, and they should. Is there metal to be mined, tin or iron? Are there caches of antiquities to be uncovered and sold? I myself have found an ancient pagan site on my land, full of silver coins, and all mine, because no one else bothered to look more closely! Is it good land for sheep or smuggling or would a road across it aid business of yours? There are hidden gifts that it would be a shame to ignore through shortsightedness."

Anna could say nothing; she was overwhelmed by the idea of evaluating a place, as if it was a person, to see how it might be made to work for her. The notion that there might be opportunities visible only to her was dizzying.

She stood behind him a while, no longer trembling, and let the ideas come and tumble, each revealing a new chance. Finally, she took a long last look around the valley and nodded. They proceeded to the carriages and began the return journey home.

"There are those who think of America as empty," she said at last, after she had calmed. "A wilderness."

Lord Grenville merely nodded and waited.

"I suppose there must be many things there, overlooked, and yet ripe for the picking, to those who might see with clearer eyes?"

"I think you are correct."

Anna leaned over, and clasped the old man's hand warmly, pressing it to her cheek. "Thank you."

One evening two weeks later, Lord Grenville came from a meeting with his son. One glance told Anna the meeting had not been cordial.

"It is my success in developing your acumen that makes me so impatient with him—if I had any other heirs, I should disown him at once," Lord Grenville said. He took several deep breaths to calm the shaking anger had brought on him. "He is determined to ruin the entire county, with his pious airs and poverty of foresight. He might hang, for all of me, and yet I won't let down my people who rely on my land."

"You must find a way to thwart him," Anna said, setting aside her correspondence. Mr. Browne's manner continued jovial, and the Queen's Arms was thriving, if Josiah could be relied upon. She had no desire to help the younger Mr. Grenville; he'd been offhand in his regard for her and made it clear he resented his father's interest in her.

"I shall." He looked at her. "And you shall help me. Anna, you are enceinte, are you not?"

It was the one thing she'd concealed from him so far. Or thought she had; perhaps now even her skirts were not large enough to conceal her belly.

"Come, come now. Do not be coy. I've watched your appetite change, I've noticed your occasional absence at breakfast, and more recently, your return. Are you expecting a child?"

"I am."

"Good. Give it to me. Back months ago, in November, you asked what I would want in return for your education. I want your child."

Anna now knew better than to react immediately, and especially not with shock or any pretense to emotion she did not feel. She thought it out, as he taught. "You want to overthrow your son with my child?"

"If you bear a son, I will ensure he will not supplant my son, but the child's inheritance will discommode him. If you have a daughter, I shall settle enough on her to make my displeasure felt to him, while still leaving my lands intact."

Again, Anna pondered, smiling gently, her mind racing. "How to effect this? You'd need the backing of the law to succeed against your son, and I'd need it to protect myself...and my baby."

"I shall marry you," Lord Grenville said, rubbing his thin hands in anticipation. "The clerical gentleman who has the living of my estate is handily quite flexible in his morals. It was one of the reasons I gave him his place: I turn a blind eye to his fornications, and he does as I say, and vouchsafes it with the word of a man of God." Grenville coughed, his lungs troubled by this excess of emotion and expression. "Of course, it shall only be a legal nicety, but I shall also make you a very good settlement as well, if you do me this very great favor."

Anna shook her head. "You know I always meant to leave, once my goals were achieved for Mr. Browne, and being reasonably sure I won't be killed instantly on arrival in Boston. More than that, I believe my education is at an end."

Grenville waved his hand. "No need to remain here, if you don't wish. This is merely a legal convenience for us and an inconvenience for my son. But let us be artful about this! You could 'die' shortly after childbirth, leaving an empty crypt behind and all the paperwork signed by me, your grieving spouse, and the parish minister. That would free you for other proposals at home and leave me an object of pity, a useful state I've seldom enjoyed. What do you say?"

"I say what you have said to me on how to conduct myself in any matter of commerce: Let us make a deal with our lawyers present."

Grenville clapped with glee.

The marriage was recorded in the Grenville estate records, observed and countersigned by the bought priest and two aged, illiterate and nearly blind gardeners. The younger Mr. Deering drew up papers to Anna's satisfaction, outlining how well her baby should be taken care of in every eventuality.

"It will be an easy life," she thought. "Far easier than mine, or any generation of my family before me." She wondered whether that comfort would make the babe stronger—with the security of a roof and board, an education and the support of his lordly "father"—or whether it would make the child lax and ungrateful, as it had with Lord Grenville's second son. The situation bore watching and consideration.

Several days later, Anna felt pangs, then agony. The baby, perhaps alerted to the fine life that awaited, was determined to arrive two weeks earlier than the midwife predicted.

Pacing, the pain was almost unbearable, and her labor seemed to take an age. Through the tears, Anna wished for Prudence and the Queen. She wished to be home more than ever before. What had she been thinking, to come all this way?

In her labor, Anna thought the smell of shit and blood and sweat would forever be in her nose. But the nurse and her assistants bustled and soon, Anna was washed and redressed, the baby swaddled and the soiled bedding whisked away. Another difference between the well-off and Anna's own upbringing: servants and spare clothes and linens and comfort.

Finally, she raised her head weakly. "What is it?"

"A boy. A lovely boy, as perfect as can be," the nurse said, putting the child on her breast.

"Well, here you are," Anna said to him. "For good or ill, here you are."

The babe screwed up his face and let out an outraged wail.

Just another in a long line of those who demand something yet don't know what, she thought, sighing. She brushed at his head, smoothing a tuft of hair, and that seemed to quiet him, she noticed with relief. She did not protest when the nurse took the babe away, and other than to make inquiries about a wet nurse and send another woman to tell Lord Grenville— who was as solicitous as any doting father—Anna paid the child no heed. Young John Grenville's happy life was already well established. She had done all a mother could, by bringing him safely into the world and vouchsafing her son's future.

She realized that her curiosity about this new creature was not enough to make her wish to stay with him. In fact, young John's arrival signaled the necessity of her immanent departure. She thought with dread that her return to Boston—and to Mr. Browne's volatile temperament—might not be put off much longer.

Only a few weeks later, Anna felt well—she'd healed quickly, ridiculously, scandalously, as if she'd been a farm animal—and was curious when the maid handed her a travel-stained letter in a hand she did not recognize.

My dear Mrs. Hoyt, It is with some urgency I write, bidding you come back with all haste to Boston. Matters temporarily calmed by the resuming of business at the customs house have deteriorated. It is this: Hugh Williams, of the day watch, has been saying how you were pledged to be his wife. Williams has moreover been much in his cups, either in anticipation of his presumed nuptials or in missing you; he has pronounced that he will soon have a nice little wife to keep him, and the living of her tavern—his tavern—appeals to him very much. You may imagine how this affects Mr. Browne, that a man like Williams—now so indiscreet and a creature of the magistrates—is to be situated so close to his business? He knew before you were keeping company with Williams, and assumed you were working to find favors from him or information or both. But to think there would be some more permanent connection caused Browne to suffer almost an apoplexy.

I do not know what your mind is, but I beg you: Return home with as much speed as you can muster. I would suggest you write Browne to reassure him, but if you do as I ask, you'll be here as soon as any letter, and that will be better for us all.

One more thing: I also have some interest in your speedy return.

Browne holds me responsible for you, as it was through me you two were introduced. He hints that I have been colluding with you against him, since I argued so strongly for your loyalty and good sense on the issue that took to you England in the first place.

Come home, Mrs. Hoyt, and help me set all this aright. I do not easily ask favors or for assistance, but I ask you now. Yrs faithfully, A. Seaver.

Anna set the letter down, her brow furrowed as she thought. The sun was setting over the harbor, casting glints of light so bright, she had to turn back to her chamber or be blinded against them.

Return to Boston, to Mr. Seaver's aid? Anna's lips narrowed and compressed; her hands clenched so hard, the letter was almost punctured by her nails. She was startled to feel her features so transformed, so suddenly. It was an unthinkable imposition.

And yet, it was time to go.

She glanced at Dolly and took a breath, feeling comfort and reassurance in the cool, brilliant gaze of the manikin. Anna's composure restored, her face almost as unreadable as Dolly's, as she found other arguments to make.

"He is offering his hand to me, as he perceives I am in trouble, Dolly, and asks for mine in return. And has there ever been such another, to do so for me? Only Mrs. King, Lord Grenville and Adam Seaver. I am not so rich in friends that I can afford to be careless with them. If he is such a rarity—a constant friend—then must I not repay him?"

Dolly was too wise to answer.

Anna set her glass down carefully, the dying sun casting a ruby glow upon the port wine that soon vanished as the sun sank below the horizon.

"Letters go astray, the perils of the sea being what they are, Dolly. Duplicates are sent by several means, and still, letters go astray. We might have never received this missive, have no knowledge of Mr. Seaver's plight or mine, and continue as we will, unaware that he desired assistance, or indeed, was in any trouble at all. Letters *do* go astray."

Dolly seemed to agree with her, but Anna began to pace the room, measuring out its length five or six times.

"My errand completed, I waited only until the brat was out of me and I could travel safely. I must go back, and with as much haste as I can muster. Bessie!" she called, sitting down at her desk and pulling forth pen, ink, paper and wax.

The maid appeared a moment later. "Yes, Madame."

"Please let Lord Grenville know that I wish to see him this evening. And take this, give it to one of the boys, and send him to the wharves to Captain Throckmorton at the *Dorcas*. Have him wait for a reply, but tell him to get back with all the speed he has. I will speak to milord at dinner. Please set out the dress and ornaments that best please him."

"Yes, madame." She curtsied and took the letter once Anna deemed the wax cool enough. Bessie closed the door gently behind her.

"And anyway, Dolly. Mr. Seaver's letters are sent with more care than most, we know that. If he should survive this and I did not come...? All would not be well with me."

She began to pack.

Chapter Eight: "A Modern Marriage"
August 1747-September 1747

On her arrival in Boston, Anna sought out Adam Seaver's home without even changing from her traveling clothes, which were now saturated with the late summer humidity. He was there, and unsurprised, as if he had been expecting her arrival.

"I have done the calculations many times," he said, "to determine when you might be here. When I had news of the arrival of your ship from a fisherman returning home, I expected—hoped—it would be this evening. Thank you for coming straight here."

"I could do no less, when I read your letter," she said. "I am glad to see you are well." She looked at him, raising an eyebrow.

"For the moment. With regards to your situation, I have managed to convince Mr. Browne that you still work on his behalf."

"Of course I do!" Anna's indignation was all-consuming. "As I have written to him—repeatedly—I have traveled across the world and back in his service. I have expanded his contacts and secured the means of an even greater fortune for him, and he has responded with enthusiasm. Has the customs officer not been cooperative?"

"Very." There was a long pause. "But you've not established the bribes in Mr. Browne's name. They are under orders to deal only with you."

She hesitated, and Seaver continued. "No, because your contact, quite rightly, put your name in his letter to Mr. Abbott."

She nodded. "It was his only condition. He did not know Mr.

Browne at all and I could not convince his lordship of that man's worthiness and abilities. He would only vouchsafe my character, make me his representative."

"This is not what Mr. Browne wanted. He is jealous that anyone—no matter how loyal—should have the control but him. You know this."

"I do!" she said. "I have written him, of course, and told him. He...he said nothing. I shall reassure him of my loyalty, in person, immediately, yet I fear he shall never be content, no matter how rich we make him." Another problem to wait for later. "What of your own troubles?"

"Browne believes I am scheming against him, what with Mr. Hammond's sudden demise. It is patently untrue, as you well know, but so far, I have been unable to persuade him otherwise."

"Certainly you explained that I had handled that matter? Or rather, Mrs. Hammond did?"

Seaver took so much time to answer, that Anna realized something shocking: Seaver was afraid. "He pointed out that you were across the ocean when it happened."

Anna recalled Lord Grenville's assessment of Browne, that his fearfulness caused him to sow dissent amongst his fellows. "What nonsense! The man is quite mad. I am horrified to think he might blame you for something I am responsible for."

"He sees conspiracy everywhere, recently; his humors have taken a turn. It seems the more power he gets, the more he wishes to create strife, to reassure himself no one will take his place away from him. Hence, his fractious behavior and his suspicions of your activities, which he perceives to be on your own behalf and not his. The situation is every bit as precarious as I wrote." He paused. "I am hoping to suggest a solution that might help us both, or at least, buy us the time we need to sort out both our situations."

Anna twisted her handkerchief. "I am happy to hear your suggestion, of course."

"I wrote to you about Hugh Williams, and that is, again, in part, what makes Mr. Browne believe you're working against him."

Anna shook her head. Surely she had proved her worth and loyalty too many times for this treatment? But it was always more, more money, more loyalty, more proof with Browne.

Seaver continued. "I suspect it is only our association—I might say, friendship—that has held his hand for this long. We are profitable for him, and in our individual ways, possessing much power over many people."

Anna nodded. It was a hard thing to think her life was held by such a slender thread as her association with Seaver. As if he must vouch for her every move—no, more. Would she never be esteemed for her own work? She buried the tiny spark that ignited within her, one more to examine at a quieter moment. She needed time...

Seaver paced and smoked a long while, the smell of the tobacco pleasantly mingling with sea air. Anna thought he had turned his mind to other problems when he spoke again.

"Perhaps that is the solution. If we married, Browne would be hard -pressed to find a reason big enough to do either of us such insult as harming the other."

The statement took Anna's breath away with its unexpectedness. "Mr. Seaver, what are you saying?"

"I am proposing another in a long line of business arrangements between us two, that is all," he said. "It is a good solution to our several troubles, and as, more and more, our interests are entwined these days, it may serve us on many fronts."

"A business arrangement," she replied slowly, her mind racing. She was too aware of her travel-stained clothing, her fatigue and confusion, and a sense of resentment and jealousy along with the idea that he might be after some of her hard-won wealth.

"Nothing more. A marriage of our business and... political interests, if you will."

"I would keep my assets my own," she replied quickly, too hotly. A ruse to get possession of her businesses? Now that she would be able to use the secret tunnel beneath the Queen regularly, she would not give it up. But she'd also learned from Lord Grenville what advantages legal alliances could make.

"We could draw up any papers you like," Seaver agreed. "With whatever legal protections you desire. I want to keep my business separate from yours, as well. We must maintain a few social fictions for appearance's sake, but I think we know when we are both well situated." Seaver laughed, and despite its mirth, it was an unsettling noise. "The great houses of Europe were founded on such principles of self-interest."

A thought suddenly struck Anna. "Mr. Seaver, I cannot have children. An illness—"

"Mrs. Hoyt, as I've said, it's a marriage in name only. You and I would keep separate apartments. There would be no children, if only because there would be none of the congress that brings them. We are friends, but I have no expectation that we would be anything more than that. It *is* an alliance, not actively against Mr. Browne, but in defense of us both."

She bit her lip, trying to fathom all the angles of the arrangement, the possibilities and pitfalls, just as she might consider the arrangement of pieces on the chessboard. Even though she trusted Seaver more than anyone save Prudence King on this side of the ocean, he was dangerous and this proposal was unexpected. It might not reassure Mr. Browne, but rather inflame his present suspicions. She also had to determine what a negative response to Mr. Seaver's proposal might get her: She could not be enemies with both him and Mr. Browne at the same time, fighting a war on two fronts.

Seaver's visage was still largely unreadable, but she knew he was afraid now, something she'd never seen before. And that worried her. Seaver cocked his head. "Anna, you are not thinking about this clearly," he said, looking directly at her. "I am proposing a way to save your life and mine. Browne's humors are fed by whim and directed by rumor more than ever, so he sees machinations where there are none. If it is nothing more than that, that is certainly enough for you to take my offer seriously. It is dire enough reason for me to ask you."

Anna nodded. There were hard realities to address, and those could only be met by creative solutions. Lord Grenville had assured her that there would be no impediment to her remarriage, as she was "dead" for all legal intents and purposes in that corner of England. In fact, she was astonished at just how useful legal manipulation was: Recording a "fact" and having it witnessed made that fact reality.

She took a deep breath and made her prettiest smile. "That is most considerate of you, sir. Thank you, I will. I think a quiet wedding, just as many as legally necessary—"

"That is my inclination as well, but I think...we need to be much more public about it. We cannot have anyone, least of all Browne, imagine we are not married, and a larger party is the way to best be seen and our connection recognized and understood."

"I understand." She sighed. "I shall look into the necessary arrangements, find a clerk, arrange the party." Anna paused before she finally asked, "What do you get from this, Mr. Seaver? It is a tremendous favor, but is it wise for *you* to *ally* with me?"

"It will confuse Browne, which I think is important. As I said before, he becomes imperious and divisive when he feels too comfortable about a situation, and so stirs up trouble to distract others. Yet, I prefer in this case that he be truly uneasy, as he is more likely to take good advice when he is uncertain, and so is more readily manipulated in our favor. That is better for all of us. It appears the man has no capacity to learn patience and see the more distant horizons of opportunity. At least this will give him pause while he tries to determine that we are not his enemies, or he will pause while he considers how to attack us both, as one foundation." Seaver paused again. "And there are other reasons."

"Such as? You were concerned he believed we were in collaboration against him."

"Perversely, he may be reassured by an outward show of allegiance. It will confirm what he believed to be true, but in a more innocent light. And..." Seaver huffed a sigh, and sat down. "Certain ladies are desirous of my attentions, and will be put off, finally, I hope, by my marriage with someone else. It seems foolish, until one finds them trailing one's coattails at very inopportune moments."

Anna remembered the appearance of a certain lady's brother, and the subsequent fight at the tavern the night of the last riot—but when weren't there riots, either fights among the Boston men or their brawls with the Royal Navy gangs? She nodded.

But Seaver was so reluctant to admit this that Anna was forced to just one conclusion: He was in love with her but could not find it in his gruff nature to say so. Many men had found her attractive, so why not him, especially when their interests were so compatibly intertwined?

"It simplifies many things," he went on, reddening. "Browne might imagine he can spy on you, through me, or curb your actions in some way, and vice versa. That will also be of use to us both."

She nodded. "I shall find a lawyer to draw up our contracts. You are agreed?"

"I am."

"And it may be that there are legal protections for both of us under cover of marriage. That warrants investigation as well. This could be an entirely new avenue to exploit. We must examine the laws for other ambiguities to explore."

Another feral grin from Seaver. "As I said. The royal houses of Europe have been working this racket for centuries."

They shook hands then.

Weary and feeling caked in salt and the grime of travel, Anna sighed and made her way home. As she walked, the ember of emotion she had put aside sprang into a blaze in Anna's heart. Her anger burned so bright, so hard, that by the time she reached her chamber, she clutched at her stomacher and tore at the hooks and laces before finally ripping her fichu away. She couldn't breathe, could barely see for the red haze before her eyes.

Why was it she must always take refuge in some man's name? Why were her alliances or misalliances what determined her prosperity, her safety, her role in life? Her father, her husband, Lord Grenville, now Adam Seaver? Even when she had her own money, made her own way in the world, and most of all, possessed the legal documents that said she was her own person, why did she require a man in this world?

How much was wasted, leashing a woman's efforts to a man, when their individual effects might be doubled? How much time was spent in remaking a woman's behavior to ensure that she had the guidance, no, the approval of so many men? It was discarding half the world, this legal foolishness.

But even if those laws governing ladies were overturned, would Anna still feel as alone as she so often did?

Even as she framed the question in her mind, she realized: It needn't be a man. *A friend, an ally, of any sort, is occasionally necessary. A dog, a child. Men happened to be the ones with the most power, the law behind them, and I have a positive advantage in being attractive to them. This is useful to me, and I should be grateful.*

While the idea that she required anyone at all rankled, she noted that the education she'd received from Lord Grenville was already proving its worth. The ability to remove such emotional confusion immediately was an invaluable asset. That resolved, she greeted her staff, shocked at how the boy Silas had grown, shooting up like a weed in the months she was absent. She spoke briefly with Josiah Ball to ascertain whether there were any issues of immediate concern. Finding none, Anna washed, ate heartily and then slept soundly.

The next morning, Anna was dressed and about early. She sent a note to Mr. Browne requesting an audience and spent the first hours of her day going over her accounts and settling her mind to address the most pressing matters that clamored for her attention during the past months.

There was now a regular, if light, traffic between the Queen's Arms and the warehouse on Ship Street. Once Josiah had discovered who owned the building that housed the other end of the tunnel, Anna had sunk a great deal of money into buying the warehouse so that she might own both ends of the tunnel. She counted it a small price to pay, for the previous owner, who could only be convinced to sell after some judicious blackmailing, had not discovered the tunnel's entrance on his property. She had fitted out the front room as a counting house, so that someone in her employ might always be watching the place. All that anyone knew, though, was that with the right password, someone might pass the bookkeepers to leave something in the back room, where it would vanish as if by magic later that evening, Josiah moving hunchbacked through the narrow ways between the buildings. Small valuable objects—papers or gold or jewels—could also be made to magically appear the same way. In this way, quite a number of transactions might be made with no one the wiser, and always to Anna's profit.

She was returning from that warehouse when she heard a whoop behind her.

Anna was taken aback to see a man racing toward her. She was already stepping back out of his path and reaching for her handkerchief filled with coins when, with a jolt of recognition, she recognized Hugh Williams. In truth, it was only by his limp that she identified him, as he had greatly changed in the past months. His beard had grown longer and bushier, and he'd gained flesh. His eyes were animated, but the rest of his demeanor suggested a long dullness unsuccessfully battled by an excess of food and drink. His clothes were ill-mended, and Anna realized with a start that he'd missed her.

She'd forgotten about Hugh except as an abstraction, merely one of her problems associated with Mr. Browne. It was strange to think they had shared an acquaintance, now; all she felt was an irritation at his effusiveness.

"Anna! You are returned!"

"As you see," she said, trying to summon up a smile.

"There were so few letters, I feared the worst!"

Anna recalled having posted at least one letter to him, giving it to the captain before they landed in Plymouth, but then wondered if she'd ever told him of her move to the country. His letters clearly had never found her, and were possibly even now, finding their way to Grenville's house, and then, back to her.

"Anna Hoyt, my dearest one! When did you return? Why did you not tell me?" Hugh reached her, and with another whoop, swept her up, crushing her in an embrace. He continued murmuring, his bristly face buried in the soft skin of her neck.

"Put me down! What are you thinking?" she hissed. She did not struggle, as that would cause even more attention to be paid to them, but her command had all the force of a whipcrack in his ear.

He set her down, the laughter vanishing slowly from his face as her words penetrated his emotion. "We are affianced, may I not even—Anna!" He stepped back, and his eyes focused on her gown. "These are not traveling clothes! How long have you been home?"

She could see confusion resolving itself in his face. It was painful to watch the slowness of his apprehension.

"You returned, and never sent for me? How could you?"

"Come with me." Without waiting to see if he followed, she all but ran to the Queen's Arms, entering through the kitchen door. Hearing the uneven creak of the steps behind her as she fled to her chamber, she knew he was still following. She pulled him into the room, shutting the door behind him. Her anger grew. Who was he to trifle with her life? Any inclination or affection for him burned away by the realization of her habit of finding a reliable man was no longer necessary. Now his thoughtlessness now placed her in jeopardy.

"What have you been saying, all the time I've been gone?" she demanded. "The whole town is buzzing with your grandiose claims, that we are engaged!"

"Anna, we are, are we not? You've given me so many signs of your love for me—"

"Fornication is no contract, nor is it a protestation of love! It is...a convenience, a release. A pastime, nothing more."

Hugh's face hardened. "You never believe such a thing, sweet!"

"Do not call me that. I never agreed to marry you, Hugh Williams, and you go blabbing all about town that I have. Do you know what you may have done to me? My reputation? There are those who do not care that we should be paired together."

"What protest can there be?" His voice grew raw with anger. "We are well-matched, reputable, we know even with respect to the..." He sputtered, blushing. "...the matrimonial bed...we are in every way compatible!"

Anna frowned, trying to determine how he had constructed so much from several careless trysts. "I am sorry you were so misled, Mr. Williams, but I never consented to be your wife, and you took liberties with my name to announce that I did." She took a deep breath; better to be done with it now, all in a moment, than to linger. "Especially since I have only last night promised my hand to Adam Seaver."

"Seaver?" William's face was as red as a cooked beet. "That...*animal*? I could abide him drinking at your place, but nothing more than that. Anna, are you mad? To make your way, with such a creature!"

"Sir, I must ask you to use more courtesy when speaking of my intended husband." The word was as awkward on Anna's tongue as the thought was in her mind, but better to break entirely with Hugh now. And better he be more concerned with her choice of husband than her other affairs.

"I will not allow this!" He turned, backhanded her and took her roughly by the shoulder. Anna, pushed beyond tolerance of Hugh Williams's fancies, kicked him in the shin of his bad leg. She caught herself before she punched him, and rather, thinking of Grenville's advice about the reputation of a lady, screamed loudly, bringing her people running. Only when Silas had slammed open the door did she slap Hugh in the face.

"How dare you! How dare you lay hands upon me in this way! How could you!"

How dare you think, much less say, "I will not allow this!" she thought. *How dare you presume so very much, and threaten my life and livelihood with it?* "Silas, please show Mr. Williams the way to the street."

"Anna Hoyt, curse you for...for a...for a damned...whore!"

The maid gasped, but Anna only smiled sadly. "Do you really think you're the first man to ever call me that, not getting what he wanted from me? Or resorted to the use of his fists? You're no longer welcome here or in any business of mine, sir. Please go, now."

She nodded at Silas, who using firm care, led the watchman out. The boy had filled out to match his height, but he knew better than to give Williams the usual unpleasant exit reserved for banned customers. There was no mistaking that, watchman or no, Silas was going to obey Anna's wish. Josiah had trained him well.

And yet Hugh Williams dragged his feet, shouting all the way to the kitchen door. "I know things, Anna! I know things about you...and Adam Seaver...and I will destroy that evil wretch!"

He suddenly realized that he'd gone too far, not only threatening Anna but Adam Seaver as well. His face went from purple rage to ashen fear in a heartbeat, and he stumbled over his next words in an effort to call his earlier ones back. "Anna! Anna...Anna, I'm sorry, I didn't mean to—"

After she heard the door shut, Anna sat. She couldn't help being rattled, and wrote a note to Seaver, who arrived very soon.

When she described what happened, Seaver's emotions seemed to ease, just a fraction. "I wondered. I ran into him—and he was staring at me with an intensity and hatred unusual for such a sorry sot. You know the fool has told me he will sue you for breach of promise, because you threw him over?"

She shook her head, uncomprehending. "I...never promised him anything."

"But, correct me if I'm wrong, you fucked him."

"Well, yes, but what has that—?"

He shook his head. "Anna, please, you are better than this. You know that such a simpleton as Williams would take that as a pledge."

Anna threw her hands up. "I was trying to keep him from pestering me with his proposals."

"He also threatened me with prosecution on several crimes he imagines he knows of." Seaver seemed unworried about this.

"And he did me—and you, again—just now." Anna gnawed her lip. "We must get him under control."

"Agreed," Seaver said. "And as soon as possible."

One of the plans that she'd begun while she was in England had come to fruition: The new house Anna had commissioned was nearly completed. On a hill above Boston Harbor, it was shocking to Anna how expensive the land was not so very far away from the Queen. The ceilings were high and the rooms regular in shape, giving a feeling of lightness that was a world away from the stolid and squat wood framing of the tavern, which now struck Anna as oppressive. While the new house was nowhere as grand as those owned by Lord Grenville, it didn't need to be, for it was quite splendid enough for Boston.

Mrs. King came visiting, and the two ladies sat talking over rum and needlework. When they visited, the ladies worked on what pleased them best, not what was needed for customers or the trifles used for show in polite company.

"Such a lovely bit of broderie perse, Mrs. King. I've always admired your gift with a needle," Anna said.

Mrs. King looked with a satisfied smile at the pattern of flowers and vines, which would be overstitched onto a stuffed coverlet. "So hard to get the printed cotton these days, Mrs. Hoyt. But I do love the richness and the color. Who wouldn't be happy to work over such beauty?"

"Imagine what you could do with a whole piece? Several yards? Or better yet, some of the India painted cloth?"

Mrs. King laughed, a noise that always gladdened Anna. They both knew Mrs. King had sold all the large bolts of that cloth Anna had smuggled for her to Boston merchants at a great price. "Well, we do what we can with what we have."

"Aye, we do. But you take scraps and make them into masterpieces, Prudence."

"That's what we do, isn't it, Anna? Scraps into masterpieces, table-leavings into fat hogs and feasts."

"Magicians. That's what we are," Anna agreed. And they both laughed as Anna saw Mrs. King to the door.

It was a rare moment of frivolity for the two women, broken when a troupe of idle children, drawn by the work being done on the house, scattered from Anna's property. She watched their blackened feet and trailing hems, and shuddered, knowing their bellies were empty. Anna thought on how carefully and hard she'd worked to avoid their fate. Such a sad misuse of hands and backs that could be put to better use than gawking and petty thieving...

She frowned, realizing these children were the unseen, unconsidered resources that Grenville had described, showing her the countryside around Plymouth. She recalled her use of George Tanner, the lamed vegetable seller, and realized she might expand on that idea, give these children, these creatures no better than alley cats, similar employment. Like Mrs. King's quilt, small remnants might be put together for greater use.

"Mrs. King, we know most of those children are orphans or if not, near enough as to make no difference."

"We do, Mrs. Hoyt. Their parents shunted back and forth, when no town will give them residence, and therefore, public assistance."

"And it is only doing charitable good to help them, is it not?"

"It is, indeed, and a neighbor's duty."

"And who notices a child running, or spying, or peeping? They know these streets as well as we do and are hardly marked by anyone at all. Excellent qualities in messengers, I think."

They shared a glance of understanding, then Mrs. King looked thoughtfully after the last of the children, who was crippled, struggling to keep up. "Were we not occasionally put to such use by our parents, when we were girls? Sent on errands of importance, but disguised by our youth and sex?"

"Such was my exact thought," Anna said with a great deal of satisfaction. "I recall Mr. Tanner has been unfailingly helpful in the marketplace, and I see a chance to expand this."

And so Anna began to let it be known that there was bread for hungry children, and they soon learned that errands or information was rewarded with small coins. Once or twice, Anna had to have one of her men roust the older beggars away who would have otherwise taken the food from the children, but she became known for her charity, and it was a situation that suited Anna and her "alley cats" very well indeed.

One day, Anna was busily at work, finalizing her orders for the wedding supper. She had at first shied away from such extravagant expense, but having reviewed her accounts several times over, could not deny that such a feast was possible six or seven times yearly if she desired, with the investments made by her while she was abroad paying handsomely and offering ever more opportunities.

Never in her life had she ever expected to have such money. Her purse gratified her and terrified her at the same time, as if the having of it ensured its inevitable loss. Yet she put that thought aside as no longer helpful. She knew how to manage herself and her funds and even if she lost it all—her parents' talk of the disastrous collapse of the South Sea Company's slaving trade still echoed in her ears—she had enough belief in herself to know she would get it back. She had resources at hand and elsewhere, to act as insurance. Therefore, she was determined to have the use of the money to do with as she would. She took Lord Grenville's words to heart, to make a splendid array for the guests with an additional special treat for those select few she most hoped to impress.

That gentleman sent word regularly about his son, and she thought proudly there must never have been such a remarkable infant who smiled so well or ate so heartily.

The new maid, Sarah, approached. "There's a lady at the door."

"I said I was not to be disturbed." Anna stretched; she felt a perfect slut, her dress wrinkled from having sat so long at her finances and her hair only hastily dressed.

"She said you'd see her. She said her name is Rebecca Charles."

Anna froze for an instant, her stomach turning to ice at the name. It was the most palpable sensation of fear she'd felt since learning that Mr. Browne believed she meant to betray him to Hugh Williams. After the icy feeling, came a slow burn, however, until Anna had gone from panic to a momentary composure to a hellish anger. There was no reason in the world for such emotion, and so extreme. The past was long in the past, and she was very nearly a different creature than she was even a year ago. And yet she could not put it aside, despite her recent successes in governing herself.

"Show Mrs. Charles to the parlor and prepare tea," Anna said, as she tidied her hair, glancing in the mirror.

"Yes, ma'am. The best china, ma'am?"

"Everyday will do for this lady, and be more than she is used to."

She swept down the stairs, cursing that she'd been caught unawares. And yet if Mrs. Charles had better manners, she would have sent a note ahead, asking.

"Madam, this is unexpected." Anna tried to keep the irony out of her voice. She realized that even if she was afraid she was less than perfectly presented, she still made a better figure than Mrs. Charles ever had or ever would. A small, churlish part of her took a savage glee, and she recognized it for what it was: the snatched triumph of one sister over the other.

The other woman was blonde and plump, but her curves were rendered blocky by hard work, which was also seen in her enlarged, chapped hands, and her hair was brittle from much time spent over a boiling kettle. When they were young, the two were thought twins and confused for each other, Anna born just eighteen months before Rebecca. She rose hastily, almost out of an unfamiliarity, made as if to embrace Anna, then extended her hand, then thought better of that. She sat back down. "I received your wedding invitation."

"Of course." Anna did not even recall what drove her to send one. Perhaps it had been some sentimental urging on Mrs. King's part, a relic of their early days together. Mrs. King herself had refused an invitation, saying she wished to keep her association with Anna as a friendly neighbor and not an intimate. Anna had reluctantly agreed to the sense of this, for both their sakes, but heartily wished her friend could be there. With a wrench, she pulled her attention to the woman before her. "There was no need to come in person to give me your reply."

She was struck by how poorly Mrs. Charles seemed, how coarse and tired, and realized, with a start, how she had once coveted the very dress the other lady wore, thinking it the epitome of fashion. It was crisply pressed and well-mended with tiny stitches, but even this couldn't hide its fading colors and spots worn shiny from years of use.

"I have not come for that. I have come to dissuade you if I could."

Anna felt her jaw tighten and eyes narrow, almost as if diminishing the sight of the lady seated before her would gentle her response. "Dissuade me? From?"

"Marrying Mr. Adam Seaver. Anna, you needn't do this. Come live with Edward and me. There's no reason to make this connection with Seaver. You know he is no proper suitor."

"He is my fiancé, not my suitor." Anna barely kept her temper in check, and her hand itched to slap the woman across from her. "I am certain it is none of your affairs to manage mine. By what right, other than pure impudence, do you come here with this bizarre presumption?"

"Anna—he is known to be...he is the worst kind of man. I hear stories everywhere. When people tell me of your business, it is always with a terrible, knowing look. They delight in bringing me the bad news of this unsavory association. You are being made a figure of fun, and worse, subjecting yourself to suspicious comment. Do not do it, Anna. Do not marry this man."

The maid came in with the tea, but Anna stood. "You may leave, Sarah. We will not be having tea."

The maid was all confusion. "I may leave?"

"You, this other lady, too, if she would. We have nothing more to discuss."

The maid turned away, but nearly paused when she heard the next words.

"Anna...sister."

"Do not dare to use that term." Anna stood, letting righteous anger have its way with her. "You no longer have the right. I am amazed you claim the connection, but no more so than your behavior today. I will not expect you at the wedding."

"Just like you. This is all to spite me, my happy marriage and my good name."

"Your dull name, bolstered with a simpering adherence to the rudimentary manners of the lower sorts, is nothing to me! I had barely remembered your name when you were announced. And there's certainly nothing left of the bond with which you might once have, with justification, offered me advice about my acquaintances, whether in business or more intimate matters."

Rebecca pursed her lips, and the two were so similar in appearance and ire, they might have been matching porcelain figurines on a mantel. "I've been told such terrible things—"

"Who?" Anna asked suddenly. "You do not go about so widely in the world, and certainly not in *my* world, that many would come to you with knowledge of my doings. Who is it told you such things?"

"There are others, worthier—" Mrs. Charles closed her mouth suddenly, having given too much away.

"Hugh Williams sent you," Anna said, understanding at last. Her violent emotions threatened to boil over. "Hugh Williams had the stones to...to...find *you* and—"

"Use whatever influence I might still have to make you see sense? What true man would not? You should have seen him, Anna—he was distraught. He is overturned with sorrow at your rejection, alternately sobbing or roaring, and he told me in what way you two were promised to each other." Here, Rebecca gave Anna another sour look. "He says terrible things about you—we can't credit them, of course, but it shows how sorrowful he is. And he's rightly horrified at this new alliance in which you entangle yourself—"

"Leave. Now. And tell Hugh Williams that if I ever see him—or you—again, you'll wish to hell I hadn't."

The other lady rose, the interview at an end. "I think you're being monstrously unwise, sister."

"And I think you're a fool to linger here." Anna turned her back to her sister. If Mrs. Charles was ever again this close to her, Anna swore to pick the eyes out of her head. Her hands clenched each other because she could not wring her sister's neck. "As for Hugh Williams..." She could feel a haze descending over her vision, which was closing to a pinpoint.

"It's as I told Mr. Williams, you never truly cared for him!" Rebecca spat acidly. Two hectic red spots burned on her cheeks. "That you eat up men's hearts and laugh at it. He won't stand for it, you know. He'll come after you. You, and the way you mock me with your fine dress and upstart house, the way you stole Thomas Hoyt from me..."

Anna laughed and glanced at her sister. "Stole? I couldn't keep the flea-bitten cur *off* me. You might have done better to keep his interest. You might have done far better to teach him some manners."

"Stole him. This family is always grabbing something away from someone else!" A crafty look stole across Rebecca's face. "You know Pa was going to take the tavern back from you, right? He never meant you to have it for long—just set you up as owner to protect his own interests. Ma told me so, right before he died, that he was going to take the Queen back. He didn't give a fig for your ambition. And here you are, all high and mighty, counting yourself clever with your numbers and books. You don't know when you have it good."

Anna knew this to be true, but as her father's scheme had fallen through, she had given it little thought over the past years. His intentions were unwelcome to hear, and Rebecca's spiteful reminder was a sharp shock to her, instantly transporting her back to that difficult time, stripping away all her composure. She ground her teeth, almost rising to snatch her sister's hair.

But Rebecca continued, maudlin. "It was too much to believe you'd found a good man who wanted you, after all these years. Poor Hugh Will—"

In the end, it was Anna's knowledge of how to needle her sister that saved her. She laughed aloud. "Oh, 'poor Hugh,' is it? You'd have him for yourself, if you could, you covetous bitch. Well, you can have him, with my best wishes."

Rebecca flushed red, indicating that Anna had found the mark.

Sighing in an exaggerated, cold fashion, Anna sat and picked up a bit of needlework and began to sew. "I think you can find your way to the door. Otherwise, I'll have my man to toss you out, like the gutter trash you are. Don't come by here again. Don't speak to me or of me again."

Rebecca was shocked. "Anna!"

She was the picture of dismissive hauteur. "You've become tiresome, Mrs. Charles. Good day."

Mr. Williams had been very busy. While he most patently did not speak to any magistrate, he spread ugly rumors far and wide, about what he knew for sure about Anna and what he could say, if he chose. He was more circumspect in mentioning Adam Seaver, whether because he feared him more or knew less than he'd claimed, Anna could not tell. She heard rumblings from her stray children and from her marketplace spies, and she knew things had become very bad indeed when Mr. Browne at last summoned her and Mr. Seaver together.

"May I offer my most sincere felicitations on your upcoming marriage," Mr. Browne said.

Anna and Seaver exchanged a glance.

"I had never expected such a situation among my associates, because of the decidedly...masculine nature of the work, and yet, I offer my very best wishes."

Before either of them could answer, Browne continued. "Now, with regards to Hugh Williams, I have not heard specifics, but that an officer of the court should show such ill-will is unacceptable."

"Mr. Browne, I assure you—" Anna began.

"Assure me nothing. Prove something to me. Before the wedding. Things can only get worse after that date if nothing is done about Williams." He returned to his letters, dismissing them.

When they left, Anna said, "We must address this, Mr. Seaver."

"Indeed, Mrs. Hoyt. I know you did not intend such consequences, but your entanglement with Williams is perhaps the most ill-conceived affection since Europa noticed the bull."

Ann could not make herself think until she heard the word "affection." "You mistake 'habit' with 'affection,' sir. Even before I left for England, I learned that I must break myself of the notion that I needed a man to get along."

Seeing his features harden, she amended her statement. "I only mean that, while we all seek society and rely upon each other in a community, the days of me relying *solely* on a husband are long past. I have proven myself and make my own way in the world."

He nodded, unconvinced.

"I have dared, and dared, and dared, and exceeded myself every time," she insisted, firm in her conviction and ability to convince him. "I have made mistakes, and I have remedied every one. This is no trivial matter, but it can be repaired."

Seaver spread his hands. "Well, what shall we do?"

"I shall tell him to meet me at the Queen, that I will run away with him—he's said he'd go away with me before."

Seaver could not contain his mirth. "I hear tell you lose many a prospective husband that way."

"Oh?"

"I heard noise from a friend in New York about a self-important blacksmith who still curses your name. I shall take care how I respond to a note from you summoning me."

"It's worked before," Anna said, shrugging. Inwardly, she was besieged by fear of what Seaver would do with this knowledge—she had thought he could not possibly know of Bram Munroe. "I must take care not to use that ploy after this. But after we have dispatched him, we shall arrange to remove his belongings and leave a note saying that he would not live here without me, and so must leave. I will ask him to visit, drug him and then do what is necessary. If you will help me with the disposal after?"

"Of course."

"And then..." A rebellious thought sprang into Anna's head. "We could...leave. We have no need to stay here, and fear Browne. After this, you and I, we may go elsewhere, and act for ourselves."

"You're mad!" Seaver said, incredulous. "We cannot run from this problem."

"I do not mean to. We should leave after we have made things right with Mr. Browne."

"No." He shook his head adamantly. "All our business, all our connections—"

"Are easily made up elsewhere, somewhere where we do not suffer the whimsies and ever-changing humors of Mr. Oliver Browne." Anna's breast was filled with excitement and awe at her plan, but also tinged with disappointment at Seaver's refusal. Even Hugh Williams would have gone away with her.

"Enough of this, Anna." There was a dangerous set to Seaver's jaw that raised the hairs on the back of her neck. "Do what you must to ready for your meeting with Williams. It must be done tonight, without fail."

Anna wrote to Williams, saying she must see him, that she would run away with him that night, and in secret so as to avoid Seaver's wrath. When he arrived at the back door of the Queen's Arms, Anna hurried him into the public room, pressing a glass of brandy into his hand as a stirrup cup and toast to their new commitment. It was well laced with opium.

He drank eagerly, then reeled, stumbling for a chair. He missed, smashing his head against the table before he half fell into the chair.

Hugh Williams moaned and stirred. Blood dripped from his temple, turning the few silver hairs there dark and the black ones glossy before seeping into his beard. "Anna, what...what has happened?"

"Shhh, Hugh. You must be still. You fell." Counting on the forgetfulness that commonly follows a sudden blow, Anna was calm. "Rest quietly, and I'll bring you a drink and clean that wound. It may need a stitch."

"Ale for me, then. Your brandy...it's too strong for me. I've given in to temptation too often lately."

Anna nodded and went behind the bar. He was still too lively; she had neglected to consider the flesh he'd added while she was away. Her skirts blocking the view, she slipped the contents of a small vial into one of the tankards, her hand shaking a little, and she returned with two mugs.

She served Hugh Williams, taking the other for herself. She raised her mug and her eyes met Adam Seaver's as he stood in the doorway behind Williams. Then she saluted Hugh.

He drank thirstily.

Anna watched until she saw his head bob, once, twice. She set down her mug. Stepped behind his chair. Drew out her bodkin—it was more difficult to use than a knife to the throat, but far better to make him look drunk or asleep until they could get rid of the body.

Hugh Williams head drooped and she moved closer, keeping her eye fixed on his ear, and nothing else.

She darted, quick and sure as a snake.

Williams's head bobbed up suddenly, and her bodkin struck his nose. Blood welled and flowed, and somewhere past the effect of the drug and the knock on his head, Hugh Williams felt the pain and screamed. His hands went up as she struck again, and bright red sprang up and ran down his palms.

Anna hesitated.

"Anna?" he said hoarsely, his voice pleading and confused. "Anna?"

"Shh, love, shhh." She seized his hair with her left hand, but pain and fear made Williams fight the poison and his struggles renewed. His desperation gave him strength, and he managed to push her hand away again.

Again a moment of hesitation, the same strange narrowing of her world to the space just between her and Hugh Williams. Anna was unsure what to do, unable to find the words to explain what was happening, to tell Williams that it would be easier if he just *died*, that all the hurt would go quickly if only he would stop fighting her...

She felt a firm hand brush against hers. Strong fingers interlaced with hers, holding Williams's head still.

The world snapped back into its proper proportions. Anna saw Seaver steadying Hugh's head, clamping down on his shoulder with his other hand. He moved with her as if doing a familiar dance, his eyes seeking hers.

Anna's wits returned, and she tightened her grip on William's hair, and, kicking her skirts up and out of the way, braced her foot against Hugh Williams' left thigh. He struggled still, but Anna's resolve was restored with Seaver's aid, and this time, with a final thrust, she stabbed the needle-like bodkin into his ear.

His body went limp, his eyes still open, something of pleading and confusion still in them. Blood bubbled at his mouth.

Suddenly Williams's body lurched forward, toppling in an ungainly fashion, chin-first onto the floor. Another well-placed kick from Seaver's boot and the corpse fell away from the center of the sitting area to the hard polished wood of the floor.

Anna frowned. There was no need, the deed was done and the matter settled. She opened her mouth to speak against this superfluous violence when a vile odor assailed her as Williams's bowels voided themselves.

She glanced at Mr. Seaver, nodding her thanks. Both were flushed and out of breath. She now understood the less blood and foulness on the chair's cushion and carpet, the less trace for anyone seeking Hugh Williams to find. It was not in Seaver to spare the upholstery for her sake, but she was glad the rug was saved.

"We had not finally determined how to rid ourselves of the remains. Your pigs or my fishermen?" Mr. Seaver said when they'd caught their breath.

"The pigs," Anna said. The wharf was closer, but the farm in Roxbury was unlikely to be visited or searched, and the cart was ready and waiting. Anna also knew that this problem was of her creation, so she felt responsible for the better part of the risk that might attend them.

"We'll check his rooms later," Mr. Seaver said. "And substitute the note we wrote for whatever he left, probably crowing about running away with you."

"Will you drink?" Anna asked as she reached for her own mug. "I am terribly thirsty, myself."

Seaver raised an eyebrow. "Thank you."

He took the mug of beer she offered him and swallowed thirstily. With a tight-lipped grin, he nodded. "Tasty."

Her own mug drained, Anna realized too late what he'd been thinking and laughed out loud. "Thank you for trusting me."

"Well, we are in this together. Also, you didn't ask me for a letter saying I was running away."

She barely smothered another smile. "Go on with you. I have no need, I have already written two or three, and keep them handy."

"And I have several in your hand," Seaver replied, also smiling. "Styled to suit the occasion."

"Well then, we are a well-matched couple." She sighed and looked down, realizing there was no time for rest or jokes yet.

Seaver gazed down at the body with disgust. "I'll get my man to help with the body," he said, wiping his hands on his britches.

"Why? I can help you. And as you see..." She spread her hands wide. "...I am even now properly attired for such work."

Mr. Seaver cocked his head and then assented. "The fewer who know, the better."

Anna found herself pleased that Mr. Seaver had accepted her assistance and spread the canvas after he rolled back the rug. She frowned, however, when he immediately drew out the cleaver and placed his hand on Williams' shoulder in preparation.

"Better to make a cut at the elbow," Anna said, unable to restrain herself. "It takes less weight, less tiring."

"Less weight, but more trips," Seaver insisted. "I can manage, woman."

"It's better for the pigs, to have smaller pieces," she said, not liking to be gainsaid. "I have always done it so." She paused. "I am well versed in how to manage a large carcass in my kitchen."

Mr. Seaver's face went blank, a sure sign of anger.

Anna kept still, bracing herself, her hand resting on her apron, close to her knife.

He took a deep breath and nodded. "For the sake of the pigs' digestion," he said finally.

"Thank you."

"Perhaps another occasion, you would indulge me by observing my technique."

"With your fishermen baiting their traps and nets with an unwelcome person? Of course. I would be honored to be so instructed."

Seaver nodded once. "Very well. The elbow, then?"

"Yes. Then moving up to the larger joints."

Anna made several trips back and forth to the barrel, not wishing to move it from where it could be readily rolled to the cart. All was done with a minimum of mess and the two worked companionably.

When it came time to change their clothing, Anna found herself at once familiarly comfortable and shy as she seldom was. After a moment, Mr. Seaver went about washing up and dressing as if they had always shared a chamber. They both had brought other clothes to change into after the dirty work.

"What will we do with these after? Bury them?" Adam Seaver did not point out that had his fishermen been the beneficiaries of his work, no one would be surprised to find bloody clothing coming off a vessel.

Anna shook her head. "No, I give them to the pigs as well. They do more than half the work of tearing them up, and then I boil them, selling the clean rags to the paper-maker. Or we can just cut them off him, with the same affect."

Seaver threw back his head and laughed. "Your economy does you credit, Mrs. Hoyt."

The color rushed to Anna's face. "It is not so easy to unlearn the habits of a frugal life, if one has not been reared to wealth."

He held up a hand. "No, no, I am in earnest. As we have discussed before, I am not partial to waste. While I would live well, I have never been an admirer of lavishness. My pleasure is at the dual benefits of your scheme, both in its economy and security. I am pleased to find such qualities in a...my...future wife."

Anna inclined her head, pleased and surprised by his approval. "The barrel, sir, I will leave to you."

Once outside of town, they resumed speaking. "The higher number of cuts does allow for a more convenient fit into the barrel," Mr. Seaver admitted.

Anna was taken aback by the compliment, still suspecting some hidden meaning in Mr. Seaver's words. "You are kind to say so."

The pigs, overjoyed to find this unexpected and opulent meal set before them, made raucous noises of eager greed and aggression as they fought over the choicer bits. Anna watched them fondly as Seaver built the fire and filled the kettle with water. The pigs having finished, Anna fetched the rags from the sty with a rake and added them to the boiling kettle along with a good deal of lye soap.

Finally, they were done. "Shall we sleep now? The chambers are always ready here in case I should arrive," Anna said.

"I could not sleep," Seaver said. "And I must be in Boston tomorrow, early."

"Then I will accompany you back, for I also have early business after we speak with Mr. Browne."

"Our lives do not allow for much recreation or reflection, do they, Mrs. Hoyt?"

"Indeed, I do not know how I should ever occupy myself in idleness, Mr. Seaver." Anna erupted in unexpected laughter, the effect of so much emotion and violent action, with too little rest.

But there was something else. Anna suddenly found herself surprisingly warm and drowsy, a great weight off her shoulders. And yet she knew that while they had so far gone undetected, they were far from safe with regards to Hugh Williams' disappearance and her previous association with him. There was no cause to relax, no reason to feel so unburdened.

Anna pondered her previous worries and found them oddly missing, like probing at a tooth that had been aching but recently extracted. Mr. Seaver seemed in every way reconciled to their plan and the execution of it. Indeed, in the past few hours, she'd developed an affection for her fiancé of a sort she'd never experienced before. His behavior most recently had been more than correctly condescending, more than politely agreeable. He had taken her opinions into account and considered them on their own merit with very little hesitation. It was a most pleasing sensation, she decided, to have a husband who was, for all his faults, a true yoke-mate in their efforts together.

But she had already caught herself in too many unguarded and careless moments, and took them as lessons. She did not trust the feeling of contentment, not entirely, and resolved to set a guard against incaution and unwariness. For the moment, however, she counted the day well ended and took Mr. Seaver's arm as he drove, resting her head against his shoulder. After a moment's hesitation, he stroked her hair then urged the horses back to town.

Chapter Nine: "A Firm Domestic Foundation"
September 1747

The day of the wedding was a blur. Anna was surprised at the nervous flutter in her stomach. This was a business transaction, after all, with a touch more sociability and more fanfare, but a business deal, no more. And yet, as excellent a social occasion as the wedding was, she realized that with the mere speaking of the minister's brief ceremony, people now viewed her differently. The ladies showed relief or approbation or another, new shade of jealousy, conversing behind their fans, their eyes riveted to her. The attitude of the gentlemen changed as well, but more subtly, in a way Anna had yet to fully understand. Was it the regret of not having bought something while it was still on the market? Were they wondering what Adam Seaver was getting that they did not see? Were they viewing her differently now that he in particular had chosen her? Anna marveled again at the power of the voice, or the signature, of some person of some accepted stature to make an idea a real thing.

Watching the guests dancing for the first time in the largest chamber of the completed new house, she laughed, taking another sip of wine, and realized that she was happy. It was strange to anticipate the future with a cheery outlook, but she relished the sensation, knowing it was not a false or misleading fancy, but sound and proved. Many problems had been solved and difficulties diminished, with her standing—and safety—intact, at least for the moment. She had found a solid footing with Mr. Browne's organization after her initial missteps and Mr. Hammond's demise. Why shouldn't she celebrate? The sword she'd given Mr. Seaver looked very well with his new coat, and she was vastly contented with the hundred bales of tobacco he'd given her. Anna approved of such a lavish and useful present. Why should she not enjoy the success she had created for herself?

Anna was en route to speak to the musicians when Mr. Browne presented himself before her with his wife.

"Madame Seaver." He bowed deeply over her hand. "Do allow me to wish you every felicitation."

"Thank you very much, Mr. Browne. Mrs. Browne." She curtsied. "Thank you for doing us the honor of joining us today, and thank you for your very handsome present." The silver tea service was an unthinkably costly gift, but a trifle compared to the fortunes Anna had brought him.

"We were very happy to see such close friends become even closer," Mrs. Browne said. She was a statuesque, stout matron, with brown hair going to silver beautifully arrayed in rose silk, which was perhaps a trifle youthful when seen against Anna's slender waist and lilac silk. "If you are looking for your husband, I believe you will find him in conversation over..." She looked around, and gestured with her fan. "Just there."

"Oh, dear," Mr. Browne said. "Someone seems to have fallen prey to temptation."

"I'm sorry, sir?" Anna asked.

"To the punchbowl. Mr. Simon Berry seems to have overindulged."

Anna looked across the room, where Mr. Seaver was quarreling with a drunken guest. Before she could say anything, Seaver seized the gentleman by the arm and the waist and led him away from the gathering.

Two more men broke into an argument, and Seaver, returning, placed his hands on the back of their necks. He drew them in closely and spoke, low and serious. Anna could not hear what he said but could not entirely suppress a grin when she saw the gentlemen gulp and shake hands, then bow to Seaver, departing hastily.

Mr. Browne chuckled. "The gentlemen are on their way to becoming the sadder for drink, it seems."

"If you will excuse me, Mr. Browne, I must find some other diversion for the guests. Thank you again for joining us."

"Oh, *Madame Seaver*—" He put such a careful emphasis on the words that Anna was immediately wary. "I would never consent to be away from such a happy occasion!" He kissed her hands, bowed, and offering Mrs. Browne his arm, left.

Anna hurried to the musicians and asked them to prepare to play a country dance.

Then she caught Mr. Seaver's eye and he hurried to her side.

"Will you dance with me, Mr. Adam Seaver?" She smiled, aware of how every eye was upon her.

Seaver's face was unreadable, but Anna thought she detected a note of reluctance. "Unless you do not care to? Perhaps you are thirsty?"

Anna cursed herself. It was possible that Seaver did not know how to dance. She had not thought to ask.

"I will dance with you...Mrs. Adam Seaver," he said with a light tone, and grinned briefly.

He led her to the floor and made a bow. While hesitant at some junctures, he danced well enough, though without some of the modern embellishments now popular in the best circles. Anna was glad she had asked for something simple rather than a French minuet. She found herself out of breath and laughing at the end of the tune as they bowed to each other and departed the floor. It had been too long since she had danced: holidays and weddings, as a girl, seldom enough while married to Thomas Hoyt, a few balls while in England.

Seaver escorted Anna to a seat and held up a finger for her to wait. He returned shortly with a glass of punch for her and she drank it thirstily. "None for you, husband?"

"No, for I mean to keep my wits about me tonight," he said with a broad wink. This was received with mocking wide eyes and raised eyebrows from Anna, and laughter from those around them.

"Well then, I shall drink to your very good health, ordered wits, and..." Anna paused as someone took her emptied glass and pressed a fresh one into her hand. "And...to firmness of purpose!"

"Firmness of purpose!" The guests roared around them with a clink of glasses while a few curses accompanied the tinkle of broken glass and porcelain.

Anna was suddenly aware that the guests' mood had moved from gaiety to hilarity and was now bordering again on raucousness. Her instincts as a tavern-keeper told her that it was high time to channel their high spirits in some useful direction, else her party might become the brawl she'd witnessed at Mr. Browne's house. She hesitated, a moment, realizing blearily that she had never hosted an event so grand before this, and while her education with Lord Grenville taught her that the better-born were not necessarily better-behaved, she was un-sure. Anna's giddiness and elevated humors were not due solely to her triumph; she had been consuming far more punch than she usually allowed herself.

She had staff she could rely upon but still pulled Seaver aside. "Perhaps it is time to signal the end of the festivities."

He seemed astonished. "Why? It is early yet, and everyone is enjoying themselves! More music, wife!"

And he seized her and whirled her again to the center of the chamber floor.

Finally, Anna was so tired and so much the worse for punch that her vision was swimming. Adam leaned to whisper in her ear. "I can barely keep my eyes open, and you are nearly asleep. Let us retreat, shall we?"

Anna nodded, and before she could protest, he swept her up into his arms. A roar followed from the crowd, and many of them seemed ready to follow the couple upstairs to the nuptial chamber. Anna had prepared for this, however, having previously arranged a bowl of punch and small gifts to be readied for the guests near the exits so that they could be led, childlike, from the house and the couple left in peace.

Anna's last memory was of feeling her face upon her pillow. She heard her new husband fall heavily on top of the silk coverlet next to her with a groan.

❋

The next morning, Anna woke, her head pounding and mouth dry. Seaver was nowhere to be seen, and with a sigh, she rolled over, away from the shuttered slats of sunlight, and dozed again.

Midmorning, Anna washed and dressed, and moved down the stairs tentatively. She took only tea and felt the better for it. Seaver was nowhere to be found, so she assumed that he had repaired to his own room, set up in the opposite end of the house, or had found himself engaged with his business. By noon, she felt enough herself to tend to her own chores, reminding herself that there was one reason to avoid the happy carelessness she had experienced the night before. It did not do to become fuddled in such company as Seaver and Browne.

After listening to the news of the streets from her "alley cats" in the back yards, she gave them orders, paid out a few coins and had the cook give them bread and some of the remains of the festive dinner. She made a list of the information she had garnered, comparing it with the papers, to see what she might learn.

The value of this was made apparent to her later, when news of another scuffle between the shipyard men resisting impressment by the navy men broke out. When she mentioned this to Silas at the tavern, he nodded, unsurprised.

Anna was taken aback. "Why didn't you tell me about this?" she said, exasperated.

"I thought you knew. Or, at least, it seemed beneath your notice, these days—"

She held up a hand, realizing that there was no excuse that Silas could give her that would explain the lapse. The blame rested on her own shoulders.

"You are overworked, and I am occupied elsewhere. I shall find you more help for the Queen's Arms, and you may better examine what comes this way in terms of intelligence. You won't work at the tavern anymore but be a messenger for me. It will require learning and hard work, but I will reward you for your efforts."

Silas continued sweeping slowly. "I would rather stay here..."

Anna frowned. "Rather stay and... sweep...and unload barrels and...?"

"Yes."

"Well, if that is your preference." Disappointed, Anna also knew that Josiah needed Silas's help, and if Silas had no higher aspirations, she would take him. She knew someone keenly interested would make a better job of sifting and relaying information to her. Silas was devoted, but really, unfit for much else but tending the Queen, and at least he understood that. She appreciated that, too.

"Thank you." His shy smile lit up and was gone the next moment.

Seaver did not come home until very late that night, and although Anna had not waited supper for him, she found herself put out. The maid had reported that he ate it cold and distractedly when he returned, long after Anna had retired.

And so it went for several weeks, when the October leaves began their colorful changes and the air grew crisp. Anna began to fear she had offended Seaver in some way. They were never so seldom in each other's company before they had married. Perhaps it was some other scheme to keep Mr. Browne's attention away from them, severally and individually.

She made a point to be up early, one morning, delaying her departure for the wharves in order to speak to him. "Mr. Seaver, is all quite well with you?"

"Yes. And you?"

"Yes, thank you, quite well. Only...you absent yourself so often. I never set eyes on you anymore."

He shrugged over his tea, his eyes on a broadsheet describing the latest outrageous acts of the Royal Navy in Boston, stirring up resentment and panic around the waterfront. "I have work, and you do, too."

"Of course." Anna felt a faint sense of relief.

"It is only as we agreed, is it not?" he asked, looking up suddenly.

"Exactly so."

"And while I have you, what shall we do about the shortage of men? The navy takes them so frequently, workers dare not show up on the streets for fear of impressment."

They sat discussing this for a quarter of an hour, then went about the day's tasks.

A few more weeks passed, and even Mr. Browne's humors seemed to balance out. He no longer hinted and provoked, and, having discovered some irregularities with Mr. Bell's latest efforts, happily focused his attention on that.

At this time, Anna wondered how she might use more of the things she'd learned from Lord Grenville. She did not believe, with her growing fortune, that she was in a position to influence the world's markets, but knew enough that she could almost sense opportunities to apply that knowledge to a more local problem. She did not have a specific plan in mind, but the notion seemed so ripe, she could not let the idea rest long without taking it out to reexamine occasionally.

She also had a letter from Grenville himself, which included a shaky but remarkably fine sketch of their son. Anna was surprised to see how good an eye the old man had, and was pleased that her son was so bonny and fat, and doing such an excellent job of ingratiating himself with his father. She thought it might be a pretty gesture to send some clothing for the child and made a note to consult with Mrs. King about a present for her "friend's infant."

Even while thinking about trade and finance, Anna struggled with the reality of her new household. A house so large as this one required two maids, a woman to come in and cook, a man to tend the heavy labor and another boy to run household errands. Anna knew that having servants freed her to attend more profitable business than washing and cooking, and she'd seen how conveniently Lord Grenville's estate was run, but she could not put the idea from her head that apart from a neighborhood girl to help her mother, Anna and her sister had always run their households. Her nerves were rankled over having to pay money to do things she could so easily do herself, but with her time more and more devoted to her businesses, organizing her home was no longer a simple matter. Anna finally conceded, telling herself that the more people in her pay, the more who owed their livelihood to her, the better.

She found herself vexed at the end of a long day of petty annoyances and greater misfortunes. Having been thwarted in a real-estate transaction and discovering that one of her shipments had been ruined by a leak of seawater, she kept an outwardly pleasant demeanor while inside she wanted to stomp her foot and curse the souls of the men who'd been so careless with her goods.

The day had been warm, and almost without thinking she changed her work-a-day gown for fine one when she descended to dinner. Again, she was alone, and the cook had spoiled the lamb.

However, wine eased her spirit, and a glass of rum after helped even more.

She waited up for Adam Seaver, well aware of the pretty picture she made over her fine needlework. "I'll join you while you eat," she said.

"If you like." Seaver was preoccupied with the day's matters. He ate absently, not seeming to notice the burnt lamb, and Anna's questions were met every time with a grunt or a shrug or silence.

"You seem troubled...Adam."

Finally, Mr. Seaver put his papers aside. "I had a talent for certain aspects of my business, but I find, more and more, that as I rise up through the ranks, I devote nearly all of my time to making sure others do their work, which was formerly my own. Those assigned to carry out my orders seem ill-suited and untrustworthy, and yet it is unseemly and taken badly if I take a hand in instructing them." He looked up. "I long for simpler days, that is all."

"Very trying," Anna said. She rose and went to his place, putting her hand on his. "Come with me."

His face went stony. "Where?"

"Our chamber."

He sighed heavily. "Anna, we had an arrangement. Why do you try to change it now?"

Not expecting this response, Anna quickly took her hand away. "I thought...we are married...Adam, we *may*. We might."

"I do not know what fancy has taken you, but...I do not need such complications and upheaval to distract me at the moment. The unease between the local men and the Crown's Navy continue and I—"

"My apologies, sir." Anna bowed. "I was mistaken. I wish you a good night."

As she left, Seaver called, "Anna, what in God's name are you thinking of?"

Shutting the door quietly behind her, Anna strode across her chamber, picked up a little vase and hurled it as far and as hard as she could. It shattered with a gratifying intensity. She reached for another, then controlled herself. She paced until her temper had cooled, then carefully undressed and went to bed. But sleep wouldn't come at all, and finally she got up to read her papers. That helped, and planning her next purchase of printed cotton was even more calming. She eventually dozed off over her books.

The next day, Anna took her sloop—she'd acquired a good one and a man to sail her—and traveled north to Salem to speak with a merchant-ship owner there about buying a majority share in one of his vessels. The transaction successful, she then toured the shipyard and spoke with some of the builders there. She was known only as an investor and thought having more than one home port might be useful, with the variations of weather and the shape of the harbors. Her business completed early, she caught the evening tide for home rather than stay overnight as she'd planned.

As she mounted the stairs, Anna heard the creak of the floor and whispers. The servants were all abed, Seaver gone for the evening.

Thieves.

She stole into her chamber and found her pistols, making certain they were primed and cocked. She was eager for violence, or at least to see the look of horrified recognition on the face of whoever was so ill-advised as to break into the Seaver household.

Tiptoeing down the hallway—she'd learned the boards in the new house that creaked less, out of habit—she paused outside the door. The noises were soft, but she was not mistaken.

She turned the knob and stepped into the chamber, her pistol raised.

It was firelight, not a lamp she'd seen making shadows under the door.

The two she'd discovered weren't burglars but lovers.

Adam Seaver stood before a seated figure, one knee upon the arm of the chair, breathing heavily but almost silently, as he was helped loose of his breeches. His cock sprung out, stiff and bobbing, and he moaned.

Before anything else could happen, he knelt down to kiss his lover, and it was then that Anna saw he was kissing another man.

She was dizzy, her head spun as if she'd been whirled around, playing blind man's buff. *No, no, no...it can't be. He's...Seaver, he can't be... Has he betrayed me to Browne? This is the end of...everything I've worked for...such a fool I've placed so much trust in him, and now, it's all for naught...all is lost...*

She gasped. The noise startled Seaver and his lover, whose eyes widened.

"No, Anna—!"

Blind with rage, sick with shame and appalled at her own stupidity, Anna could barely breathe for the emotions choking her.

And somewhere, through all of that, she almost believed she could feel the cold, dry hand of Lord Grenville's on hers, demanding that she think, think...just for a moment. She had felt murderous rage before, but acting on it before had solved something...

What will this solve? And what if I should miss? At the last minute, she shot wide of them and the ball hit the paneling, splintering the wood.

Before anyone said another word, she threw the spent pistol aside, turned and fled. She ran down the stairs and out the front door. Her stays cut into her chest as she ran, making breathing a near impossibility, and her skirts tripped her up. She found herself running, sweat blinding her, and when she could think clearly again, she stood in front of the Queen.

Her steps dragged now, the weight of her garments acting doubly on the fatigue she now felt. Something heavy and sharp hit her leg, and she realized with a start that she'd put her other pistol in her pocket. She stopped and, very carefully, removed it.

"As good a way as any I know of to shoot your leg off, you simpleton," she muttered to herself. Replacing the pistol, now secured, under her skirts, she gathered her wits.

Only after she could breathe normally did she realize that the Queen would have been long since closed for the evening—and what should she do there, in any case? She hesitated, wondering what she had seen, what it meant, unable to sort out the tumult of emotion she felt.

Across the street, there was a light on in Mrs. King's window. Anna ran over and knocked.

Mrs. King answered promptly. Anna knew her friend was often troubled with wakefulness. Without a word, she stepped back and admitted Anna, glancing up and down the street before she shut, locked and barred the door.

Only once they were safely up in Mrs. King's chamber did she ask, "Anna, what is it?"

"Prudence, I cannot tell you. I saw...something, tonight."

"Are you hurt? Your house? The tavern? They still stand?"

She held up a hand as she took a deep breath. "No, they are well. I am at my wits' end."

Mrs. King's brow was furrowed with concern. "Then it must be Mr. Seaver—"

Anna erupted into tears.

She took Anna into her arms. "What then? Whatever is it, Anna?"

In a few more moments, Anna was able to tell her what she'd seen. Mrs. King's face registered surprise and concern, and then finally, her brow cleared.

"You shot at them, but hit neither one of them? You are certain of this?"

"No, no, but...I don't know what I meant to do."

"Well, you'd best hope to find a good finish carpenter to mend the paneling, else pray you hit at the right height to cover the bullet hole with a picture or mirror." Mrs. King laughed, slapping her thigh.

Anna stared at her and wiped her nose on the back of her hand. "Prudence, how is this a joke to you?"

"My apologies, but...you were not ever truly married to Adam Seaver, were you? You'd told me all along it was a beneficial arrangement for you both, the better to survive the tempestuous seas of Mr. Browne's business? Am I correct?"

"Yes, of course, but..."

"Were—are you in love with him?"

Anna blushed, recalling the argument shortly after their wedding.

Under her friend's gaze, Anna remembered herself and thought hard. Finally, she shook her head. "I am...I don't know if 'fond' is the right word, but I do trust him, or I did. I care for him, and feel some affection toward him. But not love, not the way you suggest. Not the way I felt with Bram, or with Thomas, at first."

"There you are then."

"But Prudence, you miss the point. He's a... he prefers men!"

Mrs. King shrugged. "Anna, it's not the first time we've heard, or indeed, seen such things, is it? Not where we live, not really, at some remove from the folks who make up nice laws and then find even nicer ways to evade them themselves. It's not, is it? And even though you've moved next door to those fine folks, your heart is closer here than there, I know that. Now, are you going to run to Reverend Foxcroft and tell him?" She looked closely at Anna. "Are you going to run to the constable of the night watchmen, and tell him?"

Anna caught her breath, horrified at the suggestion. "I'm no tattle-tale!"

Prudence shook her head. "Of course not. And he was with another man—not a boy? Not one forcing the other?"

"Oh, his...the other...was definitely grown. Older than me." She recalled the gentleman Seaver had argued with the evening of their wedding and knew the truth: Seaver had been with Mr. Simon Berry.

Mrs. King shook Anna's hand and gave it two, hard little pats. "Then there is no harm done." She cackled. "Save to your wainscoting. Come now. Dry your eyes. Time to go home."

Anna raised her head, sniffing loudly. She pulled a handkerchief from her pocket and blotted her eyes. "I can't go back there."

Across the table, Mrs. King sat in silence, her lips pursed. She shoved a bottle of rum toward Anna and nodded for her to drink. "You've had a shock tonight, but you're wallowing like a child in your hurt feelings now. I never knew you to be such a fool, Mrs. Seaver. What will severing that connection do for you?"

Catching her breath, Anna heard the warning in her friend's voice. It was not a threat against the continuation of their relationship, but of something much more dangerous and immediate.

Mrs. King, seeing her hesitate, said, "It's that pride getting in your way, Mrs. Seaver. Damn me, pride is like water: too much, and you drown. Too little, and you die of thirst, a shriveled broken thing."

Anna's face cleared after a moment, and she nodded. It could still work, their arrangement, and even better, now that she knew. Nothing was truly upset by her discovery...but she must convince him of that now.

"You're right, and my thanks, Mrs. King. If I break with Mr. Seaver, I undo the protection he got for me against Mr. Browne's ire over the customs house. Maybe our marriage was to guard against Mr. Browne's curiosity about his personal life." She suddenly realized that Seaver's plan was not so much to guard against insistent female attention as to put Browne on the wrong scent. "And that protection I promised him, too. Worse, I make an enemy of him, who is my most powerful ally...a double blow. I was the one who tried to alter our agreement, not him."

"He is a dangerous man, and never forget it." Mrs. King nodded with satisfaction. "There's the woman I know. As I thought, it was only the pride of a lady's heart getting in your way, and glad I am there's nothing more than that to fight against."

A matter of sorry, wounded pride was all it was, Anna realized, mortified at how such a worthless emotion had governed her so completely. "That was a grievous indiscretion on my part, and a shameful lack of restraint," she admitted. "He is more than a friend, if not a husband to me, Mrs. King. He's offered me protection and aided me in the undertaking of my affairs, as I have aided him in his. In this, even if he beat me every day, he would still remain ten times the husband that Thomas Hoyt ever was. Look at all the two of us have accomplished together."

Anna actually laughed, feeling her spirits rise with each of her own sensible words. "I must not delay. I must make an apology immediately and try to repair this."

"Yes. And quickly. Any hesitation on your part will only compound the mire from which you must extricate yourself."

"Mrs. King, thank you for your comfort and counsel. It is, as ever, invaluable."

The other woman rose and took Anna's hand, giving her a soft kiss on the cheek. "Mrs. Hoyt—Mrs. Seaver, I mean! I know you will find the perfect means to reach a sterling conclusion. Many, including myself, have found their lives the better for your advice and assistance. I am happy to be able to return that to you in some small measure."

"But you have done as much for me, all our lives!" Anna cried. "Here, in Boston—while I was abroad, and even now! You help me steer through this complicated life of business."

"For which I have been well-paid, in addition to your generous gifts, which I know are a mark of our friendship." Mrs. King said. "That friendship that allows us two to confide in each other, in good times and bad, is another thing, and even more valuable to me."

Mrs. King escorted Anna to the back door, the better to conceal her departure, despite it being midnight with no one stirring.

✳

Anna's feet slowed as she returned to her home. She was now afraid of what she'd find waiting for her but knew her problems would be aggravated the longer she waited. As soon as she opened the door to the parlor, she found Seaver waiting for her. She almost froze, a frisson of fear overtaking her, knowing what he was capable of. All might be clarified in Anna's mind, but she still had to convince him all would be well between them.

"Why did you so immediately go to Mrs. King's house?

"How do you know this?" she asked, surprised.

"I followed you. Of course, I did. It's the first place you'd go, in any case. That you went there, and not to some judge, reassured me somewhat. You tell her everything?"

"I do. We have many bonds of friendship between us—you need not fear her having a loose tongue."

Seaver grunted.

She took a deep breath. So far, she was still alive. "I must beg your forgiveness, sir. Both for my intrusion and my...unseemly response to seeing you...both. I...I...trust neither of you was hurt, by my...outburst?"

Seaver stared at her.

She noticed a fresh scratch on his hand. "Perhaps just a splinter?"

"Madam, how comes this sudden change of feeling? Two hours ago, you might have committed murder. And now...?"

"I have been honest with you, Adam, as perhaps I have been with no other man save Lord Grenville, and damned few women, besides

Prudence King. You know most of my business, I know some of yours. In our ventures, there are few others we can trust. I have a fondness for you. I chose to marry you because it would save both our lives, perhaps, and at least strengthen our positions."

Another deep breath. His eyes were unreadable, but he was listening.

Anna continued. "We had agreed it was a business deal, and I know you well enough to believe it was clear to both of us the parameters of our arrangement. I was a victim of surprise, at first expecting burglars, and then when I realized what it was I saw, a bruised spirit."

Seaver began to pace. Taking hope, Anna continued. "Vanity, sir, was what drove my actions, nothing more. Again, I make my apologies and offer my fervent hopes that we may go on as we first proposed."

At that, Seaver sat down again, his head in his hands. It was an expression of internal disquiet, the most emotion Anna had ever seen from Seaver. He had not showed so much agitation when he'd killed two men in front of her in a London alley.

"I suppose you will not reveal me? Us?"

"No. If you thought otherwise, I might not make it to the front door alive?"

Seaver shrugged again. "Perhaps not a second time, no."

"No. But that is not the only reason I will say nothing. You have broken no promise between us, no vow shared, not that we've acknowledged. You've kept all your bargains, Adam Seaver. We could undo each other many times over, you and I, and that might be enough, but even that is not all. I mentioned trust and now I mention affection, for that is real, even if our marriage is not. We have been through so much, it seems a pity to break that now."

"Browne has been hinting about...Simon, but doesn't know," Seaver admitted. "I will need friends if he discovers the truth." Finally, he nodded. "You held your hand. Another would not have."

Anna's heart beat so quickly, she feared she might faint. The parlor took on an eerie appearance, as if darkness had fallen everywhere save around the two of them. Two lives, three lives, perhaps many more, stood in the balance.

"And how do you propose we go on?" Seaver forced himself to look at Anna. "I will not honor those false vows we took in public."

She shook her head. "You need not. We go on, as we had done, only this time with more perfect trust. No secrets between us."

"I am sure nothing like this has been attempted before," he said reluctantly. "This kind of marriage."

"But you were the one to tell me of such arrangements, and I have confirmed your words in my studies!" Anna could not restrain a loud laugh. "This *precise* sort of business-like union has been tested by the crowned heads of Europe—and most often succeeded!"

She shook her head, remembering something she'd read in England with Lord Grenville. "We are the makers of manners, Adam Seaver. We do as we wish and decide what is correct between us. No other person."

"Agreed." He offered his hand to her. She took it.

"I want to meet him," she said suddenly. She was amazed at her own inspiration, but knew it instantly to be correct. "Speak with him. Anything, anyone that affects you so closely, I need to...know."

Adam Seaver stood, as if to leave. "Impossible. What would seeing him achieve? I will not have you gawking at him like some kind of caged animal for your amusement."

"You mistake me. I need to understand. If you had confided in me, before my unfortunate observation of...you both...perhaps my dangerous response might have been averted. And..." She held up a hand to forestall his protest. "...if I had been more forthright with you at first about my hopes and expectations for our relationship, we also might have avoided the situation becoming so complicated."

"You don't know that." His eyes were hard, his glance harried.

"No, I don't. But I've learned so many things in the last year." Anna's eagerness grew as she pursued the thought. "You once said you valued my opinion when it came to observing people. I propose that any lasting...connection we form, the other must know about, to better secure our goals. To that end, I would like to meet Mr. Berry—was it not?—to know what kind of person he is. I do not mean to...pry or reveal his...yours...*our* secrets...but I would like to understand his nature."

He looked away from her. "You do not expect to...Anna, you are not proposing to observe us in our most private moments, surely?" His voice was a low growl.

"God above, no, not at all, not at all," Anna reassured him, horrified at the notion. "No. I have no doubt I am as familiar with the mechanics of your love as anyone else's. And, as with any love, someone ultimately gains and someone eventually loses."

Seaver scoffed. "That is a very bleak outlook for the species, Mrs. Seaver. Might there not be some joint happiness in any human connection?"

She shrugged. "I've found inevitably there is some sacrifice asked of one party in favor of the other, and either the sacrifice proves too much or the sacrificer is diminished. Hurt is the outcome, in every case, and I have never known it to prove otherwise, from the cradle to the grave. Which is why I suggest our current arrangement, despite these early, stumbling steps, is a more mutual and lasting expression of support."

Seaver was silent for a very long time, staring out the window; there was no sound but the crackling of the fire and sound of the rain against the windows. Anna forced herself to wait patiently, calmly.

Finally he spoke. "He is, you may well understand, a very private person."

"Of course. As am I. As are we."

"I will ask him," Seaver said finally. "He knows of you, of course, and now that there's no hiding him from you, it will require our combined efforts to repair the damage done by—"

Anna broke in. "I will apologize to him for my rudeness."

"Thank you. So I will urge him to meet you. How would you arrange it?"

"He may come to a meal, if that is satisfactory, or I will meet him wherever he is most comfortable."

"Then I will leave it up to him and inform you of his answer," Seaver said, sitting again. He closed his eyes and listened to the rain.

The next day, Anna was patient as she waited, knowing so much depended on this meeting. If she could work with Berry, all would be well. If not...then other plans must be made.

She had to wait several more days. "Simon Berry is not to be found." Seaver paced the floor in an agitated fashion new to Anna's experience of him. "He does this sometimes, when he is vexed with me.

To ponder, to lessen his emotions. He goes about his daily tasks, then hides away, making himself scarce from me until he can speak with a clear head."

"Will he...Mr. Berry...relent? Or will you find him?"

"That is my conundrum, Mrs. Seaver. If he avoids me of his own accord, I dare not seek him out. He'll send for me when he is feeling more obliging and all will be forgotten. If I go after him, he'll believe a promise between us broken, and then all will be over between us." There was a pause, then he whispered as to the wall. "I...can't bear that."

"So, as you say, he will most likely return and all mended." It was unlike Adam Seaver to be so distraught, so at sea, so uncertain of himself.

He shook his head impatiently. "But if he is not gone because he is angry with me, if he was...taken. Browne has made threats against me once before, and while I do not believe he truly knows about Berry and me or the plan formed by the three of us, it is possible. Or it is possible that Simon has not been as careful as he should be, concealing his true nature, and he was betrayed. He...he and I...we must always be careful, and if not careful, then brutal in our retaliation so that none think to come after us." Seaver paused, his face like a little child's, his voice almost the same. "Simon is very cautious, but he is not wily. He can handle himself if a private exchange becomes heated but..."

He sat and gnawed on his thumbnail. "I cannot go looking for him. Yet I cannot bear not knowing if he is well and safe."

Anna was moved as much by her own fear and confusion about Seaver's manner as she was by the pitiable quality in his demeanor. She set aside her work and tended the fire, then stood by his wing chair.

He took her hand in his, not looking at her, and crushed it in his own, as if he would wring his own misery from her fingers. Anna paused, unsure of herself, then stroked his head with the same trepidation as she might a strange dog.

Seaver began to cry, so silently, she only knew from the shaking of his shoulders. Then a noise slipped through his lips, so terrible that Anna froze. Not knowing if this was better or worse, Anna cast about desperately for some response. At last, she remembered Mrs. King holding and petting a sobbing child. She sat on the arm of the chair. Still clutching her hand, though not so desperately as before, Adam turned and buried his head into the skirts on her lap.

Anna sat, trapped, stroking his head with no sound but the fire crackling on the hearth.

A week later, Seaver returned home, and announced that he'd had a note from Mr. Berry. He had gained Anna permission to meet his beloved.

Anna walked past the counting house once, then returned, walking more slowly. She hesitated outside the window, hoping to see something that would inform her prior to her visit. The interior was rather shadowed, however, in spite of the two lit candles. She reached for the door and withdrew her hand. Appalled by her reticence, she seized the handle and entered.

"A moment, if you please," came a murmured voice.

Anna observed a gentleman, not in the first blush of youth but no older than Mr. Seaver, seated at a high desk. He was engrossed in a ledger; the hand he had raised, perhaps unconsciously, was speckled with black ink, though his sleeves were pristine.

He was not at all what Anna expected. She had anticipated one of those young boys with no beard and a mincing gait, willow-thin and pouting, waiting for their "cousins" returning from sea. Or else an overdressed fop, powdered and shining with satin and silver braid trim and paste jewels, with a stack of fines for wearing too-sumptuous apparel—bought secondhand, given, or stolen—to which he had no right by law.

No, Mr. Simon Berry was a sturdy, even well-fed man, dressed in a sober and nicely tailored brown suit. His black hair was tied back with a gray satin ribbon, and his face was round, though not fat. He had well-formed ears and his nose was perhaps a trifle wide, flanked by an agreeable, if unremarkable, mouth. The only thing Anna marked as surprising about his dress were his shoes. They were of a fine fashion that she had only seen on Mr. Deering, the elder, Lord Grenville's lawyer. The buckles were immodestly silver, with rosettes. She remembered that Adam Seaver had mentioned the quality of her shoes on their fateful meeting by the market almost two years ago. She wondered, with something like shock, if she saw his influence, or perhaps the way his taste had been informed, here, in Mr. Berry.

She glanced up again and was surprised anew by the look of Mr. Berry. Solid, studious, a gentleman. No riot of color or eccentricity of manner here, she might have passed him a thousand times on the street and made no more notice of him beyond her usual assessment of any gentleman: Was he a danger, someone to cultivate, a potential dupe? She was struck again by the incongruity of what she'd imagined and what was before her, and took it as an important lesson.

Something inside her eased and she realized, with a start, Anna sensed something slightly adjusted, as if a gear was rotated and fit properly into its place, allowing a clock to run. It took her several more heartbeats to identify her emotion as a kind of relief, mingled with enlightenment.

Anna suddenly understood that Mr. Seaver had no interest in a man who looked like a woman because he was not, just as he had honestly protested, at all interested in the fairer sex. She had nothing to be jealous of, because in no way could she contend for Mr. Seaver's heart in any capacity other than "friend."

Setting the pen down, Mr. Berry ran a finger along the last few columns of numbers, then, satisfied that all was accounted accurately, turned to Anna with a smile of welcome.

His smile faded when he recognized her, his eyes narrowing, his fists clenching. Finding himself staring at Anna, he reached into his pocket for a rag to wipe his hands. "How may I help you?" His voice deepened, grew less pleasant than before.

"I am Anna Hoyt, Anna Seaver, now, and I—"

"I know who you are and why you're here."

Anna was at a loss as to how to proceed. "Are we quite alone?"

"My associate takes this hour to dine. You may be as honest as you like, always considering you may be interrupted, either by clients or my own preference." He paused. "I also reserve the right to terminate this interview whenever I like. Do you agree?"

"I do. Thank you for taking the time to see me."

"I could hardly refuse," he said bitterly. "You hold the happiness of two lives in your hands."

"Surely three lives," Anna said. "For if we are discovered, all three will suffer."

"But we more than you, never doubt of it." His voice was suffused with unbridled resentment. "Beaten, perhaps killed. Whereas you..." Berry waved his hand dismissively.

"No, Mr. Seaver has as much power to ruin me as any you might imagine I have over him."

"Please, Mrs. Seaver, before we continue..." He turned to the accounts he had lately been studying and touched the book lightly, adjusting it so that its edge was exactly parallel with that of the desk. "Please believe me when I say I shall kill you if you ever harm him."

Berry turned back to meet Anna's gaze, holding it for a moment.

Anna had no reason to doubt the sincerity of his words, and it was almost in her to reply with a threat and reminder of who she was and of what she was capable, or merely to laugh at so bald a promise. But she had come to this meeting prepared to use every social ability she had at her command, treating her visit as if it were fraught with peril at every potential misstep. "Thank you, sir, for that information, and very direct speech. Be assured that I would do everything in my power to avoid harming Mr. Adam Seaver, for if we are not bound by conventional marriage, we are bound by far stronger ties." Anna glanced over at the stack of books, admiring them a little. Her own ledger was quite battered, but she could not bear to give it up for a newer one while it had pages left. She marveled at the neat rows of figures. "Such a fine hand you have, Mr. Berry. And I...I confess I do not quite understand your method of keeping books."

"We are not here to discuss bookkeeping—" He threw down his quill impatiently, spattering ink, dulling its tip.

"I am here to learn about you, and you me. The way a man orders his mind in his accounts may tell me very much."

"Did he feed you those words?" Berry was immediately suspicious. "Adam Seaver, I mean. Did he tell you how best to make up to me?"

She shook her head. "It is my own thought."

He stared at her, as if appraising. "I, too, find that the way accounts are kept—or not kept—reflect the mind behind them."

Anna smiled. "Then what better way than to discuss a subject of mutual interest."

Berry raised his eyebrows, frowning. "You are interested in accounts?"

"One of the two things I have studied since I was a girl. Although—" She glanced at the ruled sheets. "—mine is a daybook, and I am now struggling to keep track—"

"—of all your endeavors." Mr. Berry nodded. "It is this commercial age, Mrs. Seaver, that is complex and complicated at once, and requires new tools to go with it."

"And yet, no matter how modern the age, how quickly the innovations may follow, there are so many more opportunities than before. Opportunities for profit." She thought of her scant learning of markets and stocks, and wondered what Mr. Berry knew of them being so employed.

His smile was charming, wry. "Ah, but you may always rely on the baseness of human nature for those opportunities."

It was Anna's turn to eye Simon Berry. "Now I might ask you: Did Mr. Seaver tell you to say that? For it is a very watch-word of mine, to rely on the worst aspects of mankind."

Berry laughed sharply. "Well, there are two things we share in common."

"You said before, 'the way accounts are *not* kept.' What did you mean?"

He gestured to his work. "I work for many gentlemen, many presumed to be quite rich, who are, in fact, in disarray as far as their finances."

Anna's mind raced. "Mr. Berry, are you acquainted with Mr. Oliver Browne."

Simon Berry's face went as hard and blank as Lord Grenville's when he was in a fury. "I am."

"And you hold him in what regard?"

"Why, Mrs. Seaver, if I had it in me, I should arrange his sudden and expeditious journey to the devil." His look almost dared her to gainsay him, or protest. "But I think I know your feelings for that gentleman, if Mr. Seaver is an honest gossip. For my part, he has been nosing about matters of my personal interest that I wish he would not, and he has been hinting at Seaver about them."

Anna nodded. "I am no true friend to Mr. Browne, even if I work for him faithfully."

"My very own situation."

"And, would you tell me, is he one of those gentlemen who is orderly about his accounts, living well yet within his means? Or is he the other sort?"

"The latter." Simon Berry sat down again, resting his hand on the books before him. "He is in such a muddle that if I had the means, or the friends, I might ruin him."

Anna's heart filled with such gladness she could not help but laugh. "Mr. Berry, I am convinced we shall be very good friends, indeed."

Chapter Ten: "Masterpiece"
November 1747

Anna stared at the note with something like a premonition of doom. It was the same sort of polite invitation she'd received from Mr. Browne many times before, and yet the sight of this particular one sent a thrill up her spine. Seaver had described his mood of late as once again dangerous and uncertain, and had been going through his officers and agents searching for the cause, which was almost certainly to be found in rooted his own suspicious nature.

"Do you think he knows our plan?" They had started to siphon off Mr. Browne's wealth, using Berry's knowledge of his fortunes and bookkeeping, Anna's capital and Seaver's network of criminal connections. Berry was responsible for converting all of Mr. Browne's "cash"—in tobacco notes, letters against various crops, letters of credit, bank notes, coins from all around the world—into shillings in his own accounts. All Mr. Berry had to do was diminish his estimation of the worth of each form of currency by a small portion and skim that off. Mr. Seaver occasionally altered the destination of some the actual goods coming into port, and Anna, with her banking and trading connections, moved the money into other accounts, effectively making it vanish from sight. She and Browne oversaw those investments together, so neither had a reason to mistrust the other. If Mr. Browne had any reason to suspect Mr. Berry, he still would not have been able to trace such small amounts and exchanges readily, his awareness of such matters limited at best.

"No," Seaver said. "He is all abstraction when he discusses the loyalty or lack thereof with the men. It could be he thinks we've been pointing the navy towards his crews and men to be taken away to serve on their ships. He quite pointedly says nothing at all about you."

Anna nodded. "So we might imagine his suspicions are directed toward me, because of my relationship with the customs house?"

"It would seem so. He was like this last time he cleared house of supposed conspirators, and I rose so quickly in the ranks."

Anna realized that this was about the time just two years ago Thomas Hoyt had died. At the time, she had no idea of the machineries that surrounded her and she marveled at how her horizons had expanded since then. But now the note made her uneasy for more than the implied threat she and Seaver discussed. Browne had been at the heart of so many of her misfortunes.

The day of the appointment, Mr. Browne kissed Anna's hand, an uncharacteristically broad grin spread across his dewlaps. "I'm sure Mr. Seaver will forgive me such a liberty, but my delight in seeing you is immeasurable, Mrs. Seaver. How is your dear husband?"

"Very well, thank you."

"I do worry about him." Mr. Browne's concern was that of a comic actor. "Has he had any...peculiar turns, lately?"

"Sir?"

Browne hesitated. "He seems not to be his usual self. He is a man of rare habits."

"I'm afraid I must disagree with you. Mr. Seaver is as well as ever."

He wagged a finger at Anna. "Mr. Seaver's attention to business is waning. I fear it is due to his dedication to the pleasures of domestic life."

Anna now knew that either Browne knew the most dangerous secret in Boston, or believed he was close to it; this was the first wedge that Browne tried to drive between her and her husband. "Mr. Seaver is an affectionate husband and helpmeet, but would never neglect his work."

Browne smirked and sipped his tea. "Perhaps I am mistaken."

"I believe so."

"I am of an unquiet mind, of late, Madame Seaver, and that makes me impatient." He stood up. "You see, I know about Mr. Seaver and Mr. Berry. Confess to me what you know of their meetings, confirm what I already know, and when I've resolved the situation, I'll give you half of Seaver's shares in our work."

He said nothing specific about Mr. Seaver and Mr. Berry, neither their affections nor our plans with his accounting, Anna thought. *He knows nothing.* "I'm sorry, Mr. Browne? I do not understand."

"Come, Madame Seaver. You know what they plot. Tell me."

He knows nothing, Anna repeated to herself. *He casts about as he did with Mr. Seaver, hoping to catch something with this stingy bait. Hold fast.* "I cannot tell you what I do not know."

Mr. Browne sighed, shook his head, paced a bit and turned to her. He held his breath for a moment, as if making a decision, then spoke.

"You know, I had plans for Hook Miller. He was coming along nicely before he bungled things so terribly with you. You surprised me, and that doesn't happen. And then you continued to surprise me. But you took something from me, and despite all your ability and innovation, you must repay it. You must repay me for Hook Miller."

When she finally remembered the name, it seemed to come from the distant past. "I repaid that debt by going to London for you, sir. What were your plans for him—?"

"Please, Anna, do not play coy with me."

Refusing to accept his premise, Anna composed herself. "You want something—how can I help you?" She wondered if she would have to slay every rebellious dock worker from Salem to Charleston to satisfy Browne.

"It was the errand I sent Hook Miller on, which he never completed. The tavern. I've always had my eye on the Queen's Arms, and since commerce in this port has been growing, it has become even more attractive to me." He paused, and Anna felt the weight of his gaze upon her. "My reasons for wanting it haven't changed."

"My tavern?" She stirred her tea to cover her confusion. *Really? Still this? He might have ten taverns, far finer than the Queen...Could he know about the tunnel?*

Once again she observed that Browne had driven her to act in desperation, without her being aware of his hand in the matter.

"Come now. It has been some time since you've needed anything that place could give you. It is beneath you, now, a trifle. But a trifle that will please me and close a circle between us. For the sake of our friendship, you know I will pay thrice its value."

Most of which I shall have to return, in some equal gesture of our so-called friendship. Anna nodded. "You misunderstand my hesitation for reluctance. Your last statement took me by surprise, but you are entirely correct. It is true the Queen has been more of a distraction to me of late, and our fortunes are so intertwined now that it makes little difference whether it is your name or mine on the deed."

"So you will do as I ask?"

"Of course—but I must, you understand, discuss it with Mr. Seaver. I could hardly take such a momentous step without consulting my husband."

Browne's eyes narrowed. "I would expect no less, Madame."

"I cannot say that he would oppose the transaction, as he too complains my attention is divided between that tavern and our other affairs."

Mr. Browne nodded sympathetically. Anna knew full well he understood she had no need to consult Seaver, no real reason to pretend to care about his advice. It was a poorly concealed delaying tactic.

"But...if all goes well..." Anna hesitated. "When shall we meet to finalize the deal? For of course, I do not have the documents with me. There must be much to and fro between our lawyers."

Browne could barely conceal his glee at her discomfort. "Three weeks from today? I would prefer a quicker resolution, but understand that in dealings among such as us, we must be careful to follow the law as closely as possible, in some things." His small eyes glittered. "And I want to be very sure of this."

"I shall begin to make things ready for then." Anna rose and extended her hand. "Thank you, for so much, Mr. Browne. I eagerly look forward to this next stage of our association."

"Ah, well then, perhaps I worry too much." He kissed her hand again, and smiled, knowing he'd caused trouble and would soon see the profitable results of it.

Anna laughed. "À bientôt," Mr. Browne."

"Mrs. Seaver."

Anna walked with a light step to her carriage. She waited until she was down the long lane that led to Browne's house and some part of the way on the road before she let her mouth relax.

Browne was correct when he said she had outgrown the Queen's Arms.

He did not, however, have the privilege of telling her that he would take it from her.

Anna refused to consider the meeting until she reached her old chamber in the Queen. She looked around and met the glassy gaze of Dolly sitting on her desk.

"They never wanted me, Doll. Never wanted my talents or my energy or my goodwill, not Pa, not Thomas Hoyt, not Browne, none of them. Maybe it was the tavern or its tunnel, but never me. And now he takes the Queen to make the point? Only because he knows what it has meant to me, for I am convinced that the tunnel's secret died with Thomas's barmy mother."

Dolly said nothing, and prodded by her painted smirk, Anna took three steps crossing over the room, seized the unblinking manikin and dashed her against the floor with a sharp *crack*.

Anna reached for her old Bible—so long unread—and hurled it across the room. The covers flew open, the yellowing-white pages, lined in black and red, fluttered and spread. For a moment, the book looked like an ungainly bird about to achieve flight. A small dark object flew from the pages, catching Anna's eye as the enormous Bible hit the wall, falling with a tearing rustle and a thud. Anna crossed the room, and with a grunt, reached under the bed for it. There glinting dully through the tarnish was the ring she'd taken from Bram Munroe more than a year ago.

Her eyes filling with tears, she sat on the floor, clutching the ring, pressing her fist to her mouth. Where was he now? New York, as Seaver hinted? Or had he moved on? Why could he not have...? Anna could no longer remember how he'd consistently disappointed her, only how she missed him and longed to be caught up in his embrace. Perhaps if she was forced to give up the Queen's Arms, she would find him, make it up to him. But...

Her acquaintance with gentlemen seemed to fall into two categories, the happy and impossible or the unhappy and manageable. It was the last straw, the final indignity. Anna gave in to an unfamiliar weakness and wept for all she'd lost despite her hard work.

She could not say how much time she spent there, long after her tears dried, but shadows had appeared, climbing the wall, breeding darkness. She scrubbed at her face, feeling the salt tracks under her fingers, and raised herself painfully.

Slipping the ring on her finger, she began to pick up the shattered pieces of porcelain. Dolly's once-elegant dress was faded and worn, the lace trailing her once blemish-less arms etched with a fine tracery of craquelure. *I no longer need her*, Anna thought. *A guide once, I am capable of my own aspirations now. She is nothing to me, anymore.* And without another thought, she checked that she had not hidden anything under Dolly's dress, as she used to do, then threw the pieces out the window onto the cobbles of the yard.

She picked up the Bible and shook it gently so the pages fell straight, and replaced it on her desk with a lingering touch. So much work, so many transformations, and yet Browne had set her back to where she had been before Hook Miller had come into her life.

Out of a fond sentimentality—or was it desperation?—she let the Bible fall open where it would. She found herself reading the eighth chapter of Ecclesiastes and snorted.

"*'...wicked men may get what the righteous deserve. This too, I say, is meaningless.'*"

Meaningless? Not to those of us who get trammeled by the wicked men, she thought. *There is no answer here that I have not learned better with Lord Grenville. It seems only my death, or Browne's, will end this. So much, for no reason. Over a tavern. The root of all my wealth, the seat of my power, once upon a time, but now... Now there is so much, and he willingly overlooks the possibility of my larger holdings, however carefully I have them hid. He misses the point entirely, thinking only to hurt me this way, or that this way he can win.*

"I will not be caught up in this endless cycle of men squabbling and taking what I earn for myself," she said aloud. "My death or theirs, it ends now."

She returned home and told Seaver about her discussion with Browne. "He wants it...only because he has always wanted it," she said. "It is a childish whim, he has no practical plans for my tavern."

He listened, frowning, and then shrugged wearily. "Sell it to him, Anna. It is only a short time until we are reaping far in profit from Browne himself, in addition to whatever he does with the Queen. It is only a sad old building."

She bit back a retort at this insult, reminding herself she had felt the same way for some time now. "I shall, but how long are we to keep dancing to every tune he plays?"

"Until he is dead, or we are."

Stunned at again hearing her own words coming from Adam

Seaver's mouth, Anna was struck with inspiration. She could upend the table, end the game, change the game, as Grenville taught her.

Now it was time.

"We have enough, Mr. Seaver," Anna said, surprised at her words. She paused, realizing that even more surprising, she believed them to be true.

Until her second journey to England, Anna had believed that the only security lay in "enough." But since then she knew that every life was precarious, at every level, at every age, whether you were woman or man.

The memories of seeing her sister so recently intruded upon her thoughts. As girls, both had begun as equals, or nearly so. Now the distance between them was almost unimaginable. How had she come so far and her sister and their old friends had not?

She had learned. She had paid attention. She had changed.

But those were not the only experiences of life, Anna realized with a start. Until very recently, her experiences were those confined to the female and domestic worlds. Anna had moved beyond those and become an entirely different creature.

"We have more than we could spend in ten lifetimes," she repeated. "We have the security of a carefully negotiated truce with the other businessmen of our acquaintance, and if we are careful, that may lead to better things. We have become rich enough to consider honest business to maintain ourselves, or no business at all. Better, we could buy our way into an even better protection: the mask of respectability, which we claim by participating in civil matters, supporting politicians—the things that buy us favors and grant us access to more...we can do this, Adam!"

As she spoke the words, Anna knew it was true. Moreover, by explaining it to Adam Seaver, she was giving him the greatest gift she could give anyone: She shared what she'd learned, giving him the chance to remake himself as she had.

"What need have we of that?" Seaver frowned at Anna. "We are too well known, too notorious."

"Not to everyone," she said, becoming eager. "Those of political standing or ancient wealth or anyone who's needed dirty work done or covered up? They have concealed their connections with us, no more wanting to shine a light on us than on themselves. If we are careful, we can ascend to that most criminal of classes: the nobs, or what passes for them here in the Americas."

"Anna, you're drunk," he scoffed. "Or lunatic."

"Adam, you're not thinking at a scale sufficient to your intent. Consider: If they don't like the way something is done, they change the law. If they need goods transported, they rely on their cousin's friend's brother, who just happens to be the Crown's man in Jamaica and knows a way to pay off the pirates. They can be the pirates, if they want—all in a matter of legal niceties! Let's be the ones pulling the strings, rather than being their intermediaries. We can do it, here in Boston, where we might have more leverage, if we get rid of Browne. If you prefer, we can go someplace else, where we are less well-known. Far less trouble to move. We can remake ourselves!"

It was the same plan that she'd offered Hook Miller two years ago, but Anna realized now that it was no fanciful lure, the notion of rising in society. She knew exactly how to do it and become more than a mere merchant.

"I cannot leave Simon Berry."

"Bring him with us. Or stay—either way, it is the next logical step to securing ourselves and our fortunes. Ultimately, with Browne dictating our actions, there will be fatal consequences if we fail, but we can change this game now."

"All over an ancient, rat-infested building," Seaver said, lurching up from his chair. "I've never known you to be afraid. You were the last person I would call 'coward.'"

Anna was stung by this. "I am not! There is wealth, and then there is *power*. My plan leads to both. Yours...is only a continuation of what we have been doing."

"Which has been successful. Beyond either the scope of either of our dreams."

"Yes, but which has led to too many adventures that came perilously close to our destruction. This is not a retreat, it is the next step, and each step up has made us stronger than the last. As we ascend, we place more distance between us and these activities that might come back to haunt us."

Seaver snorted. "You would reform me? Start with yourself!"

"No," she said, exasperated. He would *not* see! "No talk of reform—we *know* how the world works. It is not elevation for elevation's sake, nor is it a denial of what we are. Adam Seaver, please, I beg of you. We lose *nothing* by moving on, ending this game."

"I do not understand you at all," Seaver said, the discussion clearly over for him. "I do not consider your talk of advancement at all useful to us. If you want my opinion, or my help, you must sell to Browne, and we will continue on as we three have planned."

He paused, confused by her passionate pleading, her insistence. Anna almost thought that might be enough to sway him or give him second thoughts, but then he shook his head. "We are done. Good night, Mrs. Seaver."

"Good night, Mr. Seaver." Anna sighed and nodded, burying the words she might have said under the appearance of acceptance.

How can he be so blind? My plan solves so many things for us. It is radical, yes, but—

He has never been so desperate as a woman, she realized suddenly. *That makes him blind to the number of avenues of escape and protection, camouflage and betterment. He, even with his curious love, has never been so desperate as I have. And now he believes he can act openly, either with our alliance or this newfound bravery, gained in surviving my discovery of his greatest secrets.*

Seaver's refusal to hear her was a betrayal of a kind, and those were common to Anna, but this was the sort she never had encountered before. After initial misunderstandings, their relationship had moved along in a smooth, comfortable and sometimes happy fashion. Why should it be so changed now? It was as though Prudence King had turned on Anna, a friend suddenly grown sour...

Anna's brow cleared. She'd found the answer. Nothing had come between them but a conflict of opinion.

That is all. But I must take steps to protect myself, she thought. *I will not rely on his decision. I must act on my own.*

The next morning, having closed the Queen and begun the removal of her personal effects prior to the sale of the tavern to Mr. Browne, Anna made time for conversation with her old friend.

"Mrs. King, we have often discussed the notion of retiring to one of the farms we've purchased, someday, far away from all this noise and disturbance here." She spoke carefully, for it was the day for Mrs. King's customers to receive their orders and Anna never knew who would be on the stair.

Mrs. King nodded. "We have often discussed the pleasures a quiet life might bring." But then she looked up sharply from her sewing. "Surely that day is far off?"

"Perhaps not," Anna said, measuring her words. "I will not always be here. No one could be more surprised than I am to hear such a thing, but it is true."

"The riots and unrest cause a good deal of concern, no doubt." Mrs. King put the work aside, nodding. "Is it such that we must begin to—?"

"I think so. You may let your neighbors know the new landlord of the Queen may not be as...affable as they are used to."

Mrs. King nodded. "I will do as you say."

"Here's money." Anna withdrew a large bundle from her basket. She placed it on the table with a heavy thud. "There's more if you need it. And while there's no need to be stingy, if you can get what we need for less, do so."

Anna placed her hand on the other woman's. "There is an equal sum here, for you, Prudence." She removed an envelope from the basket and slid it towards Mrs. King. "Drawn on my account at Mr. Gurnsey, the goldsmith's. It is to reassure you that you will always have what protection I can offer, no matter your fortunes or mine."

"Your dealings with Clarissa Jones and Mr. Oliver Browne make you wary of your true friends," Mrs. King said, frowning. "I have my own fortune, stashed away, no more than several eggs to a basket, as well secured as yours against foxes! But Mrs. Seaver, I shall take it amiss if you insist on me taking this. You do not need to buy my goodwill."

"It is not a bribe. All our lives, we have been friends, looking out for each other when we realized others who ought to would not. You have been invaluable in helping me with my recent business, and...I may not... those businesses may not survive the next month. I am engaged in a risky new campaign, in which I hazard *everything*. I want you to be able to leave, should anyone take it into his head to abuse you for our friendship. I should have said, this is to assure *me* that you have the means to escape, or bribe, or hire protection, as necessary. There may be distressing consequences of being known as my friend here, and I won't ever have you suffer for that."

"We've seen and outlived worse than you suggest, but your forethought, consideration, and kindness do you credit," Mrs. King said resolutely. "I will take it, and I will see what you ask is done, and when this is over and you are victorious, I will use it to refurbish the latest farm we've purchased."

Anna smiled broadly and took the other woman's hand.

The gradual manipulation of Mr. Browne's assets had been ongoing for several weeks now. It was astonishing to Anna how quickly the small changes effected by Mr. Berry, combined with her investments, grew steadily into more and more capital. Once or twice, there was grumbling from Mr. Browne's customers, who complained their orders were not correct, but these seemed only to be the ordinary fluctuations of business. When Mr. Browne soothed or abused them into cooperation and quiet, Mr. Seaver used his connections to circumspectly suggest other avenues of commerce, often furnished by Seaver himself or Anna.

Anna was content to watch their new accounts swell and amazed to see the ways in which Mr. Berry's advanced form of bookkeeping both facilitated their swindles and hid them. She knew, however, that eventually, inevitably, the pendulum of Mr. Browne's temperament would swing again, and some new disruption would present itself after the tavern, so she prepared against that.

It found them, as most calamities do, just over a week later, during a quiet moment over tea. A cough from the cook, signaling Anna was needed by her "alley cats" in her yard. One ragamuffin had a note for Seaver; she took it, gave the child a coin, before giving the note to her husband.

It was written, in Mr. Berry's hand, uncharacteristically blotted and smeared.

Adam Seaver read the note aloud, his face growing ashen as he did so. *"All is lost. We are lost. Some spy of B's watching me work. I think B knows that I use a different color ledger for each of our 'clients.' B wrote to me, asking about the blue ledger (that I reserved for our own private work), whether I had taken on new work and who was it? I put him off, saying it was a new merchant's account, and I would not break his confidence in me. But B pressed me to know about this new ledger and to meet with him this evening. Already I can see his carriage waiting for me—and around it, a slew of his toughs loiter. I am under no false impressions as to his intent. I do not have time to create a false ledger. I shall flee after I send you this via one of A's messengers. I hope you are able to escape as well.*

"My darling, I pray we may meet in that other, better world as we'd

always hoped. Sending all my love to you, and faithful to you in all things, I remain yours, eternally."

Seaver locked eyes with Anna, and without another word, began to arm himself from the large cabinet in the parlor. Pistols and charges, his favorite knife for close work and, after a moment's consideration, he buckled on the sword Anna had given him the day of their wedding.

She watched this in silence, knowing that nothing she could say would stop him. A surge of anticipation filled Anna, calming her and sharpening her wits. The time for contingencies was here; she had her plans in place, and he undoubtedly had his.

"I am going to Browne's—he is at his farm, no doubt, for his health has been poorly of late, troubled with gout. I will kill him, if I can, if he has done anything to Simon. Stay here; riots have been threatening for days now; the townsmen are restless and spoiling for a fight with the Crown's soldiers and sailors and their impressment gangs. If I know Browne, his men are poised to nudge a spark into a conflagration so that they may take advantage of the confusion and rob and loot his enemies. Do not go out, it is not safe for you."

Anna was moved by his concern for her. She did not say that there had never been any place safer in the world for her than Boston, and she did not fear the city or the waterfront or the men or anything else there. "Do you have money? Do you need clothing?"

"I have all I need," he replied. "Bar the door after me."

He placed his hands on her shoulders and squeezed sharply, the gesture one soldier might make to another before a battle. She nodded and watched as he left through the kitchen yard.

She did not bar the door, but wrote three hasty notes, dispatching them by three of her alley cats to the stables, Mrs. King and the man who tended her little sloop at the waterfront. She did not know what she would need, and she wanted all ready.

As she saw them off, she heard the clatter of hooves a street over. Then the slamming of a gate.

Anna was surprised to see Mr. Simon Berry standing there. She stood aside and let him in immediately without a word.

His well-made clothing was in disarray, stained with travel and sweat. A tear of his sleeve hem would never have been untended any other time. He clutched a case to his chest.

"Is he here?"

"No, he's left, gone to find you at Oliver Browne's!"

He groaned and sagged. "At other times when we thought our-selves in peril, I have always instructed him to wait for me and I would find him! Why did he go?"

Anna frowned. "He was desperate at the thought you might be in danger!"

He moaned and sagged, his head in his hands. "It's you," he said finally, his voice raw with emotion. "He's become bold, since he met *you*."

"Adam Seaver has always been a man of action, not diplomacy or contemplation," she said.

"No, he's changed, since he took up with you. Become bolder in expressing himself, in what he dares to do. Before you, he was content to follow the rules of the societies, impolite and illegal and otherwise, through which he moved. That kept us safe for a decade or more. And now, look at us! We are lost."

Anna had all she could do to keep her temper in check. "You were the incautious one, Mr. Berry, being so unwary with our work as to be seen with the new ledger."

"No! He said it was you who taught him he could change his designs and thrive. He said *you*." Berry wiped his face, inhaled deeply. "You've ruined us all."

"I am not responsible for this. I have afforded you protection, a shield for your affections." Even as she said it, though, Anna wondered if Berry might be right. It was possible she had inspired Seaver to be less circumspect, more adventurous in his dealings. When he might have threatened before, now he reasoned. Now he used more stratagems than fisticuffs, and he was not so accomplished in the first as the second. "We must find help, go to Browne's to help him. If there is trouble abroad, he can't have gotten far. We can still find him."

"You fool! I told him what I intended; ordinarily, he would have waited to hear from me, as I asked. He has not. He is overridden by his passions, and there is no governing him at all. Do you imagine he will stop once he has set out? He's going to kill Oliver Browne and now my dearest will himself be killed!"

Berry dashed the tears from his eyes. "We had prepared for a day such as this, but I always imagined we might have escaped together. I shall return to my people in Maryland."

"Wait, he may yet return! All is not yet resolved. We may all flee together."

"If you have any thought of survival, you must leave yourself." He paused a moment, and Anna was certain he would offer to take her with him. Finally, he shook his head. "You must go if you wish to outlive this night. Browne's gangs are thick on the waterfront, fanning the flames against the navy men. And I have no doubt Browne will eventually come looking for you. That is all I will say."

He turned and left. Distantly, she could hear the sounds of his horse's hooves against cobblestones.

She called out, and from the next street over, a child emerged, her thrice-turned red gown trailing behind her. "Yes, mum?"

"I have a note for Mr. Seaver," Anna said as she wrote. She scoffed, knowing that if the note found him, he would have to trust her to tell the truth, as they had joked her notes to gentlemen were often lies and lures. "If you find him, give it to him and return with an answer. Do not be seen if you can help it." She handed the child a small coin. "There's trouble abroad."

"Yes, mum."

"Check the stables and market, first." Then she held up a gold coin, and the child's eyes widened. "If you find him, this is yours. I'll be back later."

Simon Berry was right about the number of Browne's men down by the wharves, and their numbers were swelled by others who had no sense of why they were there, only that something was brewing between the locals and the Crown's men. For where there was strife, there was opportunity. She saw a few near the Queen's Arms, keeping an eye on what would be their master's newest property. Anna realized with a start that the sale of the tavern was scheduled for the next day: She had forgotten all about it in the moment.

She spoke a few words to men who were customers of hers and sympathetic, that the navy and Browne's men were close to violence, and that they should encourage it, if they saw the chance. They agreed with alacrity: The threat of impressment kept other ships from docking at Boston and that was bad for business. Then she went down the street, and making certain she was not observed, turned and slipped into the warehouse on Ship Street. In that back room, she had readied some materials useful in uncertain times, what she came to think of as her own "priest's hole," like the preparations for sieges that Lord Grenville had once described. She regarded her cache there, still untouched, took a small basket and descended into the tunnel that led to the Queen.

She was able to move quickly, the low tunnel damp but reassuringly reinforced thanks to her efforts with Josiah. She emerged at the other end, in the Queen's cellar, and climbed slowly to the main floor. The place was empty, closed for refurbishment, the bulk of goods save the liquor and ale taken away.

She had known for some time that the building itself was old and in poor repair but it had felt safe, with bones solid enough to create a haven for her. Even after her first trip to London, when she'd recognized the quaintness of the tavern, and, indeed, the squat, red-brick provincialism of Boston itself, the Queen had been like a bastion and retreat to Anna. And yet...

A memory overtook her of a day when Anna had caught herself pacing the exact dimensions of her chamber over the Queen's Arms in her new, larger chamber. She had moved beyond the confines of the Queen, even if her heart would be there, always.

Now all she could see was how the cobwebs and dust collected in the rough texture of the beams. They might not have shown by firelight, but now blowing like ragged lace curtains in the breeze from one of the cracked windows, the cobwebs gave off an air of dinginess that disgusted Anna. The creaking, uneven bare floor, worn smooth from thousands of boots and shoes, made her wary of tripping. The bar had been polished to a glossiness by decades of resting arms—sometimes heads—and glasses, mugs and bottles sliding across the wood. Anna traced a stained crack in the wood with her finger, thinking that its sturdiness no longer reassured her. Her new sensibilities were refined so far beyond those of her youth that she no longer recognized this place. She could no longer be its genius loci; it would no longer be her refuge. Her eyes and mind had changed, in such a short time. The chairs of which she had been so proud were fit only for the kindling box. As her gaze flickered from the redware and stoneware vessels on the shelf, the barrels half empty of their beer and cider flanked by the bottles of Ginevra spirits or rum or whiskey, Anna felt none of her previous satisfaction in their orderliness. She saw only trifles to be finally tallied in her ledger, before that account was closed forever.

And yet...she could not quite bring herself what needed to be done. The lesson of the Queen had been drummed into her, body and soul, and her affection for the place could not be swept aside with her recognition of what it truly was. The Queen had done its job, kept her alive and provided the time for her to learn how to stay alive in the face of adversity, by virtue of its value, and being sought by so many.

The tavern had taught her much. Anna recalled the document that made it her "feme sole merchant," and how she'd kept it in her shoe for want of any safer place. Now it was hid away, safe in the keeping of a lawyer's files. Not that she needed it anymore: Like a minister or a lord or a magistrate, she'd made the place hers by force of her character in ways no piece of paper could represent.

What had once been her world, full of riches and safety, now struck her as full of shop-worn wares and shoddy makeshift. It was time to give it up, deal in the hard currency of present necessity. The luxury of her previous fears, which had rooted her affection, pride and stubborn resistance to any path but that which would keep the Queen hers, was too costly. The land was still hers and she'd rebuild there, but for now, she needed to remove the distractions, take the Queen from the board.

Finally, it was the memory of Lord Grenville's gardens that convinced her this was the correct choice. His roses bloomed all the more for being pruned back, the sick ones removed for the sake of the rest. This was a way for her to flourish with a small sacrifice.

She remembered the text that had inspired her how to save Bram by deceiving him: *Where no wood is, there the fire goeth out; so where there is no talebearer, the strife ceases.*

She set the basket down, so carefully, and removed the napkin. She removed the bung from the small cask that sat there and picked up the cask, tipping it over. A fine trickle of black powder trickled down, following her as she moved through the building like a trail of yarn. She was careful not to get any on her gown or to step upon the line she drew and thereby break it.

From the attic chamber to the cellars, Anna wound her way through the last hallway, the gun powder trickling from the hole in the cask and leaving a path behind her.

She knew she must leave everything behind that might be looked for by the authorities; her portable valuables were long since removed to her new home and she had made a show of moving some of the finer liquor to her house, complaining her regulars didn't drink it. She recalled the Romans and their policy of burning towns and salting the arable land of an enemy. She smiled and blessed Lord Grenville again, and blessed Bram, who had taught her so much about fire and refined her use of it after she had shared her own propensity for it with him.

The place rang hollowly with her footsteps. Anna stepped a little more lightly to avoid disturbing the emptiness with echoes.

There was nothing here but memories, and the strongest of these were in every shade of distress: desperation, fear, anger, longing. Hope, then hope abandoned—and hope was a deceiving bitch, Anna thought, a sudden anger erupting in her heart. So much stock placed in a little word that promised everything from a warm meal to eternal salvation, and so seldom delivered. It was a fine word for empty promises, for preachers, for men, who were the only ones who might reliably count on some expectation in this world.

The rest of us, we must make our own expectations, she thought, *and fight to achieve them at every move.*

"Damn Mr. Browne, but he shall not have her!"

Anna picked up the now-empty cask of gunpowder and realized she could leave it there. She took a bottle of rum—cheap New England stuff she kept for the sailors who were content with it, and took a swig, feeling the familiar burn down her throat. She upended the bottle, watching the contents slosh on the floor, and then threw it as hard as she could against the far wall. She struck a flint and steel, catching the spark on a pile of straw and sawdust she had ready, and then set it to the powder before she descended into the tunnel for the last time.

She emerged at the other end of the tunnel, hems damp, but otherwise as nice as nice could be. Pausing only to arm herself, she went to the stable and mounted her horse, making for Mr. Browne's, riding as hard as she could. The tide was against her, and there was no need for a carriage for this visit. She had done what she could with her instructions to the men to encourage hostilities between Browne's men and the navy, to create distraction from Seaver and cover for him to escape, if he could. The distraction of the burning tavern would also sow confusion. Now she had her own appointment to keep with Mr. Browne.

The door to Browne's house was ajar; she heard footsteps, swearing, and screams just beyond. Summoning all her courage, Anna stepped in, her pistol raised. The floor was covered with blood and muddy footprints. She pressed herself against the wall, aghast at what she saw before her.

Several of Browne's men were dead or dying on the floor, their blood painting the place. In their midst, Adam Seaver was glorious, in his true element, as he fought two more, a welcome release after so much civilization. Browne himself watched, wounded, trying to find some way to help his men as they attacked Seaver.

Seaver grunted, taking a shallow knife wound, but then snapped the neck of his attacker, flinging the body at the other man. That one dodged away, and Browne stepped in with a knife but slipped in a pool of blood. As he fell, his knife spun away.

Anna hurried in and stepped on the blade. Then she stomped on Browne's wrist, breaking it. When he tried to grab her ankle, she fired her pistol at his other arm. He fell back to the floor, his screams lovely to her. She knelt down and seized him by the back of his neck-stock, twisting it, as he tried to cradle his two broken arms.

She looked up to see Seaver wrestling the other man, finally getting one arm free so that he could shoot him. The man collapsed.

Seaver wheeled around, a diabolical light in his eyes, covered in his blood and that of his enemies. It took three heartbeats before he recognized Anna.

"Go!" she cried. "Mr. Berry came to me, looking for you, but he has fled! There is trouble in Boston, so you may be able to catch him still—but if not, he says he is going to his people."

She waited until she saw that Seaver nodded, understanding. "And him?" He blotted a cut on his cheek, then pulled a fine white cloth from the table, scattering and shattering the china plates on it. He tore the cloth to bandages and bound his wounds.

Anna looked down at Browne, who was now blubbering, red-faced, snot mingling with his tears. He reminded her of Dolly, now only fragments scattered on the ground. "I'll deal with him."

"Thank you, Anna," Seaver said. He reloaded his pistols, and she did the same.

"Thank you, Adam," she replied. "Now hurry!"

He turned and ran out the door. Soon she heard the noise of hooves in the lane fading.

"Shh, shhh, quiet now."

Browne looked up, hope in his eyes. He snuffled.

Anna knelt and loosened his neck cloth carefully, though the blood spilled during the fight made untying the knot difficult. Pulling it away from Browne's neck, she smiled sadly, regretfully.

"It needn't have been like this. I worked honestly on your behalf, and yet you saw betrayal at every turn."

"I see that now," he blurted, snuffling again, trying to catch his breath. "I understand, how wrong I was, how I mistook your efforts...we can..."

"So much lost—and for what?" She looked around the room and shook her head. "It'd make a cat cry. Even before we'd met, before you knew my name, you were conspiring against me."

"Anna—"

She wiped her hands, used the end of his stock to wipe his face.

"No, Mr. Browne, no. It's too late. It can't be undone." She sighed and her anger at all he'd put her and so many through welled up. So much waste... "You must promise me that when you arrive in hell, you will tell everyone that it was Anna Hoyt who sent you there."

She grabbed the scruff of his hair, pulled his head back. Took up the knife again and drew it hard across his throat as cleanly as if she was slaughtering a piglet.

Anna waited until the blood stopped bubbling at his throat. She stood, a little shakily, and cast her eyes around the room. She found the secretary she'd so often admired and began to go through it. One large compartment was locked.

She heard a scream.

Mrs. Browne, in a dirt-stained work apron, ran to the corpse of her husband and cradled his lifeless head in her lap. When she could get no response, she finally saw Anna and scrambled to her feet. She held a wicked looking pruning knife at her hand and advanced.

They were a world away from when they had first met at Anna and Seaver's wedding, both splendidly garbed in their finest.

Anna raised her other pistol, halting the other woman. "I'll shoot you where you stand, I'll take the papers I want and no one will ever know I was here. They'll assume it was whoever killed your husband. Give me what I want and I'll leave without killing you. There's no need for that"

The fight went from Mrs. Browne's eyes. Not dropping the knife, she moved as a sleepwalker across the room. She paused when she reached the corpse of her husband again, and she shook her head, as if to wake herself.

"Where were you?"

The woman seemed to be in another world. "I heard horses, shouts, from the garden. I hid there until it was quiet," she said, dazedly looking about as if she expected someone to come and help her. "Apparently, the servants had the same instinct."

"The papers for the sale of the Queen's Arms—I need them." Just as Browne had been cautious about the sale, so would Anna, making sure no one would falsely sign the carefully written documents. "Is there a key?"

When the woman pursed her lips and stared silently defiant at Anna, she raised the pistol again. "I can kill you just as easily and break the cupboard open, if I have to. I don't want to. The key?"

Mrs. Browne sobbed and reached into her husband's ruined waist-coat. She pulled out a bloodied ribbon, with a key on the end, and threw it to Anna, who cautiously picked it up.

"I shall be leaving here," she said as if to herself. "I expect someone will come, anyone, but it seems that everyone—everyone but you, that is—is dead or gone. Or soon to be."

The key barely made a noise in the lock, so use to wear and so well oiled was it. Anna opened the cupboard door and saw the legal documents, the unsigned deed of sale for the Queen's Arms, on the top of a pile of books.

Oliver Browne's ledgers.

"I'll take these, too," she said, gathering them into her apron.

"There's a basket in the hallway," the other woman said, with a sob. "Take anything you want—I've done with this place, this accursed town. Just take it all, and begone!"

Anna realized that while Mrs. Browne did not show it, she was afraid of her. Long years of practice with Mr. Browne, she supposed, had trained Mrs. Browne to school her face and voice. *You don't show any emotion to a wild dog, you don't make eye contact, you don't make sudden moves.*

Anna felt that something ought to be said. "Thank you, Mrs. Browne."

Mrs. Browne snorted. "Go to the devil." But the words seemed to bring Mrs. Browne back to herself, and she shrugged. "In fact, I believe you will find your own way there, sooner than later. But you might not, if you learn from me and my mister, over there." She nodded at her dead husband. "Although we are nearly strangers, I believe you, Mrs. Seaver, to be a lady of some discernment and intelligence. Don't make the mistake of overreaching yourself. That way lies only distress and violence."

Anna, so fatigued by her day's efforts and emotions, could not restrain a laugh. "Mrs. Browne, I thank you, but I have only stayed alive these past years because I was in a constant state of overreaching myself."

"And here you are," Mrs. Browne said.

"Yes." Anna felt the other lady taking in her dirt-smeared gown, tear-streaked face and filthy hands. "Here I am, when many others, more powerful than me, are not. My state may not be impressive at the moment, but I assure you, not every effort that keeps body and soul together leaves one composed as one might wish."

"Efforts? Ha!" Mrs. Browne shook her head. "You people—all you Sommers folk—you always have pretty words and excuses for the deviltry you work. It only follows that you'd be just the same. Once your father and his partner won that damned tavern, it wasn't any time at all before your father turned on his partner—his own brother, your uncle, Joseph Sommers. Philip cheated Joe out of his share of the tavern when Joe was drunk, then faked Joe's signature on the deed. And then tried some legal rubbish to make sure Joe could never get it back. Smooth talk to hide cruel work!"

The woman spat and stepped toward Anna, her eyes hard and contemptuous.

"Stay where you are!" Anna raised the pistol. "Mrs. Browne!"

"Mrs. Seaver," Mrs. Browne mocked and stepped forward again. "No, I should say 'Anna Sommers,' because you'll never change your stripes, no matter how rich you become, no matter who you marry. You're gutter scum, a whore, a murderer and I'll make sure the world knows it!"

Anna stepped back. "I'll not warn you again!"

Another step forward. "—just like your family—"

Anna shot Mrs. Browne. Raised her second pistol, and shot her again.

The woman collapsed, dead as her husband.

Anna found a discarded pistol and discharged that into the body.

Anna reloaded her pistols again and picked up her bundle. She found her horse, and carefully stowing the basket in front of her, nudged her horse onto the road. She reached a turning and paused. She could hear the tolling bells and knew that a riot had started in Boston.

She should leave, now, retreat to the countryside as she'd planned with Mrs. King. But with Browne dead, and Seaver nowhere to be found, who should step into their shoes?

"Must I do everything myself?"

Her mother's voice carried across the small tavern, two years before, but Anna could barely register it, her hands clamped over her ears as her father, in the chamber above, coughed unceasingly with pneumonia.

Anna watched Mary Sommers mixing the medicinal syrup into the mug of tea her husband had requested. "I've lost two children, and the ones who survived are girls. I can feel the cancer gnawing at my gut, I'll not see another month, and still I'm waiting on the man hand and foot. My life has been a plague and a misery since day I fell for that bastard's sweet talk."

Anna noticed that the syrup was not of aniseed, which might have soothed her father's cough, but had come from the jar her mother kept far at the back of the highest shelf in the larder. The belladonna.

"He shouldn't have done that to poor Joe," Mary said, shaking her head. "No, he shouldn't have taken advantage of his own brother—but Philip will come to his final judgment soon enough. The minister isn't hopeful about your pa's chances of lasting week."

She cast a sharp glance at her daughter. 'Course, that means you'd have to make all the decisions about how best to run the Queen." She shook her head again. "You two—butting heads—no wonder he caught pneumonia, you worried him so with your plans—"

"Mary! My tea, dammit!" came the breathless demand from up the stairs. Another bout of wet hacking ensued, followed by a groan.

"Enough. Bring that up to him, and mind you—don't taste it, not a

drop!"

Anna stared at the brown earthenware mug, fragrant blackberry and honey wafting in the steam.

"Go on, girl! Must I do everything myself?"

The tolling bells brought Anna back to her present conundrum: She thought of the terrible men she had met in Browne's company and shook her head. They would fight and tear at each other until they destroyed themselves and the city around them. She would not have that. She turned the horse toward the smoke now rising from the city and the sound of the bells and followed them back home.

An hour later, as she watched the flames devour the old tavern, leaping from windows, and attempting to overtake the other houses on the block, tears streamed down Anna's cheeks. At first she didn't feel them, because her face was warmed by the fire and exertion, but eventually, the chilly breeze startled her by cooling her damp face. She moved back, not wishing to be consumed by the pyre, for pyre it was, the immolation of the remains of her old life. A wave of giddiness and nerves overtook her as Anna struggled to compose herself. She marveled at the beauty of the fire and efficiency with which it could accomplish her goals.

The land, the tunnels and now all the buildings around the tavern were hers, bought at great expense and with quiet patience during her sojourn in England and since then, with the help of Mrs. King and Mr. Van Meter the lawyer. She would rebuild, disguising her efforts with new brick buildings. She would operate at a remove from the new, fine tavern and seldom be seen in this part of town again, though her alley cats and her servants and her tenants would keep her quietly well-connected there. Rioters would be blamed for the fire; insurance money would pay for the new buildings, and she would never leave this place.

Some bonds may never be broken.

She had heard no word of Adam Seaver or Simon Berry—it had only been a few hours since the riot. No one had missed them yet, and there was no one else left asking if they were alive or dead. She had done all she could by creating this chaos in the center of town, to give them a chance to escape, or perhaps, if necessary, to suggest they'd perished in the fire. After the flames were extinguished and the dust had settled and the smoke had been banished by the winds off the Atlantic, she would make discreet inquiries as to whether they lived still.

It was not fear or exhaustion, and it was not relief that Anna now felt. It was anticipation of a happy sort, that Anna distantly remembered from one or two other times in her life. She was only twenty-six years old with a fortune and the wits to keep it. A new life, *tabula rasa*, and no one the wiser.

The scales had been lifted from her eyes and she could not be distracted by trifles and illusions. She knew what mattered. She had changed and survived, and others had not. She knew what mattered.

There would be work to do tomorrow and much more in the days ahead, but for now, there could be rest. Anna knew she would sleep like the dead and rise a new woman.

❋

Acknowledgments

My thanks first off to Jim Fusilli, Dennis Lehane (the editor of *Boston Noir*), and Johnny Temple (publisher and chief editor of the Akashic Noir collections) for giving me the chance to discover the character Anna Hoyt. David L. Ulin, the editor of *Cape Cod Noir* asked for a second Anna story—and encouraged me to write what I imagined to be an impossible novel. Other previously published stories appeared in *Ellery Queen's Mystery Magazine*; my thanks to editor Janet Hutchinson.

Josh Getzler, my agent, always wanted me to write the whole of Anna's story and it's the hardest thing I ever wrote. I am so proud of this book and I couldn't have done that without his enthusiasm for Anna. My thanks to him, and to Jon Cobb, for their assistance and reading acumen; a shout-out to everyone at HG Literary for their support. Clarence A. Haynes was again my developmental and copy editor, and my work is always the better for his suggestions. Errick Nunnally designed the gorgeous cover, as he has for the other DCLE books. I simply adore it.

In one of those truly weird coincidences that happen to fiction writers, after I'd written the first draft of Anna Hoyt, I saw an 18th-century doll that almost exactly resembled Anna's "Dolly" at the Concord Museum (Massachusetts). The coincidence grew even stranger when I learned that the doll's name was "Lady Anne." The owner of the doll, Anna West Winter, graciously answered all our questions.

Charlaine Harris and Toni L.P. Kelner are the best beta readers—and friends—that anyone could ask for. They've been with me (and

Anna) from the start.

With every new story, there were countless readers (including my parents) who whisper to me (and it was always a whisper), "I love Anna." Thank you, thank you, to the readers who've reached out to tell me they've enjoyed any of my work.

Much of the 18th-century setting was based on my own research and that of my colleagues in historical archaeology; I hope they'll enjoy some of the Easter eggs I left for them in "Ardent," for example. Christy (Vogt) Dolan's 1994 M.A. thesis research on the Great House /Three Cranes Tavern in Charlestown, Massachusetts, informed the idea of the Queen's Arms, which is a fictional place. I relied especially on the 1722 map of Boston by John Bonner; I have an academic's desire for accuracy, but also took a writer's liberty to shape the world to my own designs. Ellen Clair Lamb and Verena Rose helped me in understanding colonial banking—and how to turn accounting into theft. D.P. Lyle gave me advice for some of Anna's more nefarious actions. Marylynn Salmon's *Women and the Law of Property in Early America* guided me in forming Anna's unique problems. If there are any inaccuracies, most of blame rests on Anna (and her family's) peculiar interpretations of colonial law and religion. The rest is solely on me.

James Goodwin is the reason you are reading this book. He was there for me (and the book) even when Anna's decisions were surprising and alarming, and especially on those days it took me a while to shake off her point of view. My love and thanks to him for this and all things.

Dana Cameron writes across many genres, but especially crime and speculative fiction. Her work, inspired by her career in archaeology, has won multiple Anthony, Agatha, and Macavity Awards, and her short story "Femme Sole" was short-listed for the Edgar Award. Dana is best known for the Emma Fielding archaeology mysteries (now on Hallmark Movies & Mysteries) and the Fangborn urban fantasy novels. When she isn't traveling or visiting museums, she spends her time weaving, spinning, and yelling at the TV about historical inaccuracies. You can find out more about Dana and her writing on her author website and blog at danacameron.com.